JORDAN'S WORLD

JORDAN'S WORLD

ALLEN STEADHAM

Ambassador International
GREENVILLE, SOUTH CAROLINA & BELFAST, NORTHERN IRELAND

www.ambassador-international.com

Jordan's World
The Jordan of Algoran Series, Book One
© 2019 by Allen Steadham
All rights reserved

ISBN: 978-1-62020-909-7
eISBN: 978-1-62020-922-6

Cover Illustration by Christopher Jackson
Cover Design & Typesetting by Hannah Nichols
Edited by Daphne Self

AMBASSADOR INTERNATIONAL
Emerald House
411 University Ridge, Suite B14
Greenville, SC 29601, USA
www.ambassador-international.com

AMBASSADOR BOOKS
The Mount
2 Woodstock Link
Belfast, BT6 8DD, Northern Ireland, UK
www.ambassadormedia.co.uk

The colophon is a trademark of Ambassador, a Christian publishing company.

"The seeker embarks on a journey to find what he wants and discovers, along the way, what he needs."

- Wally Lamb

PROLOGUE

SEVENTEEN-YEAR-OLD JORDAN LEWIS WAS FORCEFULLY roused in the middle of the night with no warning. Sound asleep one moment, she next felt powerful arms grabbing and picking her up. Unsure whether this was real or a dream and terrified regardless, Jordan resisted with all her strength. Using both hands, she pounded against her abductor's chest, which was covered with armor of some kind, and head, which was protected by a helmet. Trying to twist out of their grip, she kicked and screamed as loudly as she could, but it did no good.

Her assailant apparently could see in the dark, never turning on a light nor having any illumination on his or her protective suit. They never said a word, either, as they stole Jordan away from her home in Colorado.

"What do you want? What are you going to do to me?" Jordan shrieked. "Let me go!"

Silence continued to be their only response. In her panic, Jordan wondered if it was even human.

"Someone! Please help me!" Jordan cried.

Passing through the living room, Jordan's kidnapper sidestepped the couch and exited through the open front door, walking over the cobblestone path to the driveway. Her eyes adjusting to the brighter moonlit sky, Jordan beheld her assailant's companion, a second abductor, who held her mother, Janice, struggling in its arms. She looked like she was screaming, too, but Jordan heard no sound.

No one can hear us, Jordan thought, horrified. *Somehow, they're blocking the sound! That's why no one has tried to help us!*

One of the kidnappers pressed a button on its wrist and a circle of bright light erupted in mid-air. It was about eight feet wide by eight feet tall. They calmly walked through the portal with their captives. Jordan's senses were nearly overwhelmed by the jarring sense of motion within this phenomenon. She didn't know how fast they were traveling or in which direction. It seemed like every direction simultaneously.

It made her feel sick and extremely anxious at the same time. Would it ever stop? Were they going to die?

Seconds, or maybe minutes, later, the abductors emerged on the other side of the anomaly, still holding Jordan and her mother just as tightly as before. They seemed unphased by the experience. Unlike Jordan, who felt shaken and dazed.

Almost immediately, her assailant gently set her on the frigid, snow-covered ground while its companion did the same for her mother. Jordan remained emotionally spent and fought to orient herself.

"Wh-where have you taken us? What do you want??" Jordan shouted with as much strength as she could muster.

Her kidnapper pointed at a light in the distance. Was that a fire? Jordan watched her foe launch some kind of flare from its wrist, using another technology she was unfamiliar with. Then both assailants walked back into the pulsating portal of light before it closed behind them. Jordan crawled on her elbows and knees to reach her mother, who had fainted. The last thing Jordan perceived before passing out was silhouetted shapes approaching them and shouts of alarm in a language she had never heard.

1

THE MOKTA

JORDAN WOKE TO THE LIGHT from the distant twin stars Hylot and Ghorot, "The Brothers" in the Mokta language. She rolled to her side, half-tempted to go back to sleep. But icy winds forced open the flaps of her tent and made her squint, holding close the furs covering her until the gust ceased. Whether she liked it or not, she was awake now. As with most mornings, she dragged herself out of her tent, stood up and stretched. The frigid air bit into her lungs as she took a deep breath. She then exhaled slowly. Moisture from the snow-covered ground and the smells of the nearby tall, slender trees and fall flowering plants greeted her. The scents of the rest of her hunting pack, still sleeping in their tents, mingled with the freshness of the morning. She ran her hands through her long, soft dark brown hair, untangling waves as she went, and then secured it into a braided ponytail.

Looking at the mountain in the distance, the birds and clouds in the sky, Jordan smiled at the wonder of another day. Soon, she and the other hunters would be pursuing a giant Sasstonn, an animal that looked like what would happen if a woolly mammoth crossbred with a cheetah, or two. It was their job to secure a meat supply for the coming months.

She performed additional stretches to loosen up her limbs and to ready for the coming challenges of the day. A tent's flap rustled, and footsteps crunched through the thin soft snow.

"Will you be performing the fire dance for us soon, Jorr-Don?" Zoska asked in the Mokta language. "Or were you intending to break your spine to avoid the hunt?"

"Neither. The stretches loosen me up," Jordan replied in Mokta. "I do them every morning and they help me."

"I eat a hearty meal every morning. *That* helps me!"

"Are you saying I do not eat well?"

Curious, Jordan turned to her friend. Zoska tilted her head slightly and raised an eyebrow.

"You eat well enough now. You used to eat like an insect. That is why it took so long to train you."

"You were a good mentor."

"I am *still* a good mentor!"

Jordan chuckled.

"Yes. But I do not understand why you parent me so much. You are only two cycles older than me."

"You are a handful, darkhair," Zoska said with a smile. "Maybe you need a second parent!"

"Maybe," Jordan said, returning the smile. "Shall we start the morning meal?"

"Why should we do that?" Zoska replied. "Let the other member of this pack make it!"

"You have tasted Reiban's cooking, right?" Jordan grimaced.

Zoska stared at Jordan for a moment. She wrinkled her nose in dismay.

"Yes. Yes, I have," Zoska said. "I will get started on the food."

Jordan pulled some kindling wood from one of the bags and started a fire for the cooking. She caught a glance of Zoska entering her tent to get ingredients. Jordan then returned her attention to maintaining the flames.

Zoska befriended me when I still did not want any friends, ties or connections to this world, Jordan thought. *She helped me out of my despair and self-pity. She listened to me and then reached out and told me what I needed to hear. I will always owe her for that.*

"Do you remember when we met, the night I arrived on Algoran, four cycles ago?" Jordan asked as she started the fire.

"Yes, I was the first to find you. You had such thin clothing and were shaking from the chill."

"Even the coldest nights where I grew up were warm compared to here," Jordan said.

She wasn't feeling frigid at the moment, but the memory made her involuntarily shiver.

"You were hurt from going through the, what did you call it —'porr-tahl,'" Zoska added. "Reiban and I were not sure you two would survive."

"I could not understand a word you said but I could tell you were worried about me and Gemta," Jordan replied, using the Mokta word for mother.

"You were strange-looking, with your light skin, brown hair, and white eyes," Zoska said. "But Chieftess had told us that your kind might be brought to us. And that you would not be prepared for life on this world. I knew I had to help you, even if you did scare me."

"I scared *you?*" Jordan chuckled. "I would never have known."

Jordan had never been frightened of the Mokta. She considered them a handsome people, with their red skin, black scleras instead of white, amber irises, pointed ears and white hair. They were about a foot shorter than Jordan and her gemta, but they were stronger and faster than any human.

"I could not tell you that. It would have been a sign of weakness," Zoska replied.

"I would not have seen it that way."

Jordan added a little more kindling wood to the small fire, watched the flames and smoke build along with the heat.

"I did not know you well then. I could not take that chance," Zoska continued.

"I am glad you told me now," Jordan replied.

Zoska smiled in response.

"It surprised me that you and your mother learned our language so quickly. It made things . . . easier."

"Gemta has always been good at languages. I guess I am, too. At least learning the Mokta language gave us time to adapt," Jordan said. "Once we could understand what you were saying to us, your gifts for storytelling helped us learn Mokta culture, history and the importance of this mountain we live on. How do the Mokta remember all those details? The Mokta have no written language."

Jordan watched as Zoska tied her own hair into a ponytail. Jordan had observed that younger Mokta kept their hair in longer styles while elders kept theirs short.

"Once we hear or see something, we always know it. We can see it in our thoughts and recite it the way we experienced it."

"Then I was right. It is a gift," Jordan said.

Zoska smiled. "I suppose you could say that. I had never given it much thought. It is a normal thing to the Mokta, like living in the village."

The Mokta tribe occupied a mountainous region which was relatively easy to defend from invaders or rival tribes. The hunters wore tough animal hides and furs. Those in other village professions wore more elaborate clothes made from woven fibers and colored with dyes.

From inside her tent near the flap, Zoska was still pondering which ingredients to use for breakfast. She looked into one of the bags and called out to Jordan.

"Do you want wibb eggs, wibb eggs, or wibb eggs?" Zoska asked.

"Wibb eggs are fine," Jordan smiled. "Oh, tell me you still have some of your spicy lahna to go with it."

"Fortune smiles on you this day, my friend!"

"Yes! Your lahna is so good, you could sell it at the market."

"My torkomm does sell it at market," Zoska said, alluding to her father. "And for a good price, too."

Jordan's smile faltered as she suddenly felt wistful and lonely. Zoska had stopped gathering eggs and Jordan could see the concern in her eyes.

"You mentioned your torkomm and it reminded me of mine. I miss him," Jordan answered her friend's unspoken question. "I was angry with him right before my gemta and I were taken. I regret not making things right."

"Forgive, Jorr-Don," Zoska said. "I did not think about my words."

"No, it is okay. I am okay. I know my family is here now . . . with the tribe."

"Tribe *is* family but not like blood," Zoska said.

"No, not like blood," Jordan repeated. "I miss my torkomm—and my younger brother, Mark."

"Do you sometimes wish he had been taken with you?"

Jordan shook her head nervously.

"No. At least he is still on Earth with my torkomm," she said. "I do not know what I would have done if he had gotten sick with the Shilvaba like Gemta."

Zoska nodded. "You are the reason she survived."

"I only stayed with her. Healer Latas gave me good instructions: when to give her the medical salve, how to handle her fever and tremors—the loss of her sight. I would not have been able to watch my brother also."

"Chieftess Kitranor would have told the tribe to help with him. And your gemta still would have lived."

Jordan put her hand on Zoska's shoulder and smiled at her.

"Thank you. I noticed you did not say *you* would have helped with my brother?"

Zoska grinned. "No, I did not. I had to parent you."

"You did. And so did Chieftess."

Zoska's expression turned sympathetic. "Your only blood relative on Algoran could have died from the Shilvaba. Many have, even during my cycles," she said. "You were so . . . lost during that first wintertime. I feared you might perish from sadness."

Jordan felt older than her twenty-one cycles. "I had to live," she said. "It was the only way she was going to make it."

Zoska nodded somberly. "But she did recover. You were able to learn the hunt, as all young ones do. And your gemta helped in the harvest fields."

"Yes. She can use her other senses well there—touch, hearing and smell. Sight is not as important."

"And because of my training, you are a decent huntress," Zoska added.

"'Decent?'" Jordan raised an eyebrow in mock offense. Zoska laughed in response.

Reiban had arisen and approached his hunting companions. He was lean for a Mokta but strong and fast. He had almond-shaped eyes, a long and thin nose and somewhat small mouth. He had his own share of hunting scars on his arms and legs.

"This hits the spot," Jordan said in English as she savored her eggs.

"Dizz hitz thah spaht? What are these words you speak, Jorr-Don?" Zoska asked.

"I think she said something in her old language," Reiban added.

"I am sorry. It, um, lost something in translation," Jordan said. "I was saying I really enjoyed the meal. Thanks."

"We will need to go soon," Reiban said. "The Sasstonns will be stirring and it is best to catch them unaware."

"For once, Reiban is right," Zoska deliberately provoked an irritated glare from the young man. "We should go, Jorr-Don!"

"Pack up your gear then, I will be right behind you," Jordan allowed the last of her eggs, which were smothered in lahna sauce, to slide off the stone plate into her mouth.

"What a beast!" Zoska taunted. "Perhaps we should be hunting you!"

The trio laughed at that as Reiban attended to the rinsing of the plates. Zoska began packing gear.

Jordan drank some water from the stream and organized her hunting gear within a handful of minutes. She looked at the silver ring on her right hand, which had a sapphire gem embedded at its center. It had been given to her by her father a year before her abduction.

Dad, Mark, I have not given up hope! I may not know where Algoran is or how The Abductors brought us here, but if there is a way for me and Mom to come home to you, I swear I am going to find it!

2
RIDING DRAGONS

JORDAN STARTLED AWAKE, PANICKED. "GEMTA? Come on, breathe! I—?"

Cold sweat covered her skin, and her heart raced. She looked for her gemta in the darkness.

"J-Jordan?" Gemta said, still half-asleep. "What is it?"

Jordan sighed in relief to hear her gemta's voice. They were inside their hut in the Mokta village, sleeping in their kelkonos, hammock-like beds made from the velvety underside of the zala beast hide and tied with the flexible bark of the Heezit tree.

"Nevermind. It was a dream," Jordan said, embarrassed.

"You still dream about that time?" Gemta replied.

Still unnerved by her nightmare, Jordan put her feet on the floor and rubbed her eyes before standing up. Then she leaned against the nearest wall. The traumas of that first Algoran winter still had a strong and cruel grip on some part of her mind and soul. Despite how much time had passed, the burden of her fears and guilt rested on Jordan as if it had been yesterday.

"Yes. It scared me more than anything, even The Abductors."

"I understand. I am reminded of it every time I wake."

Jordan was always saddened to be reminded of her gemta's blindness but was soothed by the fact that she was still alive.

"I really could not rest or sleep much during those months," Jordan said. "The Shilvaba kept you in such danger. The nights were the worst, when the fevers spiked so suddenly and often. If I did not apply the Healer's salve quickly enough, you would go into convulsions."

"You must have been a bundle of nerves."

Jordan sighed. "I was always afraid I would sleep through one of your fevers, that I would wake up and you would be . . . "

"I would be dead?"

Jordan hesitated before responding. "Yes."

Her gemta carefully exited her kelkeno. She unfastened it from the floor and let it pull back to its resting position against the wall. She grabbed her walking stick from along the wall and listened for Jordan's movement. Once she located her, she walked over and gave Jordan a much-needed hug.

"I owe you my life, many times over," Gemta shared.

"You are my gemta, I would do anything for you. I am just glad you survived."

They sat down on the floor for a few minutes in silence.

"You do not have to be so protective of me anymore, Jordan. I am stronger now, I am fine," Gemta said.

"Yes, but you are also blind," Jordan said.

"You know I have learned to 'see' with my other senses. I walk this village every day and I feel sorry for any enemy who dares to attack me."

To emphasize her point, her gemta picked up her walking stick and stabbed at the air as if holding a saber.

"Oh, do I hear *fierceness* in my gemta's voice?" Jordan teased.

"While you were on your last hunt, Chieftess asked her daughter, Miitas, to train me in defense and how to fight."

"I am impressed. Miitas has taught many the ways of combat. Zoska may have taught me but Miitas supervised the training."

Gemta laid her walking stick back down beside her. "So, you do not need to worry about me so much."

"I will always worry about you, Gemta."

"That is sweet, but you will not always be living with me. Someday, you will choose a mate and be with him. Your focus will not be on me, it will be on your new family."

Jordan sighed again. "That seems a long way off."

"You are twenty-one. Others have been mated a cycle or two. They have children already."

Jordan softly patted her gemta's leg.

"You hang around Chieftess too much, Gemta," she complained. "You are starting to talk like her."

"And you are forgetting how different the culture is here. On Earth, our people could wait until their thirties or forties to marry and have children. They could also decide not to marry at all or have any children. There were so many people and so many options. Here, life is not so plentiful and there are more dangers."

Jordan pondered her gemta's words in silence for a few moments.

"All of what you said is true," Jordan replied, her grin evident in her voice. "But I think you just want to marry me off so you can have grandchildren!"

"I will not deny that I have had those thoughts," Gemta said with a hint of a smile. "You are all I have, and I would like to see our family continue, even if it is here. And I know your children would be beautiful—even if I cannot see them."

Jordan shifted restlessly in place. "Gemta, you still have Mark, even if he is on Earth. I have no doubt that someday, he will get married and have kids."

"Perhaps . . . but I will have no way to know that. I do not like uncertainties."

"I understand," Jordan said, somewhat dejected.

"I am sorry. I just wanted to give you some perspective. You do not have as much time to decide as you may think."

Jordan rested her hand on her gemta's leg but there was no excitement or amusement this time.

"I will give it more thought, but this is *my* decision, Gemta."

"Jordan, I trust you," Gemta said with a nod.

Jordan valued her mother's trust, perhaps more than anything. "Thanks, Gemta."

Gemta prepared some hot tea for the two of them and they spent the next hour telling each other stories until they were tired enough to sleep again.

Jordan rose early out of habit. On Earth, she had never been a morning person but during that fateful winter, between watching over her gemta and her training to become a huntress, Jordan was always up and moving by first light.

She staggered out of the hut and walked to a nearby mountain stream without putting on her furs or boots, hoping the cold winds in her face and the wet snow between her toes would further stimulate her senses and trigger her adrenaline. She took a few handfuls to drink and then washed her face with the brook's icy waters.

After a few stretches, she returned to the village and put on her furs and boots. She walked over to help with the morning meal for the village, which mainly consisted of Meesta birds (Algoran's version of a chicken), eggs, cooked Shta meat, and baked bread. Jordan enjoyed assisting with the cooking, talking with those who were preparing the food along with her, and the gratitude she received from her fellow villagers as she served them their meals.

Once most of the breakfasts had been served, Jordan sat down and enjoyed her own meal. She had sampled a few items while making the food but not enough to fill her belly. She was joined by Zoska, Reiban, and Bopol, the other members of her hunting pack.

Bopol, one of the tallest villagers, was a stern and rugged young man. His facial features, broad like his massive chest and powerful legs, contrasted with his mannerisms which she considered somewhat gentle.

"Are you well, Jorr-Don?" Zoska pointed to Jordan's eyes.

Jordan could imagine the dark circles and paleness of her face. "I did not sleep well."

"You had one of those nightmares again, did you not?" Zoska asked.

Jordan nodded. "It was vivid. Gemta had the illness and I was waking to help her but somehow in the dream, I knew it was too late. I woke for real and Gemta was fine, of course. But it took a while to go back to sleep."

Reiban stood by. Jordan thought he was clearly uncomfortable with memories from that time, as he looked away or down. Once, she saw him try to smile but it was forced and awkward. In contrast, if Bopol found the conversation grieving, she noted that his flat expressions gave away nothing and he wisely stayed silent.

"Perhaps you should try to get some more rest?" Zoska offered, reaching over to put her hand on top of Jordan's.

"I could not get more rest, even if I wanted to. I need something else to focus on." Jordan replied. "Dreams like that only remind me how I almost lost my gemta."

Jordan was surprised when Reiban's eyes suddenly showed enthusiasm and he finally spoke up.

"I have an idea!" Reiban exclaimed. "After morning meal, we will go to the lake to fish and tell tales!"

"*Tall* tales, if it is you," Zoska said, laughing and gently ribbing him.

"I have many stories to tell which are completely true!" Reiban added.

Zoska's laughter was infectious. They soon began their trip to a generous lake near the base of the mountain. It took an hour to walk the distance.

———————

Reiban had been weaving his tale for some time, eliciting curiosity and amusement. The group sat in a circle on the lush grass within sight of the lake.

"—and could I help it if the Chief of that village offered his daughter to me?" Reiban asked.

"Well, since you obviously did not end up with her, what happened?" Zoska said, fidgeting with a stone. Then she turned to look at him, half-irritated and half-curious to hear his answer.

"As it happens, it was not a real village and he was not really a Chief," Reiban said.

"And it was not his daughter, either?" Bopol asked.

Reiban froze for a moment and then looked in Bopol's direction, smiling but obviously confused. "Have I told this story before?"

Zoska grabbed him by the shoulders and pulled him into a kiss.

"No, my mate," she said. "And it is a good thing, too. Please do not tell this story again."

"You do not like it?" Reiban said, surprised.

Jordan began clapping in delight.

"*I* liked it!" Jordan interjected, as much to mess with Zoska as to lift Reiban's drooping spirits.

"You have no taste for storytelling, darkhair," Zoska said.

"I have been known to weave a tale or two," Jordan said with a raised eyebrow and a smile.

"Is that so? You have been quiet for four cycles but *now* you have a story for us?" Reiban said. "This I must hear!"

———————

Jordan looked at her friends and smiled. She turned away to collect her thoughts, then swirled around to face them again.

"Once, there was a young girl who adored her torkomm," Jordan began. "He was often busy, but he loved her very much. One day, he told her 'I am going to take you to a magic place and wonderful things are going to happen!' The girl was excited and went with her torkomm to this place. When they arrived, she was amazed. There were so many incredible things to do and see. But her torkomm told her he was taking her somewhere very special: they were going to ride a dragon!"

"What?" Zoska exclaimed. "No one can ride a dragon!"

Jordan held up a finger to silence them. Then she spread both arms at her side as she continued.

"I told you, it was an enchanted place. And the girl's torkomm had a special magic."

"He was a sorcerer?" Reiban asked.

"Shhh! Let her tell the story," Bopol insisted.

Jordan smiled in amusement, making eye contact with Bopol.

"The girl's torkomm used his power to tame the dragon. It humbled itself and let them climb aboard," Jordan said. "Her torkomm crafted a special harness and saddle to allow them to safely sit on and control the beast. When they were secured and ready, her torkomm snapped the reins and commanded the dragon to fly—and it did! They flew high and dipped low, took marvelous turns, all going quite fast. And all the while, the girl was both terrified and happy, *thrilled* really!"

"What happened next?" Bopol asked, captivated by her story. His eyes expressed a childlike fascination.

"Well, the torkomm could only use his magic for so long," Jordan replied. "After several minutes, he had to land the dragon or risk it getting out of control. But the young girl would always remember, and treasure, that experience for the rest of her days!"

Now Zoska began to clap, smiling at Jordan. Reiban and Bopol joined Zoska, causing Jordan to blush.

"Who knew that Jorr-Don was such a good storyteller," Zoska said. "Or that she actually rode a dragon as a child?"

"Eh, that is one of about two stories I know," Jordan said. "And it was not actually a dragon. But I did enjoy myself and that time with my torkomm."

Jordan felt Zoska put a hand on her shoulder and rest it there.

"This is the first time I have heard you mention him without sadness," Zoska said.

"Yeah. Maybe I am getting better," Jordan said, still smiling.

3

THE HUNT

JORDAN LEAPED ONTO THE MASSIVE beast, which was at least eight feet tall and six feet wide. She grabbed onto its long fur with both hands, pulled herself up behind its head and stabbed the back of its neck with her razor-sharp twin-bladed javelin. The Sasstonn swatted at Jordan with its claws, missing her face but shredding into her left arm, knocking her to the ground. Zoska scooped her up and out of harm's way while Reiban climbed the animal and finished what Jordan had started, slicing at it with Jordan's javelin, shoving the blade in deep and leaning against its head with all his might until it gave way.

Zoska inspected Jordan's injured arm as they both sat on the ground. When she quickly determined that it was still attached, she smiled. "The bleeding is not that bad," Zoska said. "You will have some impressive scars."

"Yes, I know I will," Jordan winced at the pain and held her arm tight while Zoska grabbed some bandaging cloth from her bag.

"Will she able to travel?" Reiban asked, concerned.

"Yes, but she will probably need our help," Zoska replied.

Jordan closed her eyes and gritted her teeth to endure the burning aggravation of Zoska wrapping the bandaging cloth around her injured arm.

"She will have that," Reiban insisted.

"Why did you let her attack first?" Zoska asked.

"She took lead, Zoska. That is her right. And her strike was good, the hunt is ours."

"But now she is hurt."

"That is a risk we all take on the hunt. What are you really saying?"

Jordan relaxed some and opened her eyes, now that her arm was fully bandaged. She saw Zoska look up at Reiban. Her mouth was open and ready to say more, but evidently, she changed her mind.

"I suppose it does not matter," Zoska said, looking down. "But how will we carry all the meat now?"

"We will manage," he rebutted.

"Will it carry itself? Will your mystery princess show up with her palace guards and they will all haul a bag?"

Jordan saw Reiban's eyes narrow in a disappointed stare towards his mate.

"How can you be jealous of a princess from a story?" he asked.

"Who said I was jealous? I was just making a point."

"A very stupid point."

"Look who is talking!"

Jordan used the bickering between the two of them to distract herself from her soreness and the stabbing sensation where she had been clawed. She wished that Bopol was here. But his sister, Miitas, had needed him to help her train some new hunters while her normal assistant recovered from an illness.

She knew Bopol could have made quick work of the Sasstonn and perhaps prevented her injury. Or he would have stayed by her side until he knew his friend was doing better.

Even though Jordan had trained for almost six months to become good enough to participate in the hunt and was one of the better hunters in the tribe, that wasn't enough to prevent occasional injury. Hunting could be deadly. Each season, the tribe knew that a handful would not return.

When she felt a little better, Jordan assisted Zoska and Reiban in stripping the Sasstonn of its meat, fat, and skin. Reiban even removed one set of claws to hastily craft a crude necklace for Jordan. He handed it to her proudly.

"A trophy. How would you say, eh, 'pay-back' for your wounds?" Reiban said.

Jordan received the still-bloody gift, amused that Reiban had learned a few English words from her. She knew she would have to clean this trophy properly before wearing it but she appreciated Reiban's sentiment. Still holding it in one hand, she stood up with help from Zoska and turned towards the fallen animal. She clasped her hands together as she had been taught, making a semi-bow.

"Thank you for your sacrifice, magnificent one. It will not be in vain. Your death allows our village to live."

"Thanks for sacrifice," Zoska and Reiban said in unison, matching Jordan's actions.

Over the next hour, they secured everything and prepared to head back with their bounty.

"The Spirit of the Mountain is with us this time," Reiban said. "With the size of this beast, we have a season's meat in one short hunt!"

"How long do you think it will take to get back to the village?" Jordan asked.

Her stance was unsteady. Even her gaze and smile wavered.

"Normally, I would say three moons. But since you are hurt, we should go faster to get you to the Healer," Reiban said. "Two moons, if fortune continues."

Jordan was glad when Zoska came up to her and helped her remain standing by letting Jordan lean on her.

"Then you might have to carry me over your shoulder if I pass out," Jordan said.

"I will carry you, if need be, darkhair," Zoska assured. "My mate needs to haul our prized meat."

"You do not want me to carry Jorr-Don? You *are* jealous, are you not?" Reiban said, delighted.

"It is exercise! Carrying her will increase my strength," Zoska replied.

"Are you saying she is heavy?" Reiban asked.

"Yeah, I was wondering that, too," Jordan added with mild irritation.

Zoska rolled her eyes. "You are both stupid!"

———

When the trio arrived less than two days later, most of the village was there to cheer and praise their successful hunt. Jordan endured it patiently as the Healer thoroughly inspected her wounds to determine whether any were severe or infected. She was pleased when he pointed out that Zoska had cleaned her gashes and used the preventative ointment he had provided each hunter. Even so, she could not argue with his assessment that she would need a week's rest to recuperate from the blood loss and regain her strength. She was grateful when the Healer gave her an herbal sedative for her pain.

Jordan was glad when Gemta entered the Healer's hut. The Healer led her to her daughter's side. She sat on the ground next to her and gently put her hand on Jordan's right arm. Jordan put her own hand on top of her mother's and lightly squeezed.

"They say you fought a huge Sasstonn," Gemta said.

"We beat him," Jordan answered weakly. "And now, the village will eat well this season."

"I am just glad you survived," Gemta said.

Jordan squeezed her gemta's hand again, more tightly this time.

"I will be fine, Gemta."

"I know," Gemta seemed not entirely convinced.

"Stop worrying."

Gemta chuckled at that, in spite of her concerns.

"I am your gemta, I am going to worry."

There was a moment of awkward silence, then Jordan closed her eyes and let the natural painkiller do its work.

"She will sleep for a few hours," Healer Latas said. "I will make sure no further harm comes to her."

Janice turned towards the sound of the Healer's voice and nodded. "Thank you, Healer."

Janice walked outside the hut and listened to the sounds of life all around her. Children scurrying to and fro, playing games with each other. Adults were selling their wares and services. Birds were calling out to each other from the trees, their wings flapping loudly as they took off or landed. She could smell the community supper being prepared on the other side of the village, probably a stew or soup. Based on the aroma, she thought it probably included some of the meat obtained by Jordan and her hunting party. Small four-footed feral animals stood by curious, panting as they watched the village or scampered by, looking for their own evening meal.

A cold breeze blew past Janice. The temperatures would soon drop, possibly followed by a storm of some sort.

She joined everyone for dinner and enjoyed the stew, but Jordan was never far from her thoughts. She checked back in on her daughter one more time after the meal. The Healer assured Janice that her daughter would be fine, that she needed this rest and that Janice should do the same at home. Reluctantly, Janice agreed.

———————

The next day, Zoska helped Jordan return to the hut she shared with her gemta, where she would continue to recover. She also lingered to help Janice with Jordan and keep her friend company, when she wasn't sleeping.

"Healer Latas told me that Bopol stopped by to see you last night but you were sleeping," Zoska said.

Jordan smiled. "I wish I could have seen him. I will thank him later."

Zoska's brow furrowed in consideration. "Knowing him, he was probably very worried about you."

"Great. Are you trying to make me feel guilty?"

Zoska stood up and deliberately changed the subject. "Can I get you some water or maybe some tea? You look thirsty."

Zoska was slightly disappointed when Jordan shook her head.

"Healer Latas also praised my quick treatment and bandaging of your wounds," Zoska mused. "He said I probably saved your arm."

"Then I am grateful, seeing as how I need both of my arms."

"There is no shame in losing a limb to the hunt," Zoska added. "I have known hunters who continued after losing an eye, ear, or hand."

"But not a whole arm?"

Zoska winced in sympathy as Jordan raised her injured arm to emphasize her point and then clearly regretted it immediately.

"My grandfather lost feeling in his right arm after it was gnashed on by a kortznika," Zoska interjected.

"Okay, okay! At least my arm will be fine."

"What matters is that your mind is intact, Jorr-Don. There are ones who took wounds and lost the will to continue being hunters. They had to learn other skills, other trades. And they were no longer the same."

Jordan rested her right hand on Zoska's shoulder, a determined, resolute look on her face. "I will always be a huntress. No beast or injury can take that from me."

"That is the Jorr-Don I know!"

"Heh! Who else would I be?"

They laughed and talked for a while longer until Janice returned, and Jordan became tired again. Zoska helped her friend into her kelkeno.

"We all will choose other professions when we have passed our prime," Zoska said. "The hunt has always been for the young. For now, this is our time."

"I understand."

"I will see you tomorrow."

It took almost ten days for Jordan to regain her strength and heal from her wounds. Once she had, Jordan was summoned to see Chieftess Kitranor. Walking alongside her daughter en route to the Chieftess' large hut, Gemta had become very adept with using a walking stick and had no difficulty matching Jordan's pace. Once inside, she and Jordan sat facing the Chieftess. Kitranor appeared to be around the same age as Gemta. She was tall for a Mokta and kept her hair surprisingly long. Her face was round and friendly but her eyes were sharp and warrior-like. Kitranor had numerous scars on her arms, legs, neck and one that stretched across her nose; some were from her younger cycles as a huntress and others were from more recent battles, helping defend the tribe. Kitranor's mate, Latas, was the village Healer.

Out of respect, Jordan was silent but attentive. Latas sat nearby, next to Jordan and her gemta.

"How is this promising young hunter, Healer Latas?" Kitranor asked, wearing a knowing grin.

"Already eager to show off her new scars and trophy necklace," Latas answered with a light chuckle. "She is well and can resume the hunt."

"That is excellent news!" Kitranor replied.

The Chieftess looked at Gemta, the smile never quite leaving her face.

"Tell me, Januss, is it not time for your daughter to select a mate? She is of age and there are many ideal males to choose from."

"Chieftess?" Gemta asked, surprise marking her face.

"With respect—um, forgive, Chieftess," Jordan interjected.

Kitranor nodded in approval. "Speak."

"The hunting season is just beginning," Jordan pleaded. "Is this really the time to settle down and have a family?"

Kitranor issued a small laugh. "You still have much to learn, Jorr-Don!"

"What?"

Jordan looked at Kitranor and her gemta in confusion, with a raised eyebrow.

"This village does have other hunters, child. You can take time now to mate and bear young. And someday, you will teach your children the hunt."

"But, Chieftess, I am not of this world," Jordan's heart raced from nervousness. "Even if I were ready could I even have children with one of the tribe?"

Kitranor winked at Jordan. "Our peoples are more alike than different. And the best way to find out is to try, is it not?"

Jordan's eyes widened once she realized what the Chieftess was really saying.

"You were from Errrth but now you are on Algoran. You are Mokta and we are one people," Kitranor said. "Take your time, Jorr-Don, and pick a good mate. Then we will celebrate the continuation of the tribe!"

"As you say, Chieftess," Jordan nodded, obedient but unsure. "I will do."

4

A VIEW FROM THE MOUNTAINTOP

JORDAN AND HER GEMTA SOON left the Chieftess' hut and went their separate ways. Gemta headed to help with the village evening meal and Jordan went to find Zoska, seriously needing to talk with her good friend. It was getting dark, Algoran's three moons were rising in a staggered orbit while the temperature was steadily dropping. She passed a few children still playing outside. Jordan then glimpsed her friend hanging up some recently washed clothes to dry.

"Zoska!"

"You look well, darkhair," Zoska said with a smile.

"I am better, thanks." Jordan had appreciated Zoska's support through her recovery.

"Would you like some water?" Zoska asked. "I can make some tea?"

"I am fine. I just spoke with Chieftess."

Zoska motioned for Jordan to enter the hut and they sat down on the ground facing one another.

"Is everything all right?" Zoska asked.

"Chieftess thinks I . . . am ready to pick a mate."

Zoska's face brightened at that. "It is about time she said so! I have thought this for a long time."

"You have? Why did you not say anything?" Jordan was surprised when Zoska raised an eyebrow at that.

"I may act like a parent to you, Jorr-Don, but I am not your gemta. It was not for me to say."

Jordan nodded in understanding.

"How do you feel about it, Jorr-Don? I already have a mate, so I may feel differently about this than you."

"I am glad you are mated. I need some perspective."

Jordan picked up a stray twig and began carving lines in the cold soil.

"What do you mean?" Zoska said.

"Before Algoran, on my world, I liked the males my age, but I was kind of sheltered and, if you can believe it, shy around people outside my closest friends and family. My parents were not against my having a—er—a potential mate," Jordan said, remembering there was no Mokta word for boyfriend. "But they did not really encourage me, either . . . so I never tried. I guess what I am saying is—"

Zoska smiled. "You have no idea how to pick a mate."

"Well, I would not have said it like *that* . . . but yeah."

"There is nothing special or difficult about it, darkhair. All you have to do is open your heart and listen to your feelings. If you have never experienced love, it does not mean you cannot."

Jordan crossed her arms over her chest, somewhat defensively. Or perhaps it was self-protection.

"I am not sure I know how to open my heart or listen to my feelings," she said.

"You do it on every hunt," Zoska answered. "You open your heart to your fellow hunters when you trust us to fight with you. In that moment, you believe we will succeed in taking down the beast."

Jordan's eyes narrowed. "I do not see what that has to do with selecting a mate?"

"Do you not think you need to trust the one you are going to spend your life with, the one who you will have children with?"

"'Children?'" Jordan recoiled, starting to stand up.

"You make it sound like some terrible curse!" Zoska grabbed her hand and stopped her, laughing. "What is so wrong with having children?"

Jordan shrugged and sat back down. "Nothing, I suppose."

Jordan did not understand the knowing glance Zoska was giving her.

"You do not see yourself having any children?" Zoska asked.

"It is not that. I just do not see it for myself any time soon."

Zoska nodded at that. "How long then? A cycle? Two?"

Jordan winced in emotional discomfort. "How about ten or fifteen?"

Zoska's jaw dropped and both eyebrows raised sharply.

"Why that long?! The other females will see their children's children born before you have one of your own! And I doubt any male will wait that long, either . . . unless you choose a mate far younger than you? I mean, it has been known to happen but usually with a widowed female."

"What are you talking about, Zoska? Why does everything have to move so fast here?"

Jordan turned from her friend, feeling isolated and embarrassed.

"Do the young women not have children on the world you came from?" she asked.

"Many do. Others wait till later, till they have established well-paying jobs and experienced more in life."

Jordan felt Zoska grab her chin and turn her head to face her again.

"A part of you is still on your world then," she told Jordan.

"Is it? Am I wrong to want that life still?"

Zoska let go of her but Jordan continued looking at her.

"The real question, I think, is do you want to go back to your world?"

"Yes! I want to take my gemta back there, to be reunited with my brother and torkomm!"

Jordan could tell by Zoska's hardened gaze that the next question would not be easy. And she was right.

"If you two could go back there, would you *stay* there?"

Jordan's eyes involuntarily widened.

What would *I do?* Jordan thought. *I was born on Earth, grew up there. Should it not be normal for me to want to go back there? But what about the Mokta? They accepted me and Gemta, made us a part of the tribe. And I'm a good huntress. I—I could take a mate—if I wanted to?*

Jordan felt her pulse quicken at that possibility. The ease which she had come to that conclusion frightened her. Mentally, she ran away from it.

"Yes! I mean, I cannot speak for my gemta, but I think she would. And I know *I* would even though I would miss everyone here."

Jordan immediately knew she had spoken too soon and said too much, letting her emotions determine her words. The hurt in Zoska's eyes and frown felt worse for Jordan than any lecture or argument.

"I am glad we were in your thoughts *somewhere*," Zoska said icily.

"I did not mean—"

"You spoke your thoughts. You meant them."

Zoska had seen right through her as always, making her feel worse.

"Do not worry, darkhair. Reiban, Bopol, and I will help you any way we can."

As they walked outside, several birds departed one of the taller trees, causing a mad rustling of leaves, branches and flapping wings. In the distance, a zala beast howled as it announced its desire to find a mate. Each new sound heightened the silent, lingering awkwardness between the two friends until Jordan spoke again.

"I feel like I am making myself an outsider again," she said.

"You will never be an outsider. Both you and your gemta became Mokta when Chieftess made you part of the tribe. That will not change, even if you leave us."

Jordan nodded. "Thank you."

"I have heard your words, but they do not match what I feel from you." Zoska considered. "What are you really afraid of?"

Jordan crossed her arms again and looked away nervously.

"I do not want to make a wrong decision. I do not want my actions to hurt me or anyone else."

"If you make choices from your heart, they will not be wrong decisions."

"On my world, it did not always work like that. Sometimes your choices were based on your thoughts, not your feelings."

"You are not on your world anymore. This is how it works here."

Jordan hugged Zoska, glad for her support and encouragement.

"You already have your answers within you, Jorr-Don. You should trust–and listen–to yourself."

Jordan nodded at Zoska, not sure what else to say. Zoska went back inside her hut and Jordan walked away.

Minutes later, she saw a stream of shooting stars pass through the night sky just beyond the moons. But few if any villagers took notice of them. She visually scanned the village as she walked through it, smiling and talking with her fellow tribespeople as she passed by. She observed the ones she knew were mated and her age, noticing their infants and young children. Jordan was happy for the mates and felt a connection to them, a kinship.

Then she looked at the silver ring on her finger and stared up at the sky. She put her hand to her heart. She didn't know how she felt about her future, her own potential mate. And that troubled her.

Restless, Jordan went higher up the mountain until she was able to look at the whole village below. The winds blew harder and pushed the cold through the furs she was wearing, but she needed this perspective. She wanted an objective view of the area, a place where she could be alone and ask herself questions.

Am I just fooling myself? With everything I've learned here, do I think there is any way I can make The Abductors tell me why they brought us here to Algoran? Do I think that I, Jordan Lewis, can intimidate alien beings with world-hopping devices into sending me and Gemta back home?

Who do I think I am? I do not know how many Abductors there are or what other technology they have. They might have laser guns or remote controls that rearrange your insides! They could send me and Gemta into outer space without suits. There are so many ways they could kill us!

So, is it really worth it to try? I would be risking my life, not to mention anyone who goes along with my crazy idea. I mean, I am willing to do it . . . but do I have the right to ask someone else? Gemta? My friends?

Zoska's words returned to her: "If you make choices from your heart, they will not be wrong decisions."

But can I live with that if something goes wrong?

Jordan had no answer for that question. Approaching her cold tolerance, she slowly walked back down the mountain to the village.

5
CHOICES

JORDAN'S BROTHER, MARK, KNOCKED ON her closed bedroom door three times. She responded by throwing a shoe at it. Jordan had been lounging on her lush, full-sized bed, which was lavished in rose pink and white patterns, as she exchanged texts on her phone with her friends, Erica and Pamela. Undaunted, the ten-year old walked in anyway.

"Can you not get a hint, Mark? I'm on the phone!"

"Mom called. She wants us to make supper."

"Is she trying to make me cook again? If I give you money to buy us some pizzas, will you leave me alone?"

"Sure!"

Jordan reached into her purse and grabbed two twenty-dollar bills and fluttered them in her hand to catch her brother's attention. Mark gladly put the money into his pants pocket and exited the room.

"You know what I want on my pizza, right?" Jordan shouted.

"Pepperoni, mushrooms, bell pepper, and extra sauce!" Mark replied.

"Bingo, bro!" Jordan said. "You're the best!"

The crackling flames, combined with the aroma of the roasting fish flesh, enticed Jordan to return to the present. Her stomach also began grumbling loudly. Night had already fallen, and a moderate wind howled through their makeshift camp. It had taken all day to catch enough game for all four members of the hunting party to eat reasonably well. Before that, nearly three days had passed while they had crossed an expanse of bitterly cold and lifeless tundra after descending the mountain which housed the Mokta village.

"I think your belly speaks for us all, Jorr-Don!" Bopol laughed.

"At this moment, I live for her cooking. The smell alone keeps me from passing out," Zoska said.

"It is nice to be appreciated," Jordan chuckled.

Reiban was sitting on a thick tree branch looking down at them.

"Watch yourself, Jorr-Don, or Zoska might make a meal of your right arm!"

Jordan peered up at Reiban and raised an eyebrow, more amused than irritated.

"She is your mate, Reiban. Watch her yourself! Is that not why you climbed up there, to scout this area?"

"Yes. And I would gladly watch my mate, but I doubt that will stop her when she is hungry!"

"Bopol will protect me. *Right*, Bopol?" Jordan said.

Bopol grinned at first but then he took on a stern expression.

"With my life, if need be," Bopol replied with bravado. "But I must get the first fish!"

"Now your protection comes with conditions?" Jordan responded.

"I need strength to protect you," he added.

Jordan started to hand the stick with the largest fish to Bopol but stopped and took a bite out of the meat first, all the while looking straight at Bopol. He looked back at her angrily until Reiban laughed and pointed at him from above.

"Her meal comes with conditions, too, Bopol. She needs strength to cook more!"

"Either that or she just claimed you as hers!" Zoska said.

"Hey, I did not. I have not claimed anyone!" Jordan said, embarrassed, her mouth barely containing her food.

"Calm down, Jorr-Don, my mate was joking!" Reiban said.

"Actually, I was not," Zoska said under her breath for Jordan's ear alone.

Bopol smiled and began devouring the rest of the seared animal meat. Jordan continued broiling two more meals, suddenly feeling shy and awkward around Bopol while she joked with Reiban and Zoska. Within an hour, Jordan had made enough food for all of them. They laughed and told stories around the fire for some time. Eventually, Zoska dragged Reiban to their tent. Jordan was left alone with Bopol.

Jordan stirred the campfire and added some wood to keep it burning. Then she stared off into the distance, deep in thought.

"I know that look," Bopol said.

"What?" Jordan turned to face him.

"Jorr-Don, you are thinking of your world again, the life you were taken from, yes?"

"I had been, yes."

"Is life bad for you here?"

"No, of course not. I love my life here. I am Mokta, like you."

Bopol nodded in satisfaction but his eyes conveyed his lingering concern.

"So, what troubles you?"

"It is kind of silly, I feel foolish."

"They are your feelings, so they are not foolish," he said. "Tell me?"

Jordan crossed her arms and turned to face slightly away from Bopol. Then she sighed.

"Chieftess thinks it is time for me to choose a mate."

"She is right. You would do well to heed her."

Jordan turned and gave him a brief half-smile.

"I know."

"So, what is wrong?"

Looking directly at Bopol, her eyes shared how conflicted she felt within.

"Do not misunderstand. I could spend the rest of my life in the tribe with a mate and maybe children, but . . . "

"You want to go back to Errrth, back to your family there?"

"Is that wrong of me? I feel like I am being ungrateful. The tribe took us in, made us family."

Bopol took Jordan's hands in his and peered into her eyes.

"That is why we are out here," Bopol said. "That is why Chieftess told us to follow you, to find answers to your questions."

Jordan thought back to a week earlier when she had sought an audience with the Chieftess. She shared her feelings and concerns with Kitranor, who listened patiently. Bopol was also there but he remained silent, sitting patiently near his gemta.

"I do not know if there is a way back to your world, Jorr-Don," Kitranor shared. "But if one exists, it will be in the Tavaa region in the far Southlands. The lights of Qui Tol, the ones you call The Abductors, have been seen there many times throughout our spoken history."

"Do you believe The Abductors live there?"

"I have never been there," Kitranor said with a faint smile. "I have only lived among the Mokta, but our ancestors once lived in the Southlands. In those times, our people saw the lights, even your people, on many occasions. The Qui Tol always brought your people to our world in groups of two or three."

"Is that why you accepted us when we arrived?"

Kitranor did not immediately respond but her demeanor softened. She looked at Jordan with sympathy and a maternal air.

"Yes. The Mokta have always accepted your people. We knew they were strangers to our lands and world, that they had nothing and needed our help. In return, your people joined our tribe, lived among us and increased our numbers. The blood of your people runs in our veins now."

"That's how you knew I could have children someday with a mate?"

"Yes," Kitranor replied. "But it will do you no good to choose a mate with your heart in two places, here and Errrth. Someday, you will have to choose but not today. So, if it eases your heart to seek answers from the Qui Tol, despite the dangers of leaving the protection of our tribe, I will allow it."

"Thank you, Chieftess!"

Kitranor's expression hardened once more, more warning than anything else.

"On one condition."

"Yes, Chieftess?"

"You cannot go alone. But you cannot take your gemta, she would never survive the journey. You must take someone strong."

"I understand," Jordan nodded.

"I will go with her," Bopol interjected. "That is, if she will have me?"

Jordan nodded in agreement.

"Also take Zoska and Reiban in your hunting party. You are safer in a pack."

"Agreed," Bopol said, standing up.

"Then that is what we will do," Jordan added.

"Take minimal supplies. You will travel faster, and it is a long journey," Kitranor said. "There is plenty of game and water between here and the Southlands."

"Chieftess is wise," Jordan replied, bowing slightly in respect.

"Good hunting," Kitranor replied.

Now, so far from the Mokta mountain, Jordan and Bopol watched the fire dwindle to burning embers. Even though he was no longer holding her hands, she felt like he was still offering that kind of encouragement to her.

"Thank you for understanding me," Jordan said. "I am glad to know I have your support, your friendship."

"I have seen your many moods. I do understand you. And I will continue to help you any way I can."

"Dream well, Bopol."

"Dream well."

Jordan laid down in her tent and closed the flaps. She covered herself in a layer of furs and allowed her exhaustion to catch up with her.

"Sis?"

"Mark?"

When Jordan opened her eyes, she was in her room on Earth. It was just as she remembered, with framed original paintings by her Uncle James on the light pink walls, a large window covered by vertical blinds near the foot of her plush bed. There was also a desk against one corner with her computer, monitor and speakers. Mark was standing next to her looking concerned. The light shining through the blinds, along with her brother's clothing, told her it was a school day and morning time.

"Sis, I couldn't wake you up! Are you okay?"

"Yeah. Is Mom here?"

"Mom's at work."

"Oh, right," Jordan said, sitting up in bed, scratching her head.

"You overslept. I made you some toast but we gotta go if we're gonna get to school on time."

"Okay, I'll be right down."

After getting dressed and walking downstairs, she realized that her brother was gone.

Did he already leave without me?

The scent of the warm and buttered toast that Mark had left for her reached her, and she devoured both pieces and chased them down with some milk. Then Jordan walked briskly to the front door, but it wouldn't budge. She twisted and shook the knob back and forth to no avail. Quickly filling with anxiety, she beat furiously on the door, crying in frustration, but she couldn't open it.

"Jorr-Don!"

Bopol had his hand on her shoulder. He was leaning into her tent, eyes wide in concern. Jordan looked around. She had been dreaming. Putting her hand to her cheek, she felt tears she didn't know she'd cried. Flustered, she looked down. She pinched her arm. This was reality.

"I heard you moving around and talking in your sleep. I thought you might be having a bad dream," Bopol said. "Then you started screaming and I had to help you, but I could not wake you. Are you all right?"

"That is what my brother said in the dream," Jordan said, still looking down, her voice weak and wavering.

"You dreamed of your brother?"

"I am always thinking of him," Jordan said. "I guess it makes sense I would dream about him."

"Yes, I suppose it does," Bopol said. "What happened in the dream?"

"I was home, but I could not leave the house. My brother had gone, and I was alone, trapped inside."

"Maybe that is how Jorr-Don feels? Trapped?"

She looked up at her friend. "What do you mean, Bopol?"

"You are trapped on our world, but you wish to go home."

"Maybe."

Bopol sat with Jordan outside her tent until the morning. It comforted her that he would give up his own sleep to make sure she was okay.

Perhaps the lure of returning to Earth is what is trapping me, she thought. *Maybe I'm using memories of my brother as an excuse. I know I have everything I need to make a life here on Algoran. Am I afraid of settling down? Is that why I am pushing so hard to go home?*

She looked all around her, at the distant sunrise to the north, at Bopol and at the signs of movement within the tent of Reiban and Zoska. Jordan looked up at the receding night in the southern skies and took a deep breath. She exhaled and stood up.

"Jorr-Don?"

"I am only trapped if I let myself be trapped."

"I do not understand."

"I have a say over this, so I do not have to feel cornered like a beast. Chieftess is right, I have decisions to make," Jordan said. "What kind of life—what kind of *future* do I want? Where do I want it to be?"

"Do you have the answers to those questions?"

Zoska's words came to mind: "Tribe *is* family but not like blood."

My gemta is here. Tribe can be family and *blood,* Jordan thought. *And if I took a mate and had a child, tribe would be family and blood. It all depends on where I want my family—my blood—to live.*

She looked at Bopol, whose concern for her was still evident in his eyes. Then she viewed Reiban and Zoska's tent, feeling a reassurance. They might not be blood but they were certainly family. She trusted each of them with her safety and well-being. They had been there for Jordan and her gemta in a way no friend on Earth ever could have. Only her gemta, brother and torkomm rested deeper in her heart.

"It is not an easy decision," Jordan said, frustrated. "Whatever path I take, people will get hurt. I will get hurt. I will have to leave behind one of my families."

"I think I understand," Bopol replied, slowly and thoughtfully. "I do not envy you."

"Me, either," Jordan quipped with a brief lopsided smile, frustrated but trying to remain optimistic. She stood up and offered her hand to her friend. "Come. We have a long day ahead of us."

6

CHALLENGES

THE ARROW DEFLECTED OFF THE hideskin covering Reiban's left arm, but its impact was sufficient to make him drop his javelin. That forced him to face the charging warrior with merely his bare hands. However, this was Reiban and combat was second nature to him! He leaped up and kicked the warrior in the face, knocking him backwards. Reiban spun around, grabbed his weapon and placed its blade within an inch of the warrior's exposed throat before he could recover his balance.

"By the size of you, I would say you are the leader of this pack, yes?" Reiban breathed heavily.

"If you want to kill me, kill me!" the warrior shouted.

"I would but then the rest of your family would attack mine. We would have to kill you all. Do you want that?"

"You are on Ullvarr land. We protect it!"

"And you have done a fine job. My pack and I are only passing through. We are going to the Southlands."

As Reiban continued trying to negotiate with the Ullvarr leader, one of the Ullvarr women stealthily unsheathed a serrated dagger and carefully eyed Reiban. Zoska saw the action but was too far away to reach her. She turned to Jordan.

"Jorr-Don, aim at the dagger in front of you! Throw NOW!"

Without thinking and trusting Zoska's words, Jordan spotted the dagger and hurled her javelin in its direction with all her might. The would-be-assassin shifted and turned, trying to launch her blade anyway at the same time Jordan's blade pierced the woman's torso and knocked her off her feet. The dagger fell harmlessly from her hand as she collapsed to the ground dying. Jordan's eyes widened in horror. She'd meant only to disarm the woman.

Outraged, the Ullvarr leader slammed his considerable fist into Reiban's chest and sent him flying back. The other Ullvarr took attack postures towards the Mokta hunters. And while the Ullvarr had more people, the Mokta were stronger and better trained. Within minutes, all but a few Ullvarr lay dead on the cold ground while the survivors fled.

"If those three tell the other Ullvarr what happened, we will have no peace in their land. They will attack until we are dead or there are no more Ullvarr," Zoska said.

"Go. Do what you must," Reiban said to his mate.

She nodded and ran after the three Ullvarr with her bow and arrows.

"Some diplomat I turned out to be," Reiban mumbled to himself.

He looked over at Bopol who sat next to Jordan, his arm around her and his expression sympathetic.

Jordan paid no attention to Reiban's words. She sat on a boulder and stared at nothing, her mind replaying the carnage that had just occurred. She bore a fresh bleeding gash on her right cheek, but the rest of the blood spattered on her hair, chest and arms was not hers.

"Keep your breaths slow and deep, Jorr-Don," Bopol soothed. "And know that you are safe with us. We are one tribe and your burdens are our burdens."

She slowly turned her head to face Bopol. The adrenaline rush had worn off, and fatigue set in as she shivered from the cold.

"When we kill a beast, it is to feed the village. There's good in the sacrifice," Jordan said slowly. "But there is *no* good in what we just did. It was a misunderstanding . . . a mistake . . . and now, we have taken someone's brother, sister . . . daughter, son . . . gemta, torkomm."

"The good is that we are *alive*," Bopol replied. "You saved Reiban's life, defended Zoska's mate. You protected your tribe."

"Will that help me face my gemta? Will that help her understand?"

"She will understand," Bopol replied. "And she will be glad that her daughter is still alive."

Jordan sighed. "I know you are right. But those people . . . I killed them. We killed them!"

"It is not supposed to be easy. You will always remember this day."

Jordan saw Zoska running back to join them, her grim task accomplished.

"Zoska?" Jordan said. "Are—will you be okay?"

"I did what I had to," Zoska answered. "I . . . regret it was necessary."

"We must get away from here," Bopol said to Reiban. "The coming snow will hide our tracks."

"I agree. We need to cover at least ten *baas* before we set any camp for the night," Reiban said. "Grab a bite from our food reserves. We'll all need our strength for the trek."

Four hours later, they set up camp in a cave to protect them from the growing snowstorm. Reiban and Zoska had already fallen asleep. Jordan was still awake but had almost no strength. She was laying on the ground, using one of their bags as a pillow. Bopol sat near her, more or less guarding her and the others. His posture near-perfect, he allowed himself to relax some. He was tired as well, but he wouldn't let that get in the way of keeping his pack safe.

"Do you remember the first time you killed someone, Bopol?" Jordan asked.

"Yes," he replied.

Jordan shifted in place and scratched behind her neck.

"How old were you?" Jordan continued.

"Thirteen. A member of a rival tribe tried to kill Chieftess. I stopped them instead."

"Thirteen? That is so young."

She was surprised when Bopol smiled at her reassuringly.

"You are still learning about life here. There is much to love about this world, but life is not guaranteed. Each day we survive is a gift to be cherished."

"I understand. I just . . . I know I have lost something . . . something important."

"You are right. That is true."

Jordan looked at the ground and sighed.

"I will never get it back, will I?"

"No."

Jordan's eyes were heavy with sadness as she turned to look at Bopol. Her lips formed a weak smile. "Thanks for telling me the truth, Bopol."

"Always, Jorr-Don."

Jordan slipped in and out of consciousness the rest of the evening and her dreams were not peaceful.

Hours later, Jordan thought she heard someone shouting. It roused her from her deep sleep. As she turned to look around with bleary eyes, she noticed additional furs covering her and Reiban standing in front of Bopol, gripping the larger Mokta's upper arms and shaking him.

"Squarejaw! I am here to relieve you," Reiban said loudly.

Jordan was apprehensive when Bopol's only response was an incoherent jumble of sounds. She saw him sway a bit in Reiban's grasp, his eyes only slightly open with an unfocused gaze.

"Zoska! Wake up!" Reiban shouted in a semi-panic.

"What is wrong?" Zoska answered, squinting as she turned to look at him.

"Bopol is very ill! He is not as impervious as he thinks," Reiban said. "If we do not warm him up soon and treat his symptoms, he could get the Shilvaba!"

Jordan's eyes widened, and she helped Zoska up. They grabbed what furs and warming agents they could and ran to Bopol's side as Reiban forcibly lowered him to a lying down position. Jordan and Zoska both had to work at straightening out his legs as Reiban started a new fire next to him.

"Why is he like this?" Jordan asked.

"He took two watches and blocked you from the winds with his own body," Reiban said, having assessed the situation.

"Does he already have the Shilvaba?" Jordan asked soberly.

"I do not think so, his eyes have not changed," Reiban said. "But that could happen at any time. We have to get him through the next dayturn. If he survives that without any new signs, he should be all right."

Jordan's thoughts raced, thinking of what she'd learned of medical care on Algoran. Then she replayed memories from her childhood and early teen years on Earth, trying to find anything to save her friend. And she had an epiphany.

"This may seem strange, what I am going to do, but please assist me," Jordan said. "My body's own heat may make the difference between life and death for Bopol!"

"You may be right, Jorr-Don, but I warn you: his skin is like the snow and ice," Reiban said.

"I do not care! He risked his life to protect me. I have to do the same for him," Jordan said, quickly unbraiding her hair.

"Then do it, darkhair. He has no time to waste," Zoska said, already grabbing furs from where Jordan had been sleeping.

If I remember correctly, this is normally done with skin to skin contact, but Bopol needs as much heat as possible. If Reiban and Zoska place furs over me, that will concentrate the heat through my light layer of clothes. That should protect us both a little better . . . I hope.

Jordan laid down on Bopol, who was already lying on his back. She winced in discomfort as she came into contact with his frigid skin, feeling the stinging chill even through the garments she wore, but she didn't let the cold stop her. She turned her head and rested her cheek against his exposed chest, her hair flowing all around her.

"C-cover us both in furs," Jordan said to Reiban and Zoska. "Then sit in front of us to protect us from the winds."

She was relieved to see her friends do exactly as she requested.

"This could take a while," Jordan admitted, still adjusting to the glacial temperature of Bopol's skin, the enemy she was trying to vanquish. "I would l-love to hear some stories."

"Well then, it is your good fortune that you are with us," Reiban replied, shifting to a more positive-sounding tone of voice.

"My mate may have a flair for the dramatic, but he can weave tales like no other," Zoska added, putting her hand on Reiban's arm in a show of support.

For the next hour, Jordan listened to Reiban relate stories of places, people and creatures he had encountered. Next, she enjoyed Zoska sharing the tale of how she had fallen in love with Reiban and what an annoyance that had been when she'd realized it, which made Jordan laugh. Zoska also made it known how deeply she cared for and respected her mate, despite her frequent and spirited verbal jabs at him.

Eventually, they all fell asleep. Jordan had become comfortable on top of Bopol. And the warmth from her body, combined with the heat generated by the furs and the nearby campfire flames, had calmed her and relaxed her hold on consciousness.

A while later, Bopol's face twitched and his eyes opened. He felt Jordan's hair draped across his nose and cheeks. Her head was resting on his chest and she was breathing softly. Her arms and legs were loosely laid across his own and the furs covering them both were thick and warm.

What happened? Why is Jorr-Don—here—on me? he thought, turning his head to see Reiban and Zoska asleep nearby.

He felt a wave of dizziness wash over him and was momentarily disoriented.

I am . . . not well? I remember I was shielding Jorr-Don from the cold. Did something happen?

Bopol suddenly sneezed, startling Jordan from her slumber.

"Hey," she said with a groggy smile. "You are awake!"

"Yes. What—what happened, Jorr-Don?"

Bopol watched Jordan's smile fade as her eyes projected her worries.

"You got much too cold and could have died," she answered. "I tried to warm you with my own heat and told the others to cover us with the furs to help."

"You saved my life!"

"It looks that way," she grinned.

"I . . . am thankful."

"Are you warm enough that I can get up now?"

Bopol considered Jordan's words for a moment.

"No. I do not think so. Will you stay?"

"Okay, but only for a little while longer."

"All right," Bopol agreed. "Can you tell me one of your stories?"

7

HER FATHER'S EYES

WHEN JORDAN LEWIS WAS TEN years old, her father fulfilled a wish. He took her to an amusement park. They spent from morning till night together, waiting in lines, riding roller coasters, eating snacks and enjoying each other's company. Since Kevin worked the night shift as a manager in a twenty-four-seven call center, it was rare for him to have time to spend with his family, especially his children. That was what eventually led him and his wife to divorce.

But on that day, her tenth birthday, Jordan seemed so very happy to be with her father. She exuded the elation she felt through her starry gaze and wide grin as she held his hand tightly, as if she would never let go. There was pep in every one of her steps, a giddiness that would not be denied. This was *her* time with her Daddy. They stayed until the last ride shut down. And then they went for pizza. Even when they arrived home again, as Kevin carried her, asleep on his shoulder, inside the house, a smile radiated from her sleeping face. It had been the perfect day.

Nearly six years later, Kevin had allowed his wife to have full custody of their two children. As much as he loved Jordan and Mark, he knew the best way he could provide for them was financially due to his work hours. And the only way he could continue to do that was to remain at his current job. He felt trapped by the circumstances, but he accepted his responsibilities and their consequences.

Four years ago, Kevin sat wide-eyed and in shock on his ex-wife's couch with his twelve-year old son sleeping next to him. The police had called the disappearance of his ex-wife and daughter a kidnapping, but it felt far worse.

"What kind of kidnapper tears the front door off its hinges?" Kevin demanded.

"You'd be surprised. We've seen all kinds of crazy things," the male detective said. "Do you know if anything is missing?"

"I don't think so, but I haven't lived here in about a year."

"From the looks of it, they were taken right out of their beds," the detective said. "But they must have struggled. Their rooms are a mess."

Kevin scowled. "How can you say that so calmly?"

"Mr. Lewis, from my perspective, I'm glad there are indications they were still alive when they were taken out of here."

"I see."

"You should expect the kidnappers to contact you. They could make a call, a handwritten note or they might text or email you, for all we know," the detective said. "But it'll probably happen in the next twelve to twenty-four hours."

The detective was wrong. No one ever demanded a ransom of any kind from Kevin Lewis. Half of his family was just gone, and he had no explanation. Within seven days, a judge awarded him custody of Mark. His employer allowed him to transfer to day shift to be able to take care of his son. His boss said it was the least they could do for one of their better managers. Twelve months later, Kevin gave up hope and held funerals for his precious daughter and the woman he still loved.

Now on the fourth anniversary of their disappearances, Mark was in his room playing video games and chatting with his friends. Exhausted from a long and stressful day, Kevin had fallen asleep on the couch with the television on. There was a thunderstorm building in the distance and heading their way, but Kevin was oblivious to it.

His dreamlike thoughts were far away. He hovered above the snow-capped peaks of a mountain on a world with a jade-hued sky and two bright green suns. As his view descended, he saw a woman who resembled his ex-wife. She was somewhat different, more athletic-looking than he remembered, and her hair had grown considerably but her face was unmistakable. She was laughing with others, a strange red-skinned people who were shorter and appeared even stronger than her. When she stood up to exit the tent she was in, she used a wooden walking stick. Was she blind?

Then as if a bird, his perspective shifted, and he traveled at great speed down the mountain and through a wide and vast tundra before entering another land. Closing in on a group of four people, he saw that there was a young human woman among them. It was Jordan! She looked hardy and fierce. Her hair long and braided, she was dressed like some kind of hunter or warrior. Within minutes, the traveling quartet encountered a hostile-looking group.

Although the mood was tense, the two groups looked like they might come to some understanding. However, a woman from the larger group pulled out a dagger and stared intently at the smaller group's leader. Kevin saw his daughter throw an intimidating dual-bladed javelin to knock the dagger from the other woman's hand. But the woman turned unexpectedly, and the javelin killed her. It caused the situation between the two groups to explode violently.

Kevin watched in utter amazement at the young woman his daughter had become. He saw her retrieve her weapon and help her comrades fight off the other group, despite being outnumbered. Helpless to intervene, he could only observe as his daughter's group prevailed, having no choice but to kill or be killed. Despite feeling that this was merely a vivid dream, Kevin was profoundly saddened to behold his firstborn child covered in the blood of her foes, the anguish on her face in response to her own actions. He saw that she felt emotionally ripped to pieces by this senseless loss of life.

A loud crack of thunder startled Kevin from his dream. As he sat up, his body laced in cold sweat, he heard rain beating down in sheets against the roof and windows of his home. Lightning flashed nearby, followed by rolling thunder. Disoriented, he tried to reconcile his thoughts with the reality all around him. Did the storm induce his dream? Or had his focus on Janice and Jordan done it as he thought about the anniversary?

His thoughts were interrupted by a mad knocking at the front door. He looked at his wristwatch. It was after midnight.

"Who is it?" he called out, wondering if he was perhaps still dreaming.

There was no answer, only more thunder and rain.

Kevin cautiously walked to the door and peered through the peephole. He saw a woman wearing some dark-colored poncho or jacket and she was completely drenched. Her head was down, and she continued knocking on the door desperately. After gathering his resolve and taking a deep breath, Kevin swung open the door and was instantly lashed by wind and precipitation.

The woman spoke a language he'd never heard before, her voice a harsh whisper. When lightning flashed, he immediately recognized her face and was chilled to the bone.

"Janice?"

She pulled back, not looking at him but turning her head as if verifying a sound.

"Kevin?"

Kevin took her arm and led her inside the house, shutting the door behind them. Then he helped her to a nearby chair and he sat beside her. She looked so much like she had in the dream, it was uncanny!

The rain covering him from head to toe was cold enough, but he was shivering from his own adrenaline rush, the shock of seeing his supposedly dead ex-wife very much alive. This was real as he stood next to her, his hand on her shoulder. They were both equally impacted, neither one expecting to encounter the other. Their breaths were quick and shallow. Both seemed unsure what to say next. Then Janice broke the silence.

"Is—Earth?" Janice asked, clearly distressed. She gripped the chair and seemed to listen intently, her eyes open but unseeing.

"Yes, of course this is Earth," Kevin said, confused. "Where else would we be?"

Her brow furrowed, and her body tensed.

Kevin frowned at Janice's strong accent. How long it had been since she had last spoken English? He also wanted to know something else.

"How long have you been blind?" he asked sympathetically.

"Cycles. Almost . . . four cycles."

"Where have you been? Where's Jordan?" Kevin said, gripping her arm tightly, resisting his own frustration. "We thought you were dead!"

"Jordan . . . oh *ildas ma!* Still . . . there?"

"Still where??"

"Other . . . planet. Algoran."

8

SEPARATION AND WONDERS

THE HUNTING PACK HAD DEPARTED the Ullvarr territory and entered a mountainous region. They had begun their ascent in the early afternoon. Halfway up, the ground began to tremble.

"Landshift!" Reiban shouted to the others. "Secure yourself to something!"

Jordan tried to find a safe spot but nothing looked promising. She saw Zoska latch onto a nearby tree with her arms and Bopol ran towards Jordan to offer assistance. But then, the quaking intensified even more.

"Run! This is a bad one!" Reiban exclaimed. "Scatter! We can find each other once we are safe again!"

The violent shaking began literally cracking the ground. Falling boulders had started deadly rockslides. Each hunter was holding onto their individual bags for dear life, making mad dashes in different directions. All were attempting to survive the raging temblor, not sure if their next move would be their last.

Jordan tried to outrun the crumbling mass of land and stone. Not having the luxury of worrying about anyone else's safety, Jordan leapt over a growing chasm which tore apart the ground beneath her. That pit exposed craggy rock and natural ores as it stretched four feet across and downward at least a dozen meters. She made it to the other side with her bag still gripped tightly in her right hand but landed on her recently wounded left arm. She cried out from the blinding pain then felt herself rolling down a hill, tumbling over countless stones and branches. She came to a rest against a wide tree as blackness claimed her.

Hours later, she awoke to setting suns at the edge of a forest, a far distance from where the pack had been. She checked herself for injuries. There were some new cuts and bruises and her left arm was strained but functional. Miraculously, nothing seemed broken. Landing on her bag had probably cushioned her enough to prevent serious damage.

She called out her packmates' names. But the only response was the howling wind.

They could simply be too far away. Jordan tried to calm herself.

Or they could be dead. I have to focus on keeping myself alive more than anything else. That's the first thing Zoska taught me. Find a safe place, set up my tent, and start a fire, eat some dried rations. Stay alive through the night.

It was miserable going through the motions, knowing what she had to do and following her training. Thoughts of her friends possibly being injured and needing her help or worse, dead from the quake, gnawed at her. She forced herself to chew the dried meat and sip liquid from her water bag. However, she couldn't help but wonder if her rations could be better used to keep the others alive.

Jordan's senses sharpened with adrenaline at the sound of panting breath behind her. She gripped her dagger as the panting turned into a growl.

A zala beast! Fairly young by the sound of him.

Closing her eyes, Jordan used her hearing and sense of smell to determine the exact location of the wolf-like animal as it crouched, preparing to strike. Then with one fluid motion, she hurled her dagger with all her strength. The blade embedded in the zala beast's head, penetrating its cyclopean eye and the brain behind it. The dead creature collapsed in a heap.

Other animals howled in the distance. *This is going to be a long night!*

Before the twin suns rose, Jordan had to slay a poisonous *pidra* snake and two *mosdons* that resembled two-foot long arachnids with fangs and scorpion-like stingers. Fighting the last *mosdon*, she had taken a glancing blow from its six-inch stinger as it sliced across her leg. Now she was bleeding and walking with a limp. Somewhat lightheaded from initial blood loss, she reached into her bag and grabbed some bandaging cloths to prevent or at least slow further hemorrhaging.

I cannot stay here. I have got to keep moving, keep myself from becoming a target for predators and find the others. But where should I look? Back up the hill? Can my leg even make it? Or should I go further into the forest to find herbs for medicine, in case I took in any venom?

Or should I head back to the village and get help?

She looked past the trees into the morning sky.

Gemta, what should I do? What will do the most good?

Jordan struggled to climb the hill but her injured leg started losing strength.

I guess that is my answer. I cannot go up the hill again and I have venom in my leg. So, if I want to live, I have to go into the forest.

Jordan leaned on her javelin and used it as a walking stick as she pressed forward. An hour passed, and she managed to gather a few of the herbs she needed. Her right leg grew numb and she began to feel feverish. After another hour, she had to drag her leg and she was drenched in her own perspiration, despite the cold temperatures. Barely able to focus her eyes, she rested her back against a tree trunk and let herself slide to the ground.

I can't believe this! she thought in English. *I've come all this way and I'm gonna die—alone—on an alien world?? I'm never gonna see my mother, brother or dad again? If the others didn't make it, no one will know what happened to me. Is this really it? Is this all I was meant to do with my life?*

Jordan teetered between waking and sleeping states over several minutes as her fever continued to climb. A hoarse laugh escaped her lips as she closed her eyes.

She had been in danger before but never faced death until now. She realized she might die and could not do anything about it. She wanted to find the Abductors and make them send her and Mom back to Earth. She wanted to see her brother again. She hoped he was all right.

She wondered what would happen to her. Would she just fall asleep and then not exist anymore?

Is there a God? Is He just a God for the Earth or is He a God to the whole universe? I don't think God is gonna be limited to one planet. That wouldn't be a very big God.

Her head swirled, colors blended together until her vision went dark. She knew she didn't have much time left. She wished the others were close, so she could call for help. Then another thought occurred to her.

God, will you help me? Will you let me live? I'm on Algoran and I know I'm dying but I want to live so bad! Please help me!

Over the next few moments, the breeze died down and everything around Jordan became quiet. The insects and other animals seemed to cease their activities and even the leaves no longer rustled. A tremendous peace and stillness surrounded her.

And then Jordan heard a presence in her thoughts. It was a soothing sound and she sensed no deception. Despite her desperate condition, she was no longer alone in this place.

"Would you be willing to spend the rest of your life on this world?"

Jordan attempted to open her eyes but didn't have the strength. Still, she wanted to lift her right arm and stretch out her hand towards the direction of this presence, but her arm only trembled in response. She could feel the beads of sweat on her face and arms. All her senses seemed fluid. She was sinking.

"If it meant never seeing your brother or father again, could you handle that?"

That would hurt but . . . yes.

"Do you truly believe in the power of the God you called out to?"

Is this God?

"Do you believe that God can restore your life to you?"

Yes. Yes, I do!

"Will you trust in that power?"

Yes.

———

Sometime later, Jordan opened her eyes to a blurred world. The breeze had returned, as had all the sounds of the forest. The presence she had encountered was no longer around, although she remembered it vividly. As her vision cleared, Bopol's eyes shone with relief as he turned his head to alert the others.

"She is awake!" Bopol shouted.

"I am alive?" Jordan managed to speak in Mokta, still weak.

"Your spirit nearly took flight many times," Bopol said. "But you are still with us."

Bopol helped Jordan bring a water bag to her lips. She greedily drank as much as she could consume.

"How did . . . how did I make it?" she asked.

"We are not sure, really. It looked like you took enough *mosdon* venom to kill a Mokta my size. Perhaps the bleeding actually helped you or perhaps it is because you are from Errrth."

He put the water bag on the ground within reach, ready to offer her more when she needed it.

"Or maybe it was something that cannot be explained?"

"Yes, that could be so."

Bopol looked like he could barely contain his smile. He seemed thrilled that she was doing better.

"Is everyone else . . . okay?"

"Ask them yourself. They will be here any moment."

Jordan smiled, happy to have survived and been reunited with her friends. When she recovered, she would have many new questions about the direction of her life, now that she had been spared from death.

9

FORK IN THE ROAD

JORDAN CONTINUED TO DRIFT IN and out of consciousness, but she often overheard her friends talking. She would occasionally turn her head to see what they were doing.

"Just watch, Bopol, with all of this attention you have been showing her, she is going to think she is Chieftess now," Zoska teased.

"She nearly died yesterday," Bopol insisted. "I only want her to fully recover."

Zoska probed him with her inquisitive stare. Then she shrugged. "If you say so."

Jordan still had a mild fever, but she was no longer in danger. Her joints ached and she was exhausted, even lethargic.

Of the four of them, Bopol and Zoska had the most medical training from Healer Latas, so they took turns being in charge of her care. Reiban mostly stood guard outside the cave they had taken refuge in or he kept Jordan company and told her stories.

Jordan leaned forward and consumed some broth. After she swallowed, she made a pained face.

"What is wrong?" Zoska asked.

Jordan shook her head with her eyes closed. "Tastes like kimzana root."

Zoska chuckled. "That is pretty bad. But do not worry, your sense of taste will recover, too."

Jordan made a small cough. "I hope so. Have there been any signs of Shilvaba?"

"Relax, darkhair. Despite your fevers, your eyes never changed. You have avoided the shilvaba this time. But the poison and the convulsions they inflicted caused you much harm."

"Where are Reiban and Bopol?"

"My mate is guarding the entrance to this cave. Bopol is getting some sleep."

Jordan sighed. She tried to turn on her side but was too weak. Zoska gently pushed her to a comfortable position.

"I wish this had not happened," Jordan said. "I am keeping us from moving forward."

Zoska stroked Jordan's sweat-dampened hair, a sympathetic smile adorning her face.

"You are still recovering, Jorr-Don. We will take as long as we need to. It will be several more days before you will be able to travel. You need to get your strength back."

Jordan nodded. "I can tell. Thank you for all you have done. To Bopol and Reiban, too."

Reiban entered the cavern. "You are welcome," he said to Jordan. "Bopol has taken the next guard shift, but I will tell him when I see him again."

Zoska gave Reiban a kiss. "I will go get some rest then."

"Dream of me," Reiban hinted.

"When do I *not* dream of you?"

Pleased, Reiban cleared his throat. "And how are you right now, Jorr-Don?"

"I still feel pretty dizzy," she admitted.

"That is not surprising. Between the poison and the bleeding, you lost a lot of your fluids. Bopol has been worrying over you like a *third* gemta! Zoska keeps asking me how you bring that out in people."

"It is a gift, I suppose."

Reiban picked up a clean rag and patted away some sweat from Jordan's forehead and neck. "Your fever persists. That is also why you feel dizzy," he said. "Are you up for a story or two?"

Jordan smiled. "I always love your stories, Reiban."

"Shall I tell you about the Princess of the Fire Kingdom or the Queen of the Ocean?"

Jordan turned her head to look up at Reiban. "The Queen of the Ocean!"

"Ahhh, you have picked a fine tale! No one knows exactly how old the story is but many believe it to be true. Thousands of cycles ago, there was a kingdom beneath the ocean waters and it was ruled by a beautiful queen named Kafilana. She was rumored to be part-woman and part-fish."

"A mermaid?" Jordan asked.

"Merrrr-may? What is that?" Reiban responded.

"It is a word from my world for the type of creature you described," Jordan said. "I cannot think of a Mokta word for it."

Jordan continued listening to Reiban tell his story until she fell asleep. But even in slumber, she would sometimes jerk or shiver.

"I . . . do not understand," she said in English while still dreaming. "Is this God?"

———————

She was vaguely aware of Reiban wiping away the perspiration on her forehead, cheeks and neck. However, she could not distinguish that he was separate from what she was seeing in her thoughts and memories. Everything was blending together in a jumble until she completely lost consciousness.

"Jorr-Don, you need to drink some water," Reiban said.

He helped her lift her head and she gulped down some more of the refreshing cool liquid from the bag.

"My . . . thanks," she replied. "How – how long was I asleep?"

"At least half a dayturn. Your fever grew a few times but it is better now."

"Stubborn poison, I guess."

"No doubt. It is a wonder you live at all," he said. "Tell me, who was it you spoke of while you were sleeping?"

"I was talking?"

"Yes, it was as if you were speaking to someone as you dreamed. The parts in your old language I did not understand. But when you spoke Mokta, you asked them why you had to stay and what they wanted from you."

"I must have been remembering what happened before Bopol found me."

Jordan looked at the cavern ceiling, recalling memories. Reiban leaned forward some, clearly curious.

"What do you mean?" he asked.

"I do not understand it all, so I do not know if this will make any sense if I try to explain. I was given a choice and I made a decision."

"Who gave you that choice?"

Jordan turned her head to look at Reiban. Despite her lingering temperature, she was alert and sober. "God."

"Who is that?"

Jordan stared at Reiban in surprise.

"You mean, you have never heard of—? I guess that makes sense, this is another world. Um, I do not think I can explain right now."

"Perhaps you can explain again when you feel better?"

"I will try. May I have some more water?"

Jordan consumed more of the liquid and then rested some more while Reiban went to check on his mate. Jordan watched him exit the cavern. He gave Bopol a wink as he entered and sat down at her side. She found Bopol's presence comforting.

―――――

Days later, Jordan had regained much of her vitality. When she walked out of the cave with the rest of her pack, the glare from the mid-morning sunlight was almost blinding but still a welcome sight compared to the dark, damp den which had been her refuge recently. Reiban tossed Jordan her bag, which she snatched from the air without issue.

"Do you think you can carry it again? I'm tired of hauling it everywhere," he said with a teasing grin.

"Would you like me to shoulder *yours* as well?" Jordan returned the verbal jab.

"Do not make an offer you are not prepared to follow through with, darkhair," Zoska added as part-joke and part-warning. "He might just accept it."

"My mate has a point," Reiban said. "Though I would not have . . . this time."

"Right," Jordan replied, rolling her eyes but smiling.

The trek forward was more challenging than Jordan anticipated. Bopol matched her pace and accompanied her. She could tell it was as much for her protection as to encourage and keep her company.

"Which way will we be heading?" Jordan asked. "Between the recent quake and everything that happened afterwards, I have gotten completely turned around about where we are."

"Reiban and Zoska are both outstanding scouts. They will figure out the best route to take to get to the Southlands."

"So, you are just as lost as I am?"

At that moment, Jordan stumbled, still feeling somewhat weak. Bopol gently took hold of her and helped steady her. She nodded when she was able to continue.

"I have not been paying attention. Your health has been my only concern," he said.

"I am sorry that I worried you so much," she replied.

"Chieftess sent us as a pack for this reason. We can divide tasks and do what we are best at. Reiban is a good leader and Zoska watches out for him."

Jordan picked up on his unspoken hint, turning her head to look at him as they walked.

"So, you are watching out for me?" she smiled.

Bopol nodded. "And you would do the same for me."

"Yes, I would."

Bopol smiled back at her. "Now you understand."

Jordan nodded. "So, what am I good at?"

"You are good at hunting . . . and now, surviving."

Jordan's thoughts drifted back to her near-death experience. She mentally replayed it all again in a matter of seconds. Her smile disappeared.

"What is wrong? Did I say something to upset you?"

"No, Bopol. It is just . . . I have changed again. It happened after I killed the Ullvarr and now this, when I almost died from the poison. I am different inside, I can feel it."

"Is that bad?"

Jordan stopped for a moment and looked at the ground. Then she peered ahead of them.

"No. I feel like, somehow, this was meant to happen. I guess I wonder what kind of person I will be by the time we get to our destination and face the Abductors."

"At least these experiences have not dampened your enthusiasm," Bopol said with a smile, patting Jordan on the back as they resumed their trek.

In response, she side-hugged him. "With companions like you, Zoska, and Reiban, I feel like I could conquer anything!"

She reluctantly let go of him and pulled back. Bopol gave her another smile.

———

By early afternoon, the path before them split in two directions, winding away from one another, each potentially a way through the challenging mountainous terrain ahead. Reiban looked forward in one direction and Bopol looked in the other. After a few minutes, they rejoined Zoska and Jordan.

"Zoska and I will follow the path that leads to the east," Reiban said. Zoska nodded in agreement.

"That leaves myself and Jordan to follow the western path," Bopol responded. "Good."

"In two days, if your path still seems good, then light a fire and use the dried leepaj leaves to turn the smoke blue," Reiban suggested. "If at any time, the way is blocked or too dangerous to continue, turn the smoke of your fire red."

"What if both our paths seem good?" Jordan asked.

Reiban smiled. "If that happens, I will decide. If I believe the eastern path is safest, I will light a blue smoke fire in response to your signal and you will join us. If I do not, then we are on our way to join you and should meet in three to four moonturns."

"Agreed," Bopol said.

Zoska approached Jordan to give her a parting embrace, smiling.

"I would wish you well, but you are with the squarejaw. He will keep you safe," Zoska said.

"I know. Just as I know you will protect your mate."

Zoska chuckled. "My mate can defend himself quite well. But yes, I—how do you say it? Hm, in Mokta, I would say 'I defend him always' but in your old language, what would the saying be?"

"You have his back?" Jordan said in English.

"Havv hiz bakk! Yes! I havv hiz bakk!" Zoska said, clearly pleased.

"Be well, Zoska," Jordan chuckled.

"Until we meet again," Zoska said, hugging her friend.

———

Jordan picked up her bag and joined Bopol, who was ready to leave. Zoska watched them head westward until they were no longer visible to the naked eye. Reiban had been observing Zoska with a mixture of amusement and concern.

"You really do act like a second gemta to her," Reiban said.

"Since her own gemta cannot be here, I have to act in her place," Zoska replied.

Reiban checked one of his bags to make sure he had refilled their two water bags. He did so as they continued walking.

"Does she worry you so much?" Reiban added.

"You already know how dangerous this mission is," Zoska replied. "How many times have we all nearly died, Jorr-Don most of all?"

"We risk death waking up each morning and starting a day."

"That is normal risk under the protection of the village. Out here, we court death and invite it to dinner."

Reiban started to laugh, then realized his mate was being serious.

"Do you think we should convince Jorr-Don and Bopol to head back to the village?" he asked.

Zoska chuckled. "And miss all the fun? We are hunters! What would we do without the risk?"

Reiban kissed his mate. "You are a madwoman."

"And that is why you chose me."

Reiban nodded. "Yes. No one has fire like you!"

Zoska grinned in response to that.

Half a day passed. Jordan and Bopol stopped and set up camp for the night. She roasted some vegetables and meat for them.

"We made good progress today," Bopol said between bites of savory vegetables.

"Do you think this is the better path?" Jordan asked.

"It is too soon to tell. It may seem that way now, but we will know more tomorrow."

She turned over the vegetables and checked the meat. Momentarily satisfied, she returned her gaze to Bopol.

"You are wise," she said. "Let us be sure, or *more* sure, anyway."

Bopol looked up at the clear night sky and the three moons. A meteorite burned up as it blazed between two of the satellites.

"A falling star!" Jordan exclaimed. "Where I come from, that is supposed to be good lu—a good sign."

That surprised Bopol. He lifted an eyebrow and one side of his mouth curled with intrigue.

"Your people make stories about the stars, too?" he asked.

"Yes. We have names and stories for the planets and constellations, just like the Mokta," Jordan said. "Not only is a falling star supposed to be a good sign, some people believe that if you see one, close your eyes and make a wish, it will come true."

Bopol smiled. "Did you make a wish?"

Jordan returned his smile and gently put her arm around him. "I did not have to. I am with a good friend sharing a hot meal. What more could I wish for?"

Bopol looked at Jordan then back at the sky. "And you say I am wise?"

10

TRUST

IT HAD INITIALLY LOOKED LIKE the western path was the quicker and safer way to proceed. Then, fierce winds started a rockslide that could have easily become an avalanche. Hearing the danger in time, Jordan rushed them both out of the way. Bopol's momentum, however, took him over the side of a cliff. He had been fortunate to land on a ledge, despite it being unstable. Even so, it had given Jordan time to reach him.

She held onto the frozen rock face with all her might while stretching her hand towards Bopol to help pull him up from the fragile perch he was on. There was a gap between the two of them, more than two feet across, which she couldn't close. Inspiration struck, and she pulled her javelin from the strap across her back, held it below the blade and aimed the staff end towards her comrade, who leaped to grab onto it. Gripping her weapon in one hand with all her might, she hauled herself up with her free hand and legs to the next plateau, along with a very grateful Bopol.

"I think you have actually grown stronger, Jorr-Don!"

"Maybe you have just lost weight," she said with a grin.

They were now standing on a more stable portion of the mountain, above the devastated area they had just escaped.

"We both know that is not true," he replied, laughing. "Why do you and your gemta have trouble accepting praise?"

"Modesty is prized among my people?"

"What is modd-ess-tee?"

"It means humble in our language," she said.

"You are being ironic. Why would you pretend to be humble when that's not how you feel?"

"'What are you talking about?"

"I saw the pride in your eyes when you felt you were strong enough to pull me up. And you *should* be proud!"

Jordan blushed. "I guess a part of me is still holding onto customs from my world. But I do not need to do that anymore."

"Your life is here now," Bopol said. "You have earned your place on this world and among the Mokta."

That gave Jordan pause. She gave a sideways glance to Bopol and decided to take a chance by opening up to her friend.

"What am I, Bopol, besides a huntress? Besides Mokta?" Jordan asked sincerely. "On Earth, I thought I wanted to be an actress someday."

"Ak-Tres? What is that?"

"It's like being a storyteller but you are one of many people sharing the tale. Each person pretends to be a character, it helps bring the story more alive for everyone."

Bopol looked like he was trying to comprehend what she was saying but was still confused.

"So, you wanted to be a special kind of storyteller?" he asked.

"Um, more or less. But I wanted it for the wrong reasons. I thought, if I was that kind of storyteller, I could become famous, have wealth and make everyone love me," Jordan said. "But then I was brought here, where being an actress does not mean anything. The machines that let actors be seen by many people at the same time—they are called—"

Jordan couldn't help but notice the hopelessly lost expression on Bopol's face. He was clearly trying to comprehend what she was talking about. But without common experience and knowledge, she may as well have been speaking in English.

"Anyway, those things do not exist on this world. And storytellers have a different role here," Jordan said, smiling and blushing in a self-deprecating way. "I had to let that dream go."

Bopol brightened at the opportunity to offer a response.

"On Algoran, you may not become wealthy as a storyteller, that is true, but you could gain fame within the village," Bopol said. "I think you could become a good storyteller."

"Thanks, but I do not want to be that kind of storyteller anymore," Jordan replied. "So, getting back to my first question: What am I?"

"Why are you asking these questions? You seem different since—"

"Since I nearly died?"

Bopol nodded.

"Yeah, I guess I am," Jordan continued. "I got a second chance at life and I am looking at who I am in a new way. I was always my gemta's daughter or my brother's older sister. Now I am a huntress. But that does not feel good enough anymore. I want to know who *I* am!"

Bopol looked sympathetic. His sincere smile was disarming. Jordan could see the respect in his eyes, that he was trying to understand and relate to her.

"You are an intelligent and resourceful woman who could do anything she wishes," Bopol added. "You are kind, generous . . . and beautiful."

"You think I am beautiful, Bopol?"

"Yes. I have always thought so, ever since you and your gemta arrived on Algoran."

That surprised Jordan. "I was a weak, spoiled brat back then."

"What is spoy-uld bah-rat?" Bopol asked.

"I'm sorry, I used the other language again," Jordan replied. "I meant to say I was immature, like a child in a teenager's body. I did not understand many things, so I took a lot for granted."

"Ah," he said knowingly. "You were faikamsa. Yes."

"Above us all? I suppose I thought I was. Everything I knew was back on Earth, except for my gemta. I could not accept that so much of what I knew was gone, completely out of reach," Jordan said. "The truth is, I was terrified. When you have been faikamsa, losing everything is about the worst thing that can happen to you."

Bopol continued to listen, occasionally nodding his head in understanding.

"Why were you like that back then?" he interjected. "You are not like that now."

Jordan took a moment to make sure she was thinking in the Mokta language, so she would speak in it. The Mokta had a lot of trouble understanding English.

"I think I became angry when my parents no longer wanted to be mates," Jordan said. "They still cared about our family and each other but it was painful for them to be together. My father left our home and moved away, even though he still communicated with me and my brother. He sent payments to my gemta to help her afford our needs, but he did not live with us and I missed him. I did not understand how he could abandon us, why he did not make things right with my gemta."

"Is this kind of separation between mates *normal* on Errrth?"

"Yes. It happens a lot."

"My parents, Chieftess and my torkomm, they do not always act friendly to one another. Sometimes my torkomm angers my gemta, or she angers him. The burden of leadership can make Chieftess seem cold and far away," Bopol said. "But they are mates, and nothing can dim their love."

Jordan smiled at that. She was happy for his family.

"Your parents are *chimtaksa!*" she exclaimed.

"'High mountain?'"

"They are steady, reliable. They will be together a long time, like a high mountain."

"You are chimtaksa also, Jorr-Don."

The comparison humbled her, and she didn't feel worthy of it. Bopol meant every word he was saying but that made it even harder to hear. Since arriving on Algoran, she had made many mistakes. To be compared to someone like Chieftess or even Healer Latas made her uncomfortable, even while she appreciated the sentiment behind it.

"No," Jordan said. "But maybe someday, if I follow your parents' example."

"I am sure that is true," Bopol said.

Jordan looked at Bopol for a minute and then giggled.

"What?" Bopol said, surprised.

"We just spent all that time talking about what a faikamsa I was, but you are a son of Chieftess," Jordan said. "Why are you *not* faikamsa?"

Bopol smiled. "My gemta was not always Chieftess."

"But your torkomm was Chief, right?"

"No. In his younger days, my torkomm was a hunter like my gemta," Bopol said. "My gemta's uncle was Chief before her. There was war between the tribes in those days. While she, my torkomm and I were away to hunt, a large battle happened. Her uncle's family was killed, including her parents. The elders made my gemta Chieftess."

"That is incredible!"

"The elders had to teach my gemta how to be Chieftess. She had to learn the entire history of our people," Bopol said. "It took more than a few seasons. And in that time, my gemta vowed that her offspring would be ordinary children of the tribe, not faikamsa."

"And you are not, that is true," Jordan said. "She is a great Chieftess. You are a good son, a good man."

"Thanks, Jorr-Don."

Jordan looked at the land around them, the paths on all sides which they might take.

"So, should we move forward, Bopol, or give up and rejoin the others?"

"I think we should be bold and move forward."

"I like how you think!" Jordan said, slapping him on the back as she stood up. She offered him her hand. "We shall move forward then."

He smiled and took her hand in his, rising to join her.

11

SNOWFIRE

IT HAD TAKEN ANOTHER DAY for Jordan and Bopol to make their way past the area damaged by the rockslide. Their food and water supplies began to run low and the weather grew colder as they ascended the western route through the mountains. But they were in relatively good spirits. They had passed the time by sharing stories about childhood, hunter training and their friends, Reiban and Zoska.

The daylight quickly faded, so they found a safe, defensible position and set up their tents. Despite the difficulty in navigating around and over the rockslide debris since daybreak, Jordan wasn't as exhausted as she thought she'd be. In fact, she was restless. Bopol started a campfire and was already roasting vegetables to make a simple soup for their evening meal. Jordan sat on the ground a few feet back from Bopol. She found herself staring at the way the firelight reflected off of his physique, how rugged and handsome his face was and the way his hair was braided.

"Do you know any of the legends of the Mokta mountain?" Bopol asked Jordan.

"I know the one about the Ice Faeries and the Mountain Stream!" She noticed that he nodded in recognition but did not look up from turning the vegetables.

"Do you know any others?" he asked.

"No. I am sorry," she replied.

She watched him step back from the flames and walk closer to her, sitting at her side.

"It is all right," he continued. "I learned many tales when I was growing up. We had storytime three days out of the week and Chieftess told them very well."

"I would love to hear you tell stories!"

"Very well, Jorr-Don. Tonight, I will tell you the legend of SnowFire."

"'SnowFire?'"

"Yes. Long ago, a Mokta discovered the mountain that would eventually become our present home. He ascended it, walking past the trees, bushes and flowers seeking the peak. He wanted to claim the mountain for the Mokta and create a new tribe there. But as he thought he saw the peak in the distance, his eyes beheld what looked like a blue flame. Intrigued, he changed his course and followed his curiosity towards this strange flame."

She scooted a little closer, fascinated.

"Did he reach it? What was it?" she asked.

"That was the odd thing. Whenever he got close to the flame, it flickered out. But seconds later, he would spot it in another location, each one a little further from the peak. Still, he was now determined to find this flame and discover its secret. He pursued it for hours!"

"But he did not give up?"

"Of course not. He was Mokta! And he realized that whatever this flame was, it was trying to trick him. So, he plotted to outsmart the flame."

She wrinkled her nose in frustration as Bopol stood up to go check on the vegetables.

"How did he do that?" Her fingers dug into the dirt. She did her best to remain patient while he set the vegetables aside and started to make the soup base. It smelled wonderful, the combination of seared vegetation and spices. But she wondered if he was intentionally taking his time just to tease her.

"Since the flame was clearly trying to distract him from reaching the peak, he ignored the flame and ascended back up the mountain," he resumed. "And out of the corner of his eye, he looked behind him. Now that the flame knew it was being ignored, it began following him. Sometimes it would appear before him, trying to distract him again but he continued to pay it no attention. When he was mere feet from the peak, the flame spoke to him in his language."

"What did it say?" she asked.

"It asked him to stop. He turned around and it was a tall slender female in a red gown. Her eyes were filled with the blue flame and her hair was the same color as the flame. She had pointed ears like him but more pronounced. And she was the most beautiful being he had ever seen. He did not tell her that, though. He asked why she wanted him to stop, why was it so important that she would go to so much trouble to lead him away from the peak?

"She told him that she was the Spirit of that Mountain. If she allowed the Mokta to reach the peak, he could claim the mountain as his and she had to see if he was worthy of that. If he was easily distracted, foolish or stupid, he would chase the flame until he got too frustrated and he would leave, as others had before him. But if he was strong and brave, he would find his way to the top and make his claim."

Jordan rested her hands beneath her chin, captivated by the tale.

"So, did he go to the top?" Jordan asked.

"He asked the Spirit her name. She said it was SnowFire. And then he did something unexpected."

She returned her hands to her lap and slightly lifted her head. "Really? What?"

"He humbled himself and asked if she would take his hand and walk to the peak with him. She was so moved that she said yes, and they took a leisurely stroll the rest of the way. When they reached the top, she said that, in addition to his claim, he could ask any one thing of her and she would grant his wish."

Jordan grinned as she leaned forward in anticipation. "This is getting good, Bopol! What did he wish for?"

"He asked her to be his mate. That was all he wanted. In his eyes, her beauty, conviction and passion for the mountain had won his heart. At the same time, his wisdom, determination and attractive appearance had won her heart as well. She gladly granted his wish and their children became our ancestors."

She leaned back on her hands but her eyes never left his. The remaining campfire light danced around them.

"Wow! What an incredible legend! And you told it so well."

"There is one more part to this legend," he added.

"Seriously? There is more?"

"That Mokta was the first Chief. He and SnowFire had ten children during his lifetime. Their oldest son became the second Chief and so on. But after many years, First Chief became old and died. SnowFire was consumed by grief because she now had to spend the rest of time without her love. Her mourning was so profound that she broke into many pieces, precious SnowFire gems which were scattered throughout the mountain. And each Chief since then has kept one of the SnowFire gems as a symbol of their power and authority, the eternal bond between the Mokta and the Spirit of the Mountain."

Jordan found her eyes becoming misty, yet she was still amazed and thrilled by Bopol's story.

"That is so sad, but also beautiful!" Jordan said. "So, even Chieftess has one of these gems today?"

Bopol nodded in response. She was grateful when he poured the soup into two bowls and presented one to her. She hadn't even realized how famished she was.

———————

After they finished their evening meal, Bopol opened a pouch attached to his belt and removed a small object. It was a thin wooden circle overlaid with dark blue cloth and a glowing sapphire-like gem was mounted on it. In addition, there were two drops of red blood dried onto the gem.

"A SnowFire gem?" Jordan gazed in amazement. "But why do *you* have this?"

Bopol handed the object to Jordan but she was too intimidated to accept something belonging to the Chieftess.

"I do not understand, Bopol! What are you doing?"

"As I told you, since the days of legend, the SnowFire gem represents the authority of the Chief or Chieftess," Bopol said. "The blood is from Chieftess. It is the same as her being here with us."

"Why would that be necessary? Why would she send it with you and why would you give it to me?"

"Will you grant my wish, Jorr-Don? Will you become my mate?" Bopol asked looking completely sincere and serene.

12

TWO HEARTS

"JORR-DON, MY HEART IS FOR only you. Do I have yours?"

Jordan had always found Bopol attractive, brave and noble in his own way. Since beginning this quest, they had grown closer than ever. He had provided friendship, support and a good sounding board for anything on her mind or heart. Now he stood before her with the apparent blessing of the Chieftess in the form of a SnowFire gem in his hand. He wanted to marry Jordan and share a future with her.

"I . . . I am honored, Bopol, but I am also confused. Why me? Why is your heart mine? What did I do to deserve it?"

"You have been true to yourself and your convictions. You overcame your fears and losses and became part of this tribe. And as you proved not long ago, you are a survivor."

"That did not exactly happen overnight."

"No, of course not. But you are brave and passionate, you have become strong. I have watched your struggles and I have no illusions about you. I admire and respect you. My heart has grown to love you."

"Why tell me this now? We— we might not come back from this mission I have set us upon. Even if we survive these different lands and their peoples, we do not know what to expect from The Abductors!"

"That is precisely why now is the right time."

"I do not understand?"

"If we are to face death together, I do not want to have any regrets . . . any unspoken questions or missed opportunities. I truly love you and I want to be your mate. I can die happy, knowing I at least made my feelings clear and asked for yours, no matter what you decide."

Jordan stood there nearly overwhelmed by Bopol's words and feelings. She couldn't help but smile, even though she didn't know yet what her answer would be.

"I have never heard anything so beautiful in my life, Bopol. No matter what I decide or how things go on this mission, please know that I will carry your words in my heart forever."

"You do not have to make your choice right away," Bopol said, obviously touched by her response. "This will change both our lives from now on."

Jordan nodded and smiled nervously at Bopol before looking up at the night sky. She let her gaze slide down to the SnowFire gem lying next to where Bopol sat. She thought about her childhood and her life before Algoran, the trauma of being brought here and all she had experienced on this world. On Earth, she had felt like a child, even into her teen years. She had been sheltered, even spoiled in some ways. Aside from her parents' divorce, she had led a good life but there hadn't been any real challenges. In contrast, everything about Algoran had been a test of endurance, courage or strength. But with those trials came equal rewards, knowing she had overcome her fears and doubts, even if there were physical or emotional scars as a result.

She had been given a second chance to live. The Voice had asked her: "Would you be willing to spend the rest of your life on this world?"

She considered whether it had been God who spoke to her or one of His angels. She also wondered if God knew that Bopol would ask her to be his mate. It made her ponder the possibility that Algoran was supposed to be her home and not Earth.

More words from the The Voice circled within her mind: "Do you truly believe in the power of the God you called out to? Will you trust in that power?"

She looked at Bopol. He had never babied her or gotten in the way of her struggles. He had supported her as a friend, someone who genuinely cared about her. And now he loved her.

She didn't know how she felt. She knew they shared a friendship and the hunt. But those by themselves were not enough. They could not be considered justifiable reasons for spending a life with someone or possibly bearing their children. She knew she needed a stronger validation for her choice. She didn't want either of them to regret it, as her parents had.

Even when he wasn't looking directly at her, she saw the look in his eyes and comprehended the depth of his declared feelings. Tears began welling within her eyes.

In the distance, Tisa birds screeched, and Jordan turned to behold them flying together in formation. They weaved throughout the night sky, graceful yet swift and precise.

Could that be me and Bopol? Could we make each other happy and be in-sync like that? Is this just another challenge, like facing a Sasstonn for the first time or climbing a mountain? When I faced each test, I did not think about it, I knew what I had to do and I went for it.

She closed her eyes and put her hand on top of her chest. Her heart beat a strong but fast rhythm and she listened to the music of her pulse. When she opened her eyes again, she had her answer.

"Bopol," she said, turning to face him. "Come here."

She was pleased at how quickly he closed the distance between them, staring at her in innocent anticipation.

"This is my response," Jordan took his hands and kissed them. "My heart has answered, and it is yours."

Bopol smiled. He pulled out the Snowfire gem and put it in her hands. This time, she accepted it.

"What do we do now?" Jordan asked.

"This is a Jakalat. As you guessed, the blue crystal is a SnowFire gem. And this is Chieftess' blood."

"Why did she do this?"

"As I said before, this blood is the same as Chieftess being here. If we add our blood to hers, we will be joined as mates forever in the eyes of the tribe. It will also join you to Chieftess and my family."

Jordan gasped. "But that also means . . . ?"

"Yes," Bopol said smiling. "If anything happens to Chieftess and me, *you* may become Chieftess."

Jordan was somewhat frightened by that possibility. It meant committing to staying on Algoran.

The words from before echoed in her thoughts: "Would you be willing to spend the rest of your life on this world?"

Peering at Bopol, her heart stirred, and her worries melted away. Looking at the warmth in his eyes and smile inspired confidence and acceptance. This tenderness and joy was nearly overwhelming . . . a longing she'd never experienced before. It could be satisfied only with one person, his presence. It was wonderful and terrifying simultaneously.

It was then that she comprehended how deeply in love she was with Bopol. It felt so good to acknowledge the beauty of that simple truth. As she stood close to him, she felt as if she were floating off the ground, a smile never leaving her lips.

I just want to explore this relationship with him. Is that wrong of me?

Then she looked down at the silver ring on her finger, the one her father had given her.

But what about the mission? Jordan wondered. *We've come so far. What about the lives we—I—took? Was it for nothing? I will not accept that.*

"We have to go on, keep moving forward," she said. "I don't want the lives that were lost to be in vain."

"I understand," Bopol replied. "We will see this through to the end, along with Reiban and Zoska."

Jordan took off the ring and placed it in one of her bags. Then she faced Bopol once more.

"Good," she responded. "Even so, let us begin our life together . . . as one."

She pulled her dagger from its sheath on her belt and made a quick cut across her palm. Then she let a few drops of her blood drip onto the SnowFire gem. Bopol extended his hand and she gave him the blade. He made a similar cut across his palm and let his blood drip onto the SnowFire gem. Then without prompting, they put their hands together and stared into each other's eyes.

"Thank you for joining your life to mine, Jorr-Don of Errrth!"

"For better or worse, in sickness and in health, through thick and thin," she said, still in the Mokta language.

"A saying from your world?"

"Yes, for when my people become mates."

"How does it end?"

"'Till death do us part.'"

Bopol smiled. "It is a good saying."

Jordan nodded. "Yes, it is. It's usually followed by another saying."

"Oh? And what is that?"

"'You may now kiss.'"

And that's exactly what they did.

13

SHARED MEANING

JANICE HAD NOT SPOKEN TO her ex-husband in nearly five years. Now she was in the living room of the house he'd bought in the interim, their sixteen-year old son upstairs in his room, completely unaware that his mother was even alive. The storm continued to rage as if to share with the region all the suffering Janice had endured while away from the world of her birth. The house shook and rumbled with thunder, rain lashing against every surface as winds howled and shrieked.

She heard Kevin's heavy footsteps as he walked from the kitchen to the living room with two cups of liquid that were shaking slightly on their saucers. She was sitting on the couch and drying herself with a large towel which Kevin had given her. She startled slightly when she heard the clinking noise of one of the sancers making contact with the glass coffee table in front of her, then she took in a whiff of air.

"Chamomile?" she asked, pronouncing it a harsh "kahm-MOmeel."

"Good sense of smell," Kevin said.

"I . . . rem—rem—*know* it," Janice replied with frustration. Her words were stiff, unfamiliar. It added a level of anxiety to the awkward nervousness she was already feeling.

"You should probably get out of those clothes, Janice, you'll catch a cold," Kevin said. "You're welcome to anything of mine. I can bring down some from my room. You could change in the bathroom?"

She understood about half of what Kevin was saying. He was speaking perfectly normal English, but she could no longer process all the words.

"Thanks, Kevin."

She heard him walk across the carpet and ascend the stairs. Moments later, a door closed and she counted the fourteen steps Kevin took returning to the ground floor. She felt his gentle touch on her shoulder before he pressed some thick and soft clothes into her hands, which were resting on her lap.

"It's just a long-sleeved flannel shirt, some black sweatpants, and pair of socks," he said. "But they should fit and it's the best I can do for now. If you take my hand, I'll guide you to the restroom to change."

"Okay," she responded. "Thanks."

Janice had forgotten how strong his grip was as he helped her stand up. Her pride wanted to resist his attempt to guide her but she reminded herself that she did not know this house. She needed his help.

"It's not far," he added. "About twenty feet in the direction we're going. Then we're going to enter a hallway and take a right, okay?"

"Okay," she repeated.

"Will you need any help once you get to the bathroom?"

"No. I can put on the clothes. Thanks."

"Sure. I'll hang up your wet clothes to dry after you're done."

"Okay."

Once Kevin closed the door, Janice felt around in front of her and quickly located the sink counter. She dropped the clothes to the floor and leaned against the counter with both hands. She took in several deep breaths and released them slowly.

"Easy, Janice," she said in Mokta. "You are alive, you are all right. Safe. You can figure out the rest later."

She took off her drenched clothes and put them in the sink. Holding onto the counter with one hand, she reached down and felt around on the floor until she found the new clothes and grabbed them. She put on the shirt first. She was briefly confused when it opened in the front but remembered that Earth shirts often buttoned together. It took a couple of minutes but she recalled how to correctly line up the buttons with their corresponding holes. When she put on the sweatpants, she had to tighten them slightly to keep them from falling or hanging down in an odd way.

"Janice, is everything all right?" Kevin called through the door, his concern evident.

"I am . . . fine," she replied in English. "It is . . . time taking."

"Oh, okay. Well, let me know if you need any help."

"Okay," she answered with a slight grumble.

Handling the socks was perhaps the most awkward part of her clothes transition. She located the toilet by feeling around, made sure the lid was closed, and then sat down on it. She wasn't sure whether they were inside out or not and really didn't care. She pulled them over each foot and up each leg until they felt snug.

"I . . . am done," Janice said.

"May I come in?" Kevin asked.

"Yes."

She was still sitting on the toilet lid when he opened the door and entered. She heard him wring out her clothes over the sink. He carefully stepped past her and she could hear him lay the clothes across a surface.

"It'll take a while for them to dry hanging on the tub but that's probably safer than running the dryer in a thunderstorm."

Janice had to remind herself what a dryer was. "Okay, Kevin."

"Your, um, boots will take longer. What are they made of?"

"Sasstonn—skin."

"Sasstonn? What's that?"

"An animal."

"Hm, okay. Well, take my hand. I'll get you back to the living room."

She reached out and felt him take her hand. He helped her stand up and led her back to the couch. He sat down beside her.

"Help me understand this again, Janice," he asked calmly. "What happened to you and Jordan the night you vanished?"

She took in a deep breath. "We were . . . ab—ab—taken—at night."

"Taken? By whom? Who took you?"

"No faces. Suits . . . hel-mets," Janice said. *"Pozwi grem!* Fought them! They—*kojpa*—strong. Took us . . . Algoran."

"The other planet?"

Slowly and very carefully, Janice did her best to choose words to describe Algoran and its colder, harsher climate. She went into great detail about the sympathetic and friendly Mokta tribe who had adopted her and Jordan. She explained how she and Jordan were able to eat and drink the foods of that world and survive that first severe winter. And she related how the same had cost her sight and nearly her life. She shared how the healer, Jordan, and Chieftess had worked so hard to keep her alive.

She wondered out loud if maybe her illness had robbed her of her memories of English but somehow made the Mokta language easier. Neither of them had an answer for that. Kevin had listened patiently.

"It *is* hard to believe, Janice, but I trust you," Kevin said. "As amazing as it all sounds, it's the only thing that explains your absence, your changes, your clothes, and the language thing."

"Kevin is . . . wise," Janice said with a hint of a smile.

"This may sound strange, too, but before you showed up, I was having a dream about you and Jordan."

"'Dream?'"

"First, I saw you in that village you described. The people looked just like you said. You were blind and walking with a stick," he said. "And then I saw Jordan. She was with three other people, all dressed alike. Two men and another woman. They were a long way from the village."

Janice gasped. *"Ziss Kalla!"*

"Excuse me?"

"Forgive. Mokta words. They mean living dream," Janice said. "What Kevin see . . . real. Jordan, hun-ters go . . . look for . . . Abduktorz."

"'Abductors?'"

"Mokta call them 'Qui Tol', 'strange ones.' Jordan call them Abduktorz."

"I see. So, I was seeing you two on that other planet through a dream? How could that be possible?"

"Mokta . . . belief. We . . . tied to . . . ones we . . . love . . . in ways . . . not seen. We know they . . . hap-py . . . sad . . . or if in dan-ger. Dream . . . them. Say more? You . . . see Jordan?"

"There was a fight between Jordan's group and some other people. A male from Jordan's group spoke with a male from the other group."

"Reiban."

"Ray-ban? Like the sunglasses?"

"He . . . talk to . . . people," Janice continued. "Good at . . . talk."

"Some woman from the other group was about to throw a dagger at Ray-ban but—"

Janice could sense Kevin's reluctance to continue.

"Kevin? Tell."

"Jordan threw a spear at the woman," he said a moment later. "I think she was trying to knock the dagger out of her hand but the woman turned, and the spear got her."

"Kill?"

"Yes. Everything went crazy. Jordan's group held them off. Actually . . . they killed all of them."

"*Kushaba!*" Janice felt a chill run down her spine. "How Jordan? She . . . no kill people . . . ever."

"In my dream, she was—Janice—she was devastated. It was like watching something out of a movie. Jordan had some pretty bad cuts though she wasn't very hurt. But she was covered in the blood of the ones she had to fight. One of the males was trying to calm her down."

"Tall? Like . . . Jordan?"

"Yeah."

"Bopol. Chief-tess son. Jordan friend."

"That's when I got woken up by some thunder. I didn't see any more. I'm sorry."

"With Bopol . . . Jordan . . . fine," Janice said, sounding relieved. "Jordan safe."

"He's that protective of her?"

"Dream is true . . . of Jordan and Mokta. Family are connected. We know what happens to each other."

"Hey, don't change the subject. What's the deal with this Bo-Paul guy?"

"Good . . . strong . . . loves Jordan. Wants Jordan to be . . . mate."

"An alien wants to marry our daughter?!"

"Kevin, calm! Mokta good people."

Janice heard light footsteps on the stairs. The footsteps slowed until they stopped about halfway down. She heard a creak as the person leaned on the stair rail.

"Mom??"

"Mark?" she replied, turning her head towards the sound.

Janice had not expected her son's voice to be so deep and strong. But he had been a pre-teen when she'd been taken. He was past puberty now. She wished she could see him, trying to imagine how tall and handsome he had become.

———

Kevin found himself wishing he'd taken time to go upstairs and prepare Mark for this or at least warned his son. Instead, he was torn by the shock, confusion, and re-lived grief he saw on Mark's face. Since he couldn't shield him from these feelings, all he could do was speak the truth.

"Yes, Mark. This is your mother," Kevin said, attempting to remain calm himself. "Come on down."

"Dad, how can Mom be here?" Mark asked, his speech still pained and his face pale. "We buried her and Jordan years ago!"

"You thought . . . us dead?" Janice asked in disbelief.

"After a year with no leads, we—I had no choice," Kevin said. "We both needed closure."

"Under-stand," Janice said tenderly.

"One of you gonna tell me what's going on?" Mark demanded, his eyes teary.

Kevin stood up, turned, and looked at his son. He could see the confusion and hurt in Mark's body language, how the young man refused to move. It would be difficult to explain in a way Mark would accept, especially since he was still trying to process it all himself.

"Your mother and sister didn't die, Mark," Kevin said. "They were abducted."

"Someone kidnapped them? We didn't get any ransom demands," Mark frowned in skeptical confusion. "Why is that?"

Janice stood up, using her hand to help balance herself against the couch and turn around. He watched as she looked in the direction of her son's voice.

"Taken . . . far away," Janice said.

"Why do your eyes look like that? And why do you sound like that?" Mark said. "I know you're my Mom but why are you so different?"

"People . . . change," Janice said, mustering a smile for her son. "Eyes . . . blind."

"You can't see? What happened?" Mark said, now sounding concerned.

"Sick . . . was . . . ve-ry sick," Janice said. "Survived but . . . not see. No sight."

Kevin felt helpless. He understood his son's skepticism as Mark gazed at his mother, probing for any sign of deception, any weakness in her story. Janice wasn't faking her blindness, but he could tell his son wasn't sure. Kevin watched Mark study Janice's frustration in choosing her words, the difficulty it was causing her. He saw his son's uncertainty transform into compassion.

"It sounds like you've been through a lot . . . Mom," Mark said. He looked around expectantly. "Where's Jordan?"

"Far away," Janice said, somewhat wistfully before she allowed herself a smile. "But . . . free . . . strong . . . happy."

"Will she come back home like you?" Mark asked.

"I hope . . . yes."

14

TOGETHER

JORDAN SAT ON THE EDGE of a cliff and enjoyed a scenic view of the lands awaiting her. Her untied wavy hair flowed freely in the soft cool breeze. She clasped both of her arms in happiness and amazement at her decision. Two days ago, she had chosen Bopol as her mate and their lives were now entwined. She didn't regret the choice at all, but she knew it would have far-reaching consequences, both positive and negative. She reached up and touched the SnowFire gems, which Bopol had crafted into a pair of earrings, to remind herself that this had really happened and wasn't a dream. They were mates now and all would eventually know this.

She heard movement behind her: a quick and light-footed dash past the trees. Whoever they were, they were good, but the terrain was too rough for their efforts to go completely unnoticed. Jordan smiled.

"Hello, Zoska," Jordan said without turning around.

"*Wostaz*, Jorr-Don! I can never sneak up on you!"

"That was a good try," Jordan said. She stood and turned to face Zoska. "I am glad you saw our signal fire, I have missed you."

Her friend immediately noticed the earrings. "SnowFire? Chieftess must have—wait, does this . . . ?"

Zoska sprung a grin that spread from ear-to-ear. She pulled Jordan into a bear hug. When she released her, Zoska was still holding her by the shoulders.

"You zala beast! When did you and the squarejaw become mates? This is wonderful!"

"Two moons ago."

"Oh!" Zoska said with some surprise. "Plenty of time to be alone together!"

Jordan smiled knowingly and looked down blushing. Then she returned Zoska's gaze and nodded.

"As it should be," Zoska said, looking up at her friend with admiration and joy. "Perhaps by this time a cycle from now, our children will play together."

Jordan raised an eyebrow at that. She knew her friend would not say such a thing for no reason.

"Zoska, are you pregnant?"

Zoska took Jordan's hand and pulled it towards her belly. Jordan spread her fingers across her friend's abdomen, feeling a very slight curve as she ran her hand downward. Jordan grinned and then hugged Zoska.

"I am so happy for you and Reiban!" she said. "But will you be able to continue on our hunt to find The Abductors?"

"My child is many months from birth, Jorr-Don. We will reach the Southlands long before then. Besides, no one is more dangerous than a huntress gemta defending her own."

"Especially if she is Mokta!" Jordan said, winking.

"There, you see?" Zoska said with pride. "I will be fine."

Jordan put her hand on Zoska's shoulder and looked in the direction Zoska had come from. "Reiban must already be boasting of how strong and talented his son will be," Jordan added.

Zoska chuckled slightly and looked at Jordan with amusement. "I am sure he is boasting to your mate as we speak, but I think he wants a daughter."

"Really? That's a surprise."

Zoska looked back towards the woods and rested her hand on her abdomen, contented.

"I am always surprised when it comes to Reiban," Zoska said. "It is one of the reasons I chose him."

Jordan's eyes widened a bit at that. "I thought he chose you?"

"That is what I *wanted* him to think," Zoska said knowingly.

Jordan nodded with a grin, pointing her index finger at her friend, her thumb aimed skyward. "I knew there was a reason you are my best friend!"

Jordan watched as Zoska pulled back and tilted her head with mock offense. "You mean besides my keen intellect, charming wit and prowess as a huntress?"

"Sorry, Mama!"

Zoska raised an eyebrow at Jordan's reference. "Mah-mah? Why do you call me that?"

"If you have to explain the joke . . . " Jordan said, sighing.

"You are not making sense, Jorr-Don."

"I am sorry. It is an Earth term for gemta. It was a compliment."

Jordan was relieved to see Zoska relax with new understanding, patting Jordan on the shoulder.

"Ah. Your Errrth language is strange," Zoska said. "But you speak Mokta like you were born to it, so I forgive you."

"Thank you, Mama!"

At that, Zoska playfully smacked Jordan on top of her head. Jordan lifted her hands in mock surrender, smiling and laughing with her friend. They sat down and drank from the water bag.

"How excited are you about having the baby?" Jordan asked.

"I am eldest child in my family. I helped my gemta raise my brothers and sisters," Zoska said. "You would think that would make me wary of having children so soon. And yet, I have wanted my own for years. When I chose Reiban, I could have focused solely on the hunt, waited a cycle's time. Custom allows for that with hunters."

Jordan crossed her arms, curious.

"But you did not want that?" Jordan asked.

"No. And truthfully, neither did Reiban," Zoska said, smiling. "I think he wants to raise an army just from our brood!"

"If anyone could do that, it is you two!" Jordan said, laughing.

"I know my limits," Zoska said, shaking her head. "If we were like Menjah and Hosp back home, I would never have a moment to myself!"

Jordan started counting on her fingers.

"Did they not stop at seventeen?"

"No. Hosp is carrying one or two more," Zoska said. "But Menjah is the best fisherman in the region and when Hosp is not chasing her brood around, she is a fine craftswoman."

Jordan raised an eyebrow and showed her amusement through a lopsided grin.

"And apparently, the gemta of the next generation of Mokta?" Jordan added.

"The village could do worse. She and her mate love our tribe almost as much as they love their children."

Jordan sat down and nodded. She looked nervous and a bit reserved now. Zoska sat down beside her.

"It is still difficult to imagine myself having a child someday," Jordan said, closing her eyes and shaking her head. "Then again, I did not imagine Bopol asking me to be his mate, either."

"Was it a hard choice to make?"

"No," Jordan opened her eyes and looked up at the twin stars in the sky. "My heart had already made its choice. I just listened to it."

"You have become wise then, my friend," Zoska said. "I made Reiban pursue me another month. He could have chosen another in that time."

"There was never anyone else for him," Jordan responded with a grin.

"I know that, and you know that, but he is stupid," Zoska said with furrowed brow. "Brave and decisive but stupid."

That surprised Jordan. She leaned forward towards Zoska. "Why did you choose him then?"

"He has a magnificent heart, Jorr-Don. *No one* could ever love me as he does!"

Jordan and Zoska heard footsteps approaching near them. They turned to see Bopol and Reiban carrying bags and looking happy.

"My mate and the gemta of my child speaks true!" Reiban shouted.

"He has spoken of little else for the last two hours," Bopol said in a loud voice. "The gemta of my child this and the gemta of my child that! If he weren't carrying the bag with all the food for our mid-day meal, I would have killed him for talking so much!"

Reiban lightly punched Bopol on the right shoulder, smiling in jest.

"You will be the same way on the day you learn that Jorr-Don bears your first, Squarejaw!" Reiban said.

Bopol stopped and turned his head to look at Reiban. There was no humor in his eyes.

"Do not call me squarejaw."

Reiban was not intimidated and his smile never diminished. He rested his hands on either side of his waist. His stance was humorous but there was an underlying defiance in it as well.

"I have called you that since we were all small," Reiban said. "I do not intend to stop now!"

"I would make you cook all this food—"

Zoska stood up and pointed a finger at Bopol accusingly.

"Please do not, Bopol. I wish to survive to have this child," Zoska joked.

"I caught the food—" Reiban said.

"Not by yourself," Zoska interrupted.

" . . . so someone else should cook it."

Jordan stood up as well, her hands at mid-level in front of her as she tried to diffuse the building tension.

"I will cook it," Jordan said. "In honor of the new life Zoska bears."

"Well said!" Bopol said, picking up on Jordan's cue.

"Or . . . perhaps lives, in case you—" Zoska added as she looked at Jordan, earning a playful return smack on the head from her best friend.

"Until I learn otherwise, you are the only gemta between the two of us," Jordan said, smiling. "And now, you are going to help me make this food, Mama!"

Bopol and Reiban looked at each other in confusion and mouthed the word Mah-mah. Both men shrugged.

A short time later, most of the seasoned meat was cooked into a stew which they shared. And the remainder of the meat was packed away for a future meal or snack. The hunting pack voraciously devoured their meals until Zoska was not the only one with a slightly bulging abdomen. Jordan and Bopol went for a walk, hand in hand, to enjoy the scenery and talk.

"I hope Zoska didn't trouble you with her teasing," Bopol said. "I think she just wants someone to share in her experience. I remember when my gemta carried some of my younger siblings. It was challenging for her at times."

"No doubt," Jordan said. "But Zoska knows I will support her, regardless of whether I share her condition."

"Does the thought trouble you?"

Jordan caressed his cheek and smiled. "Of possibly being pregnant right now? It would not be the best time, but I would not be upset."

"You want to find The Abductors first and get your answers," Bopol added, a subtle disappointment hid in his tone.

"Now listen here, my mate," Jordan put her hands on his shoulders and looked into his eyes. "Our lives, yours, mine and any children we may have someday, are more important to me than this mission or any goals I had before we became as one. Do not ever forget that."

Bopol's expression relaxed and he smiled back. "You are right. I did not mean to doubt you."

Jordan sighed and embraced him, resting her head on his shoulder. "You could not have doubted if I did not give you some reason to. Forgive?"

"Always. Love."

"Love."

15

WHERE YOU CAME FROM

HER FIRST FEW HOURS HOME had been emotionally exhausting. As Janice slept, her mind returned to the moments before she found herself on the world of her birth once again.

On Algoran, it didn't often rain on the mountain where the Mokta lived. It snowed frequently, and the wind was always blowing, but in the summer months, there was the occasional rain shower or storm. This evening, she had been invited to learn how to craft wooden children's toys from a villager named Hosp. When she heard the woman's voice as she drew close to the marketplace, Janice stopped.

"Hosp!" Janice said, holding out one arm to request a hug.

"Januss!" Hosp replied enthusiastically.

When the other woman, who was a little younger than her, walked over to embrace her, she heard the woman's quick, heavy footsteps. In the embrace, Janice felt the shorter woman's long hair which flowed freely down her back. She could also easily tell that Hosp, who had always been plump, was very pregnant.

Janice heard how actively Hosp interacted with her many children, who surrounded her and ranged from toddlers to teenagers. There were intermittent sounds of wood being carved by Hosp using sharp tools, yet all the while Hosp would acknowledge one child's request, answer another child's question or tell two others to shut up and mind their manners. Some of the youngest ones merely craved her attention, calling her name, asking for a hug or a kiss or just crying.

"When are you due to be delivered?" Janice asked.

"Oh, these two should be here by harvest time, Januss."

Janice felt around with her walking stick until it made contact with one of the chairs Hosp had made. She sat down in the chair and turned to face her friend's voice.

"Sixty moonturns, huh?" Janice said. "May I ask you something else?"

"You just did," Hosp replied with amusement. "Let me guess, you want to know why I have such a large brood?"

"I am sure you get asked that a lot."

"Yes, but I do not mind giving the answer," Hosp said. "I came from a small family, just me and my parents. We lived on the edge of the village then."

Janice noted Hosp's voice trail at the end of the last word followed by silence. The younger woman's breathing slowed and deepened, as if she were trying to remain calm. Then she sighed.

"This part is always hardest to tell but it is important," Hosp said. "A rival village sent a force to wipe out our village and take the mountain. My torkomm heard them coming and sent me and my gemta to hide in the woods. But they saw us, and my gemta took an arrow intended for me. Before she died, she told me to keep running and hide. My grieving torkomm held off half of their number, making enough noise in the fighting to alert our village before the enemy overwhelmed and slew him. I hid but I saw it all."

"Hosp, that's horrible!"

Janice felt Hosp put her hand on her arm, as if to silently reassure her.

"Why? My parents protected me and the whole village," Hosp said proudly. "However, even as a child, I realized that if I had died, my whole family would have been destroyed that day. So, I vowed to myself that when I was old enough to take a mate, I would have such a large family that it would not be possible to kill it."

Janice put her hand on top of Hosp's, which was still softly holding her arm.

"I do not know what to say," Janice said. "You are an amazing woman. I only have two children."

"There is no shame in that. I envy you, actually," Hosp said warmly. "You have children on two worlds! Your family will go on as well."

"I suppose that is comforting," Janice said with a small sigh. "I miss my boy every day."

Janice felt Hosp release her grip on her arm as the younger woman turned to pick up one of the small children. Janice heard the little girl's precious giggle.

"I understand. But your daughter is a good huntress and young woman," Hosp said. "She will choose a mate soon and give you grandchildren."

"I just want her to be happy. Sometimes I wonder if she is really happy here."

Hosp snorted. "Do not worry, Januss, she is happy. I have watched when she returns from the hunt. There is fire in her eyes and contentment with her fellow hunters. She is strong, fast and healthy, a credit to your family."

Janice nodded slowly. She heard Hosp exhale with some exertion as she carefully set her daughter down.

"Bopol asked Chieftess and me for blessing with Jordan," Janice added.

"Bopol is also strong and has a good heart," Hosp said with excitement. "He will make a good mate. He will be wise one day, maybe even Chief. I know why Chieftess gave blessing. Jorr-Don is like another daughter to her."

Janice nodded again. This time, she smiled as well.

"I gave blessing, too. I like Bopol. If anyone can stand toe to toe with my girl, it is him."

"Well said, Januss!"

A few minutes later, Janice heard Hosp put her crafts away. Then she said goodnight and left with her sizable family. Janice decided to take a walk through the village. And that's when the shower began. At first, it was a peaceful mist then a light rain. When the thunder grew close and the ground became muddy and slick, Janice started heading back to seek shelter in her hut.

But as Janice neared what she knew was the edge of the village, she heard a shrill humming sound and felt a radiating heat close to her. For an instant, there were no other sounds besides the hum and she no longer felt the rain or the wind. It was as if she was inside a warm cocoon. Then that sensation was gone and the storm was worse than ever! The rain-infused winds lashed at her and the thunder was close enough to reverberate through her. Janice knew she was in danger!

She felt around with her walking stick and was surprised that the terrain was so flat. She had been on an incline only moments ago. The ground was grassy like a field, not the well-tread rocky trails that led to and through the village. Her stick tapped against something solid—a wooden fence! She walked around it and found the side of a building.

Janice knew something wasn't right. She also knew there were no huts this size and definitely none made of wood, as this one was. She wondered where she was.

As the storm raged on and she was getting completely soaked, it became imperative to escape. She found what seemed to be an entranceway and knocked repeatedly on the wooden door. About a minute later, she heard it unlock and open.

"I'm sorry to trouble you but I need shelter from this storm, at least until it's over, please!" Janice said in Mokta, her voice a harsh whisper in her desperation.

Whoever had opened the door didn't immediately reply to her request. She picked up the scent of a cologne she vaguely remembered. A man's cologne. But how was that possible? The man acted a bit confused, as if not sure what to say. Instinctively, Janice lifted her head in the direction of the man's movements, even though she couldn't see him. However, he could see her.

"Janice?" the man asked hoarsely.

English? He spoke English, and his voice! It can't be! Wait! That strange humming and feeling surrounded by warmth, was that the portal again? Did The Abductors send me back to Earth? If so, why?

And what do I do now?

16

DIPLOMACY

JORDAN HAD NEVER SEEN ANY of the Kastadi people before, only heard Mokta legends about them during this journey. As her hunting party walked past the tall wooden entrance gates to their village, she was both impressed and intimidated by the sheer size of its inhabitants. The children were taller and stronger-looking than her, and the adults were easily ten feet tall. Their skin was light gray, their hair was close-cropped and dark red. They had tusk-like canine teeth and adorned themselves with various tattoos and piercings.

The hunting party was led by one of the Kastadi guards, a female in her late teens or early twenties, to the center of the village where its Chief and two elders awaited them. Bopol walked in a stately manner at Jordan's side while Reiban and Zoska walked ahead of them following the guard. They all stopped several feet ahead of the Chief when the guard went down on one knee bowing. The hunting party bowed their heads in respect to the chief as well.

"These strangers seek counsel with Chief Teebor the Mighty!" the guard proclaimed.

The words were in the same language as the Mokta but with a different dialect and inflections. Still, even Jordan understood her.

The Chief was attired in a brightly colored robe made of what looked like snakeskin and wore a headband made of silver with a ruby-like gem in its center as his crown. He was an elder, perhaps in late middle age, and fairly stout but sufficiently muscular that he probably still participated in combat. His advisors, a male and female, both looked significantly older. They were observing the hunting party very closely but said nothing.

"What is your business here, Mokta?" the chief demanded.

"Mighty Chief, my name is Reiban. My hunting party seeks only safe passage through your lands."

"Where are you going?"

"The Southlands."

"Why?"

"We hope to find information from the people there to aid our comrade, Jorr-Don," Reiban said, pointing at Jordan. "She was brought to us from afar."

Teebor nodded his head. "She does not have the eyes of a Mokta. But she is tall, for one of you, and fair to look on. She is trying to go back where she came from?"

"She wants to know why she was brought here. But she is mated to Bopol, son of Chieftess," Reiban said.

"Ah! So, she has a brain, too. That is good to know."

"Yes, Great Chief. Please know, whatever you say, we will do. The Mokta wish only peace with Kastadi."

The Kastadi Chief considered Reiban's words carefully and spoke privately with his advisors before responding. He approached Reiban with a neutral expression.

"I cannot grant you passage through our lands, Mokta," the Chief said.

"May I ask why?" Reiban said, his head bowed.

"In hunting The Ones Who Bring, you seek death. The Southlands are all but deserted now and The Ones Who Bring have mighty talismans to open the sky and bring fire," the Chief said. "You yourself said this Jorr-Don has joined your Chieftess' family. She has chosen her path. She should walk it. I regret this, but it is for your protection . . . and hers."

"We will do as you have said, Great One," Reiban said, his displeasure evident even underneath his kind and respectful voice.

As Jordan slowly turned to leave, she noticed Chief Teebor and his advisors watching the Mokta hunting party. She was trying hard to walk with dignity despite her obvious disappointment. She overheard as the Chief's male advisor spoke with him.

"She will make a formidable Chieftess someday," the advisor said.

Jordan tried not to react but the advisor's words startled her.

"You saw that as well?" the Chief replied. "For speaking no words, her eyes shared much."

"You made the right decision, Mighty One."

Bopol offered his arm for support to Jordan but she batted it away. Her angry stare told him "Do not. I can handle myself right now," so he let her be. They continued heading out of the gates.

"Do we have any alternatives?" Zoska said.

"Not really. We have no ship to travel the Eastern Sea and we don't have enough food and water to make it past the Western Wastes," Reiban said. "The Central Plains are vast, and we dare not anger the Kastadi. We have had peace with them for twenty generations and they significantly outnumber us."

"Then that is it," Jordan said, her eyes downcast. "We go home. At least we tried, so . . . thank you."

"Jorr-Don—" Zoska started to say.

She was interrupted by three ear-piercing screeches that happened simultaneously. As Jordan turned, time seemed to slow to a crawl. Astonished and terrified, she saw three black dragons descend from the nearest mountain, heading straight for the Kastadi village. Each dragon was taller than any Kastadi with wingspans of twenty feet. As they neared the village, they unleashed black fire from their mouths which incinerated anything, and anyone, it touched!

"Deathwings!" Horror laced Zoska's voice. "A whole family of them! Run!"

"No!" Jordan said resolutely. "I saw those giants. They are strong but slow. If we do not help them, they will all die."

"You are suggesting four small Mokta hunters are better suited to take down Deathwings than a village of Kastadi warriors?" Reiban asked.

"That is exactly what I am saying!" Jordan replied, pulling her javelin from her backstrap as she smiled.

"I like how you think, woman!" Reiban answered with a smile of his own. "Let us go before there is no village left to save!"

With speed unique to the Mokta, the hunting party closed the gap between themselves and the Kastadi. Working as a team, Zoska found cover and shot arrows at the closest Deathwing to distract it while Reiban and Bopol assisted the villagers in attacking the other two Deathwings. Jordan ran and leaped onto the closest dragon as it dove low to avoid Zoska's arrows and climbed its back as it tried to shake her off. Undeterred, she shoved her dual-bladed javelin into the creature's left eye then ripped it back out. A nearby Deathwing saw its mate's distress and shot fire at Jordan, who flipped backwards in mid-flight and grabbed onto the dragon's tail with both arms and legs. Jordan released a sigh of relief at the success of that maneuver.

Then she steeled herself. This fight was far from over. When the other Deathwing unleashed more flames, Jordan leaped forward, bounced off the dragon's back and landed at the base of its neck rather abruptly. Then, one-handedly, she impaled the Deathwing's head, piercing through its brain.

As the dying dragon fell to the ground, Jordan blindly leaped away. The nearby Deathwing apparently saw an opportunity to destroy the little one that had killed its mate. Jordan squinted her eyes and tried to protect her head with her arms, knowing it would do little good against a dragon's flames.

A huge boulder struck that Deathwing in the head and broke its neck. Jordan fell into a strong pair of arms. It was jolting and she nearly lost consciousness, but she was alive. When she was able to open her eyes again, she was staring into the face of Chief Teebor, who looked relieved.

"I see why Kitranor's son favors you," the Chief said. "You are as insane a hunter as his gemta was!"

"I will take that as a compliment, Chief," Jordan replied through her aches and wooziness. "Is your village safe?"

"Yes, thanks to you hunters working with our warriors," the Chief added. "Our losses are few when they could have been total. Buildings can be rebuilt."

"How are . . . my hunters?"

"They fared better than you, child. Now rest."

Jordan woke the next morning with the rest of the hunting pack at her side. They had been allowed to stay together in a large hut. Jordan had a lot of bruises and some deep cuts from riding the dragon, but nothing was broken.

"You are determined to have the most battle scars, aren't you?" Zoska said. Her tone was lighthearted, but her eyes indicated a deep concern for Jordan's well-being. "You already got your mate, you know! You should stop trying so hard."

"Save your words, Zoska," Bopol interjected. "Jorr-Don is no longer collecting scars. She is just reckless!"

"You have him trained well already, Jorr-Don. Now he speaks for you."

"He knows me well," Jordan replied with a pained grin.

"Taking on a Deathwing by yourself was beyond foolish," Reiban said. "But you did manage to impress the Chief."

"I did?"

"He is letting us have access to the Kastadi Central Plains, but not until you recover," Reiban said.

"Why did he change his mind?"

"He said you reminded him why the Mokta and Kastadi have had peace for so long. The Mokta defend the Kastadi when no one else will and the Kastadi will always return that kindness. I am also pretty sure he was amazed by you personally."

"It just goes to show, once again, that a weapon is the best diplomat," Zoska said.

"In the hands of the right hunter," Reiban agreed.

"It looks like we will be enjoying Kastadi hospitality for few weeks," Bopol added.

"A few weeks? Was I really hurt that badly?" Jordan asked.

"Had the Chief not interfered, you would have died," Bopol said. "But holding onto a moving Deathwing did nearly as much damage."

"On the other hand, you earned an awe-inspiring nickname. You are now Jorr-Don, Deathwing Rider!" Reiban said. "You will be famous among the Kastadi forever."

"And our people as well, once I tell Chieftess," Bopol suggested.

"You too, husband?" Jordan asked, wincing. "My mother is going to get gray hairs from this story!"

"She will be proud of her daughter," Bopol replied. "Like she always is."

Jordan smiled. Bopol's words were true. Saving the Kastadi village had felt good for its own sake. Now, the hunters' good deed had restored the possibility of finding The Abductors and obtaining the information they were after. It gave Jordan hope and that was more healing than any bandage or salve.

17

ADJUSTING

THE LAST MONTH HAD BEEN difficult for the Lewis family, especially Janice. Out of necessity, she had accepted her ex-husband's offer to live with him and their son, at least until she adapted to being back on Earth. At her request, Kevin had been slowly and quietly reaching out to relatives and friends to tell them Janice was alive and doing well, all things considered. But she didn't want many visitors, only her parents, siblings, and closest friends. Janice did not tell any of them about being taken to another world, only that she and Jordan were abducted and taken far away, that both of them had escaped but were separated. They had not had contact with Jordan since then. That raised many questions which they did their best to answer.

Kevin had spoken at length with his son, in Janice's presence, about how they would broach the topic of Janice and Jordan to others. They had agreed to keep things as simple as possible. This was the only way they could resume some form of a normal life together.

Prior to Janice's mysterious return, Kevin told her it had taken years of heartache, but he had eventually gotten used to her not being a part of his life. Now she was back but blind, English was no longer her native language and she was accustomed to a tribal culture. Aside from her appearance, she was almost a stranger. And she needed much more of his attention than ever before.

The simplest things were the most frustrating for Janice. She had known her way around the Mokta village and the mountain. She had traversed those paths with her walking stick, familiarized herself with the area's scents and patterns. Now, she was learning this new house. Occasionally, she still got lost or bruised from bumping into things.

The outside world was an unknown now and it scared her. The air smelled different, the sounds of the birds and insects were different. She had forgotten how loud domestic canines were.

Janice had frequent indigestion, with occasional constipation and nausea, from eating the prepared foods of Earth. Even the store-bought vegetables and fruits seemed to lack the taste and texture of those grown in the fields of Algoran.

She also became irritated with most technology after not using any for so long. She had gotten used to relying on her senses, strength and communicating directly with people, even strangers. Before Algoran, she had gone online to websites and clicked on products to buy them. Thinking back to those times, Janice could understand the convenience of internet shopping but there was no adventure in it, no fun. It took away the human experience of bartering, asking direct questions, and the opportunities to make friends.

Janice preferred going to clothing stores with Kevin or Mark, having them or the sales people describe the attire before she tried on each piece. She was still getting used to being taken to the grocery store with its mass selection of inferior foods.

Kevin had purchased some CDs to help her re-learn the English language but that was a different challenge. Repeating what a recording said helped restore some of her English vocabulary and familiarize her with word pronunciations. But it gave her almost no context, so the words themselves didn't mean much, even when she remembered them. She felt like a barbarian attempting to communicate in her old language.

In contrast, Mokta was a simple language that flowed like water off her tongue. She decided to ask her teenage son, Mark, to help her with English conversation. In turn, she taught him some Mokta common words and basic phrases. Janice was surprised that he was eager to learn her adopted language. This helped in several ways. It allowed her to re-bond with her youngest child and gave them motivation to assimilate both languages. The more they learned, the better they could understand one another. Over several weeks' time, they had already made good progress.

"Compliment," Mark said, reading a word from a flash card.

"'CommPluhMint," Janice repeated.

"Right! Now use it in a sentence."

"She gave him a . . . CommPluhMint."

"Yes! That's great, Mom! Your turn."

"Hooshah."

"Hoo-shaw?" Mark repeated, prompting a nod from Janice. "Meat?"

"Right! Now . . . sen-tence."

Mark leaned his head back and put his index finger to his temple. "Moy rip ku veus hooshah!"

"Yes, Mark! Funny!"

"What did I say, in English?"

"You never . . . serve us . . . meat!"

"Very cool, Mom! In a year, you'll be speaking like a native again."

"Year? You mean like cycle?" Janice asked, motioning her hand like a planet traveling around its star.

"Yes, exactly."

"Maybe so . . . son."

Janice's thoughts drifted back to her college days and the last time she'd had to learn a language.

During her sophomore year at the community college, twenty-year-old Janice Markov sat down on the steps outside Building 2A and sighed in frustration. Her best friend, Cora Johnson, sat down next to her.

"What's got you down, sunshine?" Cora had asked.

"I can speak Russian, some Hungarian, and English. Why am I so awful at French? I mean, isn't French supposed to be easy?"

"Who told you French was easy?"

"Hannah Cole."

"Oh, you got tricked, Jan! Hannah and her family spent four years in France before they moved here."

"What? The next time I see that girl, I'm going to blister her ears in Russian!"

"Make sure to tell me when, I'd love to see that!"

"Do you think it's still early enough in the semester to change courses?"

"What would you take instead?"

"Russian, of course!"

"Isn't that kind of like cheating?"

"If anyone asks, I'll just say I'm learning more about my family's old tongue?"

"That works for me. I certainly won't tell."

The two stood up and began to walk across the campus toward a wooded area, passing other students along the way. It was a cool and overcast autumn day.

"So, who's the new guy I've seen you with? He's cute!" Cora said.

"Who, Kevin? I met him in Calculus and we started studying together."

"And going on dates?"

"Maybe a little more than dates."

"Jan, really? You're into each other that much?"

Janice nodded and sported a goofy grin. "I wouldn't be surprised if he popped the question soon!"

"Seriously? And if he did that, how would you answer him?"

"I'd ask him how many kids he wants."

"What? Wait, I don't get it."

"If he says he doesn't want kids, my answer is an automatic no. If he says he wants a lot of kids, then it's no again. But if he says anywhere between one and three, then I'll definitely say yes!"

"You had that much figured out already? You're scary, Jan."

"I know what I want. Is that wrong?"

"No, I suppose not."

"Don't you know what you want in life, Cora?"

"Sure. I want to get my degree and start my career as an English teacher. If I find Mr. Right along the way, that's a bonus."

"And kids?"

"You can have your little bundles of joy, Jan. I think I'll wait, if I have any at all."

"Your loss."

"If you say so. Wanna grab some lunch?"

"I can't. I'm meeting Kevin for lunch in an hour. Rain check?"

"Sure. But now, every time I see you, I'm gonna be expecting to see a ring on your finger."

Janice had playfully slapped Cora's shoulder as she walked towards the campus parking lot and her own car.

The memory faded. Janice smiled at how her reverie had made her feel.

"What is it, Mom?"

"Good thoughts. An old friend. Cora."

"Do you mean Mrs. Randolph?"

"Yes. Can you . . . call her for me? I . . . miss her . . . but still am . . . learning English. You tell?"

"Okay, Mom," Mark said. "I'm friends with her daughter. I'll call their home number."

Janice heard the sounds of Mark dialing the number on his mobile phone. Then she heard the phone ring three times before there was a click and someone answered.

"Hello, Mrs. Randolph? This is Mark Lewis. I, um, actually I wanted to speak with you."

Mark proceeded to explain her circumstances to Cora Randolph as he had been told to before. Janice couldn't tell what the other woman said in response but a couple of times, she heard excitement and amazement in Cora's occasionally raised voice. She heard Mark explain that his mother had changed, that she was now sightless and had some challenges with speaking. But he also conveyed Janice's request that Cora visit her as soon as possible.

"Mom, she wants to speak with you," Mark said. "Is that . . . okay?"

Janice nodded. He placed the phone in her hand.

"H . . . Hello?" Janice said, sounding like "heh-low-wuh."

"Jan, is that you?!"

Janice could hear the tears in her old friend's voice. She inhaled before speaking again.

"Yes. It is me," she said.

"We thought you—I mean, we went to your funeral!" Cora exclaimed. "This—how is this possible?"

"Long story."

"Wait! What about Jordan??"

The thought of being separated from her daughter gnawed at Janice. "She is . . . not here."

"Is she all right?"

"Yes."

Janice mentally pushed past her distress and tried to focus on the positive. "Come. Visit me . . . Co-ra?"

"Of course! I wish I could zoom over there right now but I'll make time tomorrow morning. Is ten o'clock okay?"

Janice tried to remember time-telling on Earth, that there were twenty-four hours in the day. She understood that her friend wanted to visit her the next morning, that was satisfactory.

"Yes. See you . . . then," Janice replied.

"All right. It's so good to hear your voice again—"

Janice smiled as she remembered Cora's nickname for her. "'Sunshine?'" Janice added.

"Yeah. Good night—oh, and Jan, I can't wait to see you!"

"Night."

Janice ended the call and handed the phone to her son.

"Are you okay, Mom?" Mark asked.

"Yes, I am fine. It was good to . . . speak with her," she said with a smile. "I had forgot-ten how much . . . she once meant to me. She will vis-it after the sun rises."

"She's in for a shock."

"About my . . . changes? Yes. But Co-ra and I . . . know each oth-er . . . beyond language. She was . . . like a sister to me."

"Then things should go well."

"I hope so."

18

IN ABSENCE

IT WAS EXTREMELY RARE FOR the Chieftess of the Mokta tribe to lead a search party but this day, Kitranor would not be denied. Her closest friend, Januss, gemta to Jordan, was missing! The rains were fierce, but she barely noticed them, her sights were on the surrounding woodlands, anything that would give a clue to the whereabouts of the fair-skinned woman from Errrth. For a Mokta, Kitranor's night vision was unparalleled. If her friend was injured or taken by some enemy, Kitranor would find her.

Well into the night, one of the tribe's scouts brought a traveler to the Chieftess. He was from the Ullvarr lands and friendly.

"Bim of Ullvarr, can you tell the Chieftess what you told me?" the scout asked, pointing towards the Chieftess.

"Chieftess, I passed by your mountain not long before the rains started. I saw an unusual woman in Mokta clothes, a woman without sight and hair was like the vee flowers," Bim said. "I was respectful and asked what she was doing outside the village. She said she was taking a walk. I thought nothing of it and wished her well. She did the same. But soon after, there was a strange sound and a bright light like a tall circle coming where she had been walking."

"Go on," Kitranor urged.

"I thought it the work of the Heelos and got as far away as I could! I didn't slow down until your scout found me," Bim said. "When he said a woman like the one I had seen was missing, I knew I had to help. She was kind and fair. May the Twin Stars guide her if the Heelos have her!"

Virtually every tribe and people on Algoran were aware of the Abductors and had their own name for them. The Mokta called them Qui Tol, the Kastadi called them The Ones That Bring, and the Ullvarr referred to the mysterious ones who used circles of light to bring and take as the Heelos.

"Thank you, Bim. The Mokta will remember your kindness," Kitranor said. "Peace and safe travels."

The Chieftess watched the older Ullvarr man walk away until he faded into the distance. Rain began to fall and Kitranor couldn't tell whether it was mocking or perhaps merely trying to console her.

"What shall I tell the search party, Chieftess?" the scout asked with his head and eyes lowered.

"We will return to the village and sound the alert," Kitranor said. "Our sister is not out here, and we do not know what those fiends want. We must all be on watch for them to come back. They may look for Jorr-Don now, thinking she is in or near the village."

"You think it is Qui Tol?"

"It cannot be anyone else," Kitranor said. "Perhaps they have finally sent Januss home to correct their mistake."

"It was not a mistake, Chieftess." Latas walked up from behind her. "You know she and her daughter were sent to us for some reason. The Qui Tol do not act without purpose."

"You are right . . . as always," Kitranor said, silently pleased that her mate was close by to offer support. She would need it this night. "Stay by my side."

"As Chieftess wishes," Latas said, confidently running his hand through her hair. Her eyes smiled, even though her lips did not.

Three months passed for the village. A season changed, some mates were chosen, and several children were born, including Hosp's twins. There were also three deaths, two from illness and one from hunting. Professions were taught from parent to child and life continued as it had for generations. But the absence of both Jordan and Januss was keenly felt. Some of the younger Mokta wondered how far Jordan's hunting party had traveled and speculated whether the huntress had yet to take a mate. A few adults and elder Mokta expressed hope that Januss and Jordan were well, wherever they were. They periodically told stories of Januss' skills in the harvest fields or Jordan's accomplishments with the rest of her pack.

One evening, Kitranor decided to take a stroll through the village at sunset. She made sure to project the calm and happiness which she genuinely felt being among her tribe to put the village at ease since the presence of the Chieftess could also signal that there was a problem.

It was a mild night with a cool breeze. She enjoyed the silhouettes of nearby trees and the mountain as she passed huts lining both sides of the main path through the village, pausing sometimes to speak with her people, taking a genuine interest in their lives and accomplishments. She smelled the roasting Sasstonn on the spit and enjoyed a generous sample that was offered. Kitranor especially loved answering questions from the young children and their parents.

Suddenly, there was a shift in the air and an odd humming noise. Kitranor turned in time to see a circle of light appear in mid-air. The villagers fled from the phenomenon, not wanting to be taken from their homes by Qui Tol. Kitranor stood her ground and stared at the glowing portal. A tall and thin figure emerged from the portal, completely covered by a dark suit, their head obscured by a helmet and dark faceplate. The Qui Tol stared at Kitranor for a moment then lifted an arm to chest level, a separate beam of light shooting from its palm to form a hologram of Jordan's head.

"You took Januss and now you have come for her daughter, Qui Tol?" Kitranor shouted, enraged. "She is not here, and we will not help you find her. Go back to where you came from! We do not want you here!"

The Qui Tol reacted with surprise to the Chieftess' hostility. They took a couple of steps back, as if not sure what to do. They fidgeted with a device attached to their left wrist, pressing a couple of buttons, which caused the light in the portal to shift and change color to slightly golden. They turned around as if to re-enter the light portal.

Infuriated and appalled by the callous nature of these Qui Tol, who took innocent people, as if it was their right, never talking nor giving explanation, Kitranor would obtain her own answers right now! She would not let this opportunity pass. Kitranor extended her right arm to the side and opened her hand expectantly while still staring at the Qui Tol walk through the portal.

One of the tribe handed her a javelin and survival pack. Kitranor made eye contact with her mate and her second oldest son, Rizok, who were a dozen feet away. She nodded at them, and they nodded in reply. Everyone understood what was being communicated.

As the portal began to close, Kitranor ran with all her might and leaped into the portal to follow the Qui Tol.

19

QUEEN OF SORROWS

THE FREEZING WINDS AND SNOW lashed hard against the hunting pack. They had just emerged from a place of relative calm, where time and erosion had carved a path through part of a mountain wide enough for their group to walk through. There had been air currents in that natural tunnel, but they had no strength or fury, only the lonely echoes of a barren land. Exposed now to the full elements, the group was being pummeled relentlessly by the screaming gusts, whose bite they felt even through their thickest hides and furs. Reiban had ordered Jordan and Bopol to join him in a protective formation around Zoska, despite her insistence that she receive no special treatment. Jordan spotted what seemed to be a structure perhaps a half mile ahead. From this distance, it only appeared silhouetted through the storm, but any kind of shelter was preferable to where they were standing, so they pressed ahead. As they grew closer to it, she saw movement. Several figures walked towards them. They were taller than her and wore dark hooded robes made of somewhat thin-looking cloth. They also did not appear to carry any weapons. The closest one gestured for the hunters to follow them.

Several minutes later, a tall building made of stone, a castle amidst a world where she had only seen villages with huts or wooden walls and homes came into view. The structure was at least four stories tall and had three towers, each with its own defenses: ports for archers, reinforced doorways, and rooftop weaponry. Clearly this wasn't just a castle, it was a fortress.

The leader of the robed ones made a shrill cry towards the keep. A moment later, the massive main double doors slowly opened with a deep rumbling noise louder than the attacking winds. Jordan saw Reiban looking at the rest of the pack with an expression like "Are you sure this is a good idea?"

In a move Jordan agreed with, Zoska harshly slapped his arm and pointed insistently at the castle. Jordan and Bopol nodded their agreement with Zoska.

The robed ones led them through the gates and out of the storm. Once inside, the hunters saw two more robed ones, perhaps guards or sentries, push the hulking doors closed again. The three who had initially met them outside lowered their hoods and the pack did the same with their own fur hoods. The robed ones appeared albino-like to Jordan.

Their skin was so pale, it was virtually white. Like the Mokta, they had black scleras, but their irises were lavender. Standing easily six feet tall, they were lean but strong, even in their faces. Their noses were thin and long, and their ears were taller and more pointed than the Mokta's. They all had long white hair which was well-groomed, straight, and lustrous.

Their leader was the only one with a visible imperfection, a jagged narrow scar that ran from above his right temple to his chin. He wore a white patch over his blind eye. With thin lips, he smiled at the hunting pack.

"You are Mokta! I will speak in your tongue," he said. "Welcome to Fortress Gortecka. I am Yami of the Onchei people, protector of this place."

Jordan moved aside and took a subtly defensive stance near Bopol and Zoska as Reiban stepped forward.

"Thanks for kindness, Yami. I am Reiban, leader of this hunting pack."

"A hunting pack? I thought as much," Yami added with delight. "What a pleasure."

"With me are my beloved mate, Zoska," he boasted, turning his head briefly to look at her and smile. "And my friends, Bopol and his mate, Jordan."

"Wonderful! It is my honor to meet you," Yami replied. "These are Minth and Kuta, fellow protectors."

Jordan and the others gave a small half-bow to their hosts. Then Yami led the pack to a hall with a long table and many chairs.

"I will have our cook prepare a small feast," Yami said. "It will take a little time, but it will be well worth it. I know you must be tired from crossing the storm. We have named it Torment Without End in our own language."

"May I ask how you learned the Mokta language?" Reiban mentioned. "Have our peoples met before? I have never heard of the Onchei."

"That is probably because I am the only Onchei to encounter your people and survive," Yami said. "And that was nearly three hundred cycles ago."

Jordan noticed how that admission startled Bopol. She put her hand on his shoulder and looked in her mate's eyes to see what was wrong, but he shook his head. She became concerned about the worried look on his face, but knew better than to force the matter.

"I will go and alert the Queen. She will join us for the meal," Yami said.

"The Queen? What is this land, that it has kings and queens?" her full attention now focused on Yami.

Yami appeared angry for a second as he whipped his head around to train his eye on Jordan. She watched him school his features over several seconds from a grimace to a tolerant smile.

"You are not . . . from Algoran, but you are Mokta," Yami said. It was a statement, not a question.

"That is true," Jordan replied, resulting in a considered nod from Yami.

"This land is not well-traveled due to its harsh climate and the Mokta rarely leave their mountain," Yami said. "So, I am not surprised you have not heard of it. You are in Kinaspa, ruled by the benevolent Queen Amstar."

"Thank you," Jordan gave him another respectful half-bow.

Satisfied, Yami left the room. Servants provided them with water as they waited for the meal.

"Speak up, Bopol," Reiban said. "You know something about these people?"

"There was an old story about a pale-skinned stranger, but it's been so long, I don't remember all the details," Bopol said. "It was a tale of caution."

"Relax and let it come back to you, squarejaw," Zoska said. "Of the four of us, no one knows the stories better than you."

"Do not call him that," Jordan warned.

"We have *always* called him that," Zoska replied.

Jordan raised an eyebrow and defiantly rested her hands on her hips. "And now, it is time to stop."

"You are no fun, Jorr-Don," Zoska chastised.

"I think your warning is wise, Bopol," Reiban said, attempting to redirect them. "Although we have only been shown kindness, something does not sit well with me about this place."

"We will have to stay the night but tomorrow, we should go," Bopol said. "And I do not think I will be sleeping."

"Once the evening's activities are done, take first watch," Reiban said. "I will relieve you after a half-moon."

"And I will share his watch," Jordan added. It was not a request, so Reiban nodded.

An hour later, the cooking staff brought out the meal, which consisted of roasted meats and vegetables as well as something resembling salad and a few different types of bread. The white robed staff did not speak and had neutral expressions. Jordan had the impression they had been harshly trained and disciplined to have such uniform dispassion which they combined with professionalism. They were excellent at their jobs but something about them made Jordan feel sympathy.

Minutes after all the food had been placed and arranged on the table, Jordan viewed Yami walking proudly into the room. He looked over the display of the feast and appeared satisfied.

"My new friends of the Mokta tribe, please accept our hospitality! I think you will find this meal a rare treat."

"We are honored," Reiban replied with a gentle nod.

"Now, it is my honor to introduce you to Her Majesty and my daughter, Queen Amstar!"

A woman that was Jordan's height walked into the room wearing a dark red satin-like gown. She was strikingly beautiful to Jordan but in a disturbing way. She was not entirely Onchei. She had the hair, ears, and facial structure of an Onchei, but she was curvaceous and stronger-looking than any Onchei in the castle. Her skin had a light red tint to it and her irises were amber.

Jordan stifled a gasp as she realized the woman was half-Mokta!

Even more unusual, she appeared to be only slightly younger than her father. To Jordan, she seemed to be a woman in her early forties. She was composed to the point of looking humorless but not like the cooking staff; this was a woman who took her royalty seriously. She clasped her father's hand, walked to the head of the table and graciously sat down. She looked at her guests and allowed a slight smile to briefly cross her lips.

"You are my gemta's people. Welcome. You may call me Amstar or Queen," she said in the Mokta language, her pronunciation having a lush eloquence. "I am pleased to meet you."

20

IGNORANCE IS NO EXCUSE

"THIS IS A MOMENTOUS DAY, Queen," Reiban said. "First, we learn of the Onchei people and now we know that we have shared blood."

"What an interesting way of phrasing things," Queen Amstar said. "But as far as we know, I am the only offspring between an Onchei and a Mokta."

That surprised Jordan but she remained silent, preferring to let Reiban speak for the group.

"May I ask why that is?" Reiban asked.

"The Onchei are a proud people," the Queen said. "Mating with outsiders is not only against law and tradition, it is considered treason."

The whole room fell silent with the Queen's last sentence. The Queen, however, was amused.

"I know your next question, one-named-Reiban. If mating with outsiders such as the Mokta is considered treason, how am I here, adult royalty in a majestic fortress such as this?"

Jordan watched as Reiban nodded silently. He had unintentionally broached a razor-sharp topic. The Queen's feigned amusement was chilling. Jordan could sense the fury behind it.

"My torkomm was the King of all the Onchei territories, a ruler over many and loved by all," Queen Amstar continued. "He even took his forces into battle personally, against his advisors' recommendations.

And he went with a small force to conquer the Mokta mountain, thinking it an easy victory. But your people were not what he expected. My torkomm was injured in that battle and barely hid himself to avoid being captured or killed like the rest of his party.

"A Mokta woman found him and nurtured him back to health. She fell in love with him and protected him from being discovered. He came to care for her, too, and they became secret lovers. A year later, I was born. Eventually, the Onchei located him and his new family and brought them all back to the kingdom. Because my gemta had saved the king's life and hid him from her own people, her life was spared. But we were all sent into exile. So, you see, I am a Queen of a wasteland and this fortress is my prison."

Jordan sympathized with Reiban, who appeared extremely uncomfortable.

"But wait, I have a wonderful idea! Fortune smiles this day, my distant kinsmen," the Queen asserted.

"Daughter, be careful what you say," Yami warned.

"Is it not clear, Torkomm? These Mokta present me with a fantastic opportunity!"

"Hold your tongue, Amstar! These are guests."

"We may never get another chance like this! Forgive my desperation."

"What is this way you think we can help you, Queen Amstar?" Reiban asked with some trepidation.

"I need one—or both—of you male hunters," the Queen spoke frankly. "Grant me your seed and our children will one day lead a battle that will destroy the Onchei kingdom, so we can make a new one that will be open to both our peoples!"

"Are you crazy?" Jordan demanded as she stood up, prompting Bopol to stand next to her.

The Queen's eyes narrowed as she beheld Jordan. "I will forgive your insolence if you tell me where you are from. You are not Mokta, though you are dressed as Mokta."

"I am from a world called Earth," Jordan replied defiantly. "The Mokta took me and my gemta into their tribe when we were brought here several cycles ago."

"Earth? That is a children's fable. There is no Earth."

Jordan was stunned by that. "If you really think that, how do you explain me?"

"Perhaps you are the result of the Mokta breeding with another people of this world."

"Nice try," Jordan answered in English, pointing at herself as she spoke. "You want to try and explain my language then?"

The Queen was clearly taken aback. She looked at her torkomm, who was also surprised, and then she turned her gaze back to Jordan.

"I do not know the tongue you speak," the Queen admitted. "But that changes nothing."

"This is probably not an ideal time for this kind of discussion," Yami interrupted. "There is a feast before us. Let us enjoy it. I apologize for any misunderstandings."

Jordan nodded. She noted that the Queen's only response to her torkomm was a cold stare before she began consuming what had been prepared for her. No one spoke for the duration of the meal. Jordan and the others then discreetly excused themselves to their rooms for the evening, led by the stolid servants.

Bopol and Jordan leaned against opposing walls, facing each other outside of Reiban and Zoska's room.

"I do not know what to think of the Queen's behavior," Bopol said. "It was as if someone had died."

"Yeah, if the mood were a person, he would be very deceased," Jordan agreed. "Then again, depending on how long she has been forced to stay here, I suppose that could make anyone, well, grim."

"Grim is one thing, Jorr-Don. Completely insane is another."

"I was trying to be nice."

Suddenly, the torchlight blew out with a cold gust of wind through the corridor.

"Oh, you do not have to be nice with me, child," the Queen said as she walked closer. "I would prefer things be more honest."

"How can we help you, Queen?" Bopol stepped in front of Jordan protectively.

"I see you are a noble, boring one," Queen Amstar waved her hand. Bopol's eyes took on a glazed appearance and he stopped moving. "That is all right. I only need a child from you, not intellectual conversation."

Jordan stepped in front of Bopol to protect him. Unimpressed, the Queen grabbed her by the throat more quickly than she could see, much less react to. She shoved Jordan back against the stone wall, pinning her.

"Foolish girl, I only need your blood!"

Jordan could feel the Queen's vise-like grip slowly contracting, her fingers threatening to crush her throat, snap her neck like a twig or both. Worse, she had felt the sting of the Queen's fingernails as they cut deeply into her flesh. Jordan knew she was bleeding quite a bit from those small but painful wounds. And as she looked to her mate with rapidly blurring vision, he was as motionless as a statue, unable to help her.

No! I won't die this easily! Jordan desperately hung onto consciousness and fought her terror. *I have survived worse than this—and now, I have too much to live for!*

Jordan mustered enough strength to ram her left palm into the Queen's face and kneed her as hard as she could in the abdomen. It felt like striking stone, but it succeeded in forcing the Queen to let go.

Jordan dropped to the floor.

"You have spirit! I like that," the Queen said with a thin smile. "But if you are looking for your friends to intervene, they will not. They are in the same condition as your mate. You know, it almost seems a shame to kill you."

"Why?" She coughed. "Why do you have to kill me?" Jordan said, her throat still sore and bruised inside.

Jordan was both frightened and impressed with how cold and confident the Queen came across to her.

"I told you, I need your blood," the Queen replied.

"My blood? Why?"

"The Onchei are extremely long-lived but the Mokta are basically mortal. My father has lived for nine hundred cycles and is only now considered something of an elder," the Queen said. "I began to grow gray and wrinkled at two hundred cycles. But my father possesses knowledge from long ago, when elder Onchei maintained their youthful appearance by imbibing the blood of the young. For my sake, he researched and perfected the long-forbidden ways. I am Onchei enough that I am restored by such a sacrifice. I have lived over four hundred and fifty cycles."

Jordan felt revulsion and anger build inside her. "You are a monster!"

"Will that matter, when you are the one who will be dead?"

As the Queen moved towards her again, Jordan did her best to back away. Her SnowFire earrings began to glow brightly and the wall torch relit itself with blue flame. A distant voice began to speak in echoes in a language Jordan didn't understand.

At first, it was in whispers. But the hushed sounds grew louder until they permeated the corridor at such volume that both women had to cover their ears and squint their eyes. Even while doing so, blue light pulsated all around them.

When the cacophony faded, Jordan barely managed to open her eyes again for a few seconds. In that brief moment, she saw a tall woman with long blue hair, pointed ears, and eyes glowing like the hottest blue flames standing between herself and Amstar. The azure-haired woman was slender but appeared formidable and bore a merciless expression as she turned to focus on the Queen.

"Who *are* you?" the Queen asked, sounding impressed and a bit frightened.

"I am the one you do not wish to meet, Obscenity of the Mokta," she said in the Mokta language. "I am Snow and Fire."

Jordan closed her eyes and fought to hold onto consciousness. She wanted to hear every word and forced her eyes open once more.

"That cannot be! My mother told me of you, told me the legends, but they were only stories!"

"Like this one's world is a story to you?" SnowFire said, pointing at Jordan.

"Earth is real?" the Queen responded, sounding genuinely surprised.

"You are about to learn what real is, Amstar, Queen of Nothing!"

"Wait! Why are you here? Why are you defending that girl?"

Jordan heard the other woman breathe in sharply, then relax into a chuckle. But it was filled with disgust, not humor.

"This has been a long time coming, ever since your torkomm attacked my descendants. I permitted your people to live, to see if you would be worthy of your heritage. Sadly, you have become a detestable creature, intent on attacking both Onchei and Mokta."

Jordan was quickly growing cold from her blood loss. Her weakening eyes could see blurs of blue light and the hazy silhouettes of two people.

"This girl was adopted by the Mokta. Since she is under their protection, she is under mine as well," SnowFire declared. "But more than that, she is mate to the son of a Chieftess. She wears the SnowFire gems. That means to attack her is to attack me!"

"I—I did not know any of that!"

"The child from Earth did not know what you are and that nearly cost her life. Do you think your ignorance of me will save you?" SnowFire said. "Little Queen, this day, she will live and you—*all of you*—will die."

————

Some time later, Zoska and Reiban emerged from their room, groggy and confused. Reiban woke Bopol and Zoska went to wake Jordan. Zoska startled when she saw her friend. She shook Jordan awake. When Jordan groaned, she helped her sit up.

"Wh-what is it, Zoska? What happened?"

Zoska touched Jordan's hair briefly and then pulled her hand back uncomfortably. "I am not sure where to start. You have changed, Jorr-Don."

"Changed? What are you talking about?"

"Your hair, it is as blue as the SnowFire gems!"

"What?!" Jordan exclaimed, running her hands through her hair and pulling it over her shoulder. She stared at a mane with strands as cerulean as the deepest ocean.

"And your eyes, they are no longer brown," Zoska stared in fascination. "They are the color of the ice." Amazement and fear rushed through her. She also felt sympathy for Jordan, who appeared dumbfounded and unsure. Then Zoska noticed something new.

Zoska gasped. "Y-your hands, Jorr-Don?!"

Zoska watched as Jordan inspected the backs of her hands. They were the same color as before. But then as Jordan turned them over to look at her palms, Zoska confirmed what she had seen before: that the small SnowFire gems which had been tenderly crafted into earrings by Bopol were now embedded in Jordan's palms, fused with her body!

"Do they hurt, Jorr-Don?"

"No," Jordan answered softly and with fear in her voice. "The skin near the gems on each of my hands is numb."

Zoska peered wide-eyed as Jordan poked and probed each palm with her hands.

"When I press against the gems, my hands feel warm for a moment," Jordan continued. "Then it cools back down."

Zoska watched as Jordan suddenly stood up and felt the skin around her neck. Zoska stood up also.

"There are no cuts or bruises – but the Queen grabbed me by the throat," Jordan remembered aloud. "Her nails dug in and drew blood—but—do you see any wounds?"

Zoska shook her head, suddenly filled with dread and she didn't know why.

"I am completely healed," Jordan considered as she turned to face her fellow hunters, who looked as astonished as Zoska. "But how is that possible?"

Zoska had no idea. She feared for her friend.

"What does all of this mean?? What *am* I? Am I still human? Why has this happened to me?" Jordan staggered backwards.

Zoska grabbed and steadied her but she could only sympathize. She had no definite answers for her friend, only possibilities.

"It could have been the SnowFire gems," Zoska offered. "Perhaps they protected you, but they also altered you. Bopol, has anything like this happened before in Mokta legend?"

Zoska was disheartened when she observed Bopol staring at Jordan, his expression slack. Despite his strong body, he looked to Zoska as though a breeze could topple him at the moment.

"Bopol?" Jordan pleaded.

Zoska's heart went out to Bopol. Before she could reach out to him, he closed his eyes and covered his face with his hand, hiding his sorrow. His tension was palpable to Zoska. She was relieved when Jordan stood in front of Bopol and gently pulled his hand down, revealing tear-filled eyes.

"I failed to protect you," Bopol lamented. "I am not a good mate. I should release you from our bond."

"No! Are you crazy?" Jordan replied, desperately grabbing his shoulders as her own eyes became teary.

"You were injured, changed. You could have been killed!"

"I am—I will be fine," Jordan soothed. "I was not killed. We will figure this out somehow."

"I would do anything to make this right, Jorr-Don."

"I know," she said, resting her head on his shoulder.

Zoska felt helpless, unsure how she could help her dearest friends.

"Perhaps we should be grateful we are all alive," Reiban interrupted, attempting to be optimistic.

"Yes. You are right," Jordan concurred. "But wait—the Queen, where is she?"

A few moments later, Jordan half-stumbled out of the corridor and began descending the stairs. She suddenly stopped and gasped. The cry she wanted to let out froze in her throat at the ghastly sight before her. The others rushed to her side and were equally horrified.

The Queen's corpse was impaled mid-chest into the stone wall by a large Onchei two-handed sword. Her blood had flowed down the wall beneath her body and pooled onto the floor, where it was still slick. The stairway was overlooking the great hall where they had dined earlier that night. And there, every single Onchei was dead and burned beyond recognition on that floor.

Jordan and the other three hunters stood motionless at the sight, chilled at the grim and grotesque scene before them. It took time for her to comprehend it, much less process its implications. This was a mystery, a dire enigma with no answers at present.

"The servants, and Yami, they didn't harm us. They weren't like the Queen," Jordan uttered, her voice strained and quivering. "First, Amstar attacks us, then we are saved by—something. I look like this now and everyone but us is . . . "

Jordan looked first to Bopol then Zoska and Reiban. She needed an explanation, something that could make sense of this tragic loss of life. But no one had answers or even a hint of what to say. The castle had become a charnel house, an open mass grave.

Staggered by the sheer enormity of the circumstances, Jordan collapsed from the stress. Bopol swooped in and took her up in his arms before she could hit the ground. She felt lightheaded and dizzy, so she closed her eyes. But she could still hear them speaking.

"We will leave here now," Bopol stated to the others.

"Agreed. Even the storm is preferable to this place," Reiban added.

"The sooner we leave, the better," Zoska concurred.

21

CONCERNS

IT STARTED WITH A FEW drops and developed quickly into a light shower. Bopol looked up, felt the water bounce off his cheeks and smiled.

"At last! I never thought I could be so happy to experience rain again!" Reiban interjected.

"Compared to the blizzard we traversed over the last two days to escape that cursed kingdom of Kinaspa—" Bopol began.

He felt his mate's elbow jolt him in the side as they walked.

"Don't even *say the name* of that terrible place!" Jorr-Don hissed.

Bopol made an apology to her with his eyes and a slight tilting of his head. She accepted it with a barely noticeable nod.

"Well, compared to what we just passed through, a light rain shower is actually refreshing, yes?" Bopol finished his thought.

He saw Zoska pull her hood over her head. She made eye contact with him and Reiban before speaking.

"I think we should set up our tents until the rain passes," Zoska said. "Besides, I know darkha—er, *Jorr-Don* has not slept well recently."

Jorr-Don had been withdrawn and listless, easily irritated. Bopol was still getting used to the changes in her appearance but there was no mistaking her personality.

It only took minutes to set up their tents to wait out the shower. Bopol knew that everyone else in the hunting pack had been worried about, and somewhat afraid of, Jorr-Don.

She sat on the ground inside their tent, hugging her knees and leaning forward, as if trying to roll herself into a ball. He knelt on his knees and looked compassionately at his beloved.

"You should take this time to calm your thoughts and catch up on your rest," Bopol suggested.

"I want to but I keep seeing them when I close my eyes," Jorr-Don replied, her voice somewhat muffled by the proximity of her knees.

"Who? The Queen?"

"The Queen, the person I think was SnowFire, and then all the bodies. I can't get them out of my head."

Bopol tenderly touched Jorr-Don's cheek with his fingers. He gently lifted her head to make her look at him.

"I cannot possibly imagine what you must have experienced, facing the Queen," Bopol said. "And I cannot tell you how sorry I am that I was unable to help you."

"You do not have to say that again. I am just glad she was not able to have her way with either you or Reiban while the two of you were under her spell," Jorr-Don said gruffly. "I am thankful for all of you, who have risked so much during this mission."

"You know how we feel about you."

"Yes," she replied with a contrite smile. "Sometimes, I do not think I deserve those feelings, but I am grateful for them."

Bopol leaned forward and kissed her. When he began to pull back, she grabbed him and gave him an even more spirited embrace. Bopol was pleased that his actions had the intended effect, lifting her spirits somewhat, if only for a moment. But when she noticed her blue hair flowing over her shoulders, the recent haunting events revisited her expression and she looked self-conscious again.

"So, I may as well ask," she said, pulling her knees closer, as if trying to shield herself from the answer. "How do my changes affect you?"

"I will miss the way you looked before, if this is a lasting change. I had never seen brown eyes or hair on anyone before. So, in that way, they were special. Your hair and eye colors now are striking. However, they are no less beautiful on you."

"Striking," she repeated. "Is that another way of saying I look like a freak?"

Bopol felt conflicted. Jorr-Don's resemblance to a legendary figure did set her apart from anyone else on Algoran. So, in that regard, her assessment was correct but it also did not help her for him to acknowledge that.

"No," he answered. "I am not sure I have the right words to describe my feelings."

"Does my appearance frighten you? You can be honest."

Her unworldly stare cut through him like a dagger. It was unsettling.

"I do not fear you, but your eyes are intimidating."

"Intimidating? Great, I am scary now."

He did not mean to hurt her with his words. He pulled back and lowered his head with regret.

"You told me to be honest."

"Yes, I did," she said with a slight chuckle as she looked away and shook her head. That told Bopol she regretted her own choice of words. "And the palm gems?"

"They are fascinating. Though I admit, I do not have any idea what the full ramifications of this will be."

Jorr-Don sighed. "Me, either."

Bopol was momentarily alarmed when Jordan pulled out the dagger from her belt and attempted to poke under the gem fused into her right palm. The blade passed through her hand as if it wasn't there. He watched with wide eyes as she repeated the effort four or five more times, with each conclusion the same.

He watched her put her right hand to the ground and against her leg. Then she pushed it against his chest, eliciting confusion from him. Each time her hand came into contact with a surface, it was solid and met resistance but when she thrust the knife towards the gem in her left palm, it exited the other side ghostlike, inflicting no wound. Her eyes met Bopol's in amazement.

"What does this mean?" Jorr-Don said, her voice hushed, almost a whisper.

Bopol looked at her trembling hands and held them in his own before returning her gaze.

"I have never seen magic before, but could the gemstones be enchanted?"

She pulled her hands away from him in frustration. He didn't know what to do as Jordan stared intensely at her palms once more.

"Why?" she wondered aloud. "To protect them? Prevent their removal?"

"I do not know."

Jorr-Don sat down in a huff, frustrated. "Me, either. But I was hoping if I could remove the gems from my hands, then maybe I would return to the way I was before."

Bopol sat down behind his mate and gently rested his hand on her back. "I admit I was shaken by your changes at first. But I can accept that this is how you look now. And you are just as desirable and ravishing to me."

He patiently waited as Jorr-Don looked down and managed a brief smile in response. He watched her run her hands through her hair as a growl of irritation grew in her lungs. He was unsure how to react when she slumped forward, leaning on her hands.

"I wish it was so easy for me to accept these changes," she replied. "It would help if I knew what they meant and if maybe some good could come from all of this."

Bopol scooted forward and hugged her from behind. "Some good has already happened," he consoled. "You are alive."

Jorr-Don nodded her head slowly and chuckled. "You are right, I am alive and that is good. It is what we do *not* know that makes this frightening."

"We have all faced the unknown before," Bopol offered. "Every time we went on a hunt."

"True, but we never changed physically," Jorr-Don replied, shifting to face him.

"I disagree. We have finished hunts with scars and injuries."

"Not quite the same as—" she held up a tuft of her blue hair, giving an emphatic look with her eyes and a tilt of the head.

"We are mates and I will stand with you for life," Bopol ran his hand through her hair.

"As I will stand with you," Jorr-Don added, taking his hand and kissing it. "No matter *what* I am."

As Bopol closed the flap to their tent, Jorr-Don laid down to rest. He put his arms around her to provide comfort.

———————

Nearby in their own dwelling, Reiban and Zoska had shared a small meal and talked for some time. Zoska had kept a watchful eye on their friends but now returned her full attention to Reiban.

"Finally! I was wondering when the squarejaw would take Jorr-Don's mind off her worries!" Zoska said.

"He is the only one who can do so," Reiban said. "I am happy for them both."

Zoska narrowed her gaze at Reiban.

"She *does* have reason to be worried."

"Yes. It is a miracle she survived against the Queen."

Zoska shook her head, her eyes never leaving Reiban's.

"Not if SnowFire intervened and healed her injuries," she pondered.

"Do you really think that is what happened?"

Zoska took a sizable bite out of the bread in her hand and washed it down with a swig from her water bag.

"Do you have a better explanation?" she asked. "Jorr-Don looks much like how our legends describe SnowFire! I know she is still Jorr-Don, but . . . "

She shifted the way she was sitting, one hand holding her swollen belly as she did so. Reiban leaned forward, ready to help her if she needed it, even though it wasn't necessary this time. Her hand remained on her abdomen, tenderly rubbing it as she contemplated.

"We know almost nothing about the gems," Zoska continued. "I had always assumed they were just a natural substance, that the legends were just that: stories."

Reiban nodded. "And now we must consider that there may be more to them."

"We have to consider that everything may have changed."

She could see that what she said was alarming to Reiban, but it was how she felt. She would not take it back.

"What do you mean, everything?" he asked.

"Our mission, our relationship with her, even what she is."

"How can you say that about your best friend?"

She grabbed his hand and gripped it tightly, then she pulled it to her stomach and looked at him, filled with determination.

"I have not kept both of us, and now our unborn child, alive by blindly trusting circumstances, Reiban! I have done so by observing, analyzing facts, and acting carefully."

"I know."

Zoska released her grip and her countenance softened some.

"I love Jorr-Don as my own sister, but she is not the same after what happened in the Onchei fortress. She is trying to figure this out, but it may be too much for her. I have to say, this would probably overwhelm even me."

Zoska felt torn. She didn't even want to be having this conversation with her mate. Yet these things needed to be discussed, even if it hurt to say them.

"What should we do?" Reiban sounded miserable. "We cannot just abandon her . . . can we? We are packmates."

"No," Zoska responded. "But we will be very, very cautious and continue to watch. If I tell you we need to leave—"

"I understand. Very well."

———————

Jordan opened her eyes and was confused to find herself standing alone at the top of a mountain. Her huntress instincts kicked in and quashed her fear, rooting her in place. She positioned her arms and legs in a defensive stance while she looked around slowly, trying to figure out where she was and what was going on. The skies overhead were dark gray, and lightning dashed to the ground in a heartbeat, followed by a distant rumbling. The winds were cold and biting, blowing her hair and pulling at her furs. Light snow began to fall.

"Thundersnow?"

She had seen the weather phenomenon once before, as a child in Colorado. Then, she had her father to bring her back inside their cozy, warm house, where the two of them could start a gentle fire and tell stories to pass the time while her mother listened, tending to her baby brother. Now, on Algoran, she stood directly in the raw intensity of this weather. There was an element of menace to it, a harshness in the air.

Out of the corner of her eye, Jordan saw what appeared to be a person about one hundred yards away. With snow flurries obscuring her vision some, Jordan couldn't determine whether it was a man or a woman, only that they were covered in thick furs. The person beckoned Jordan to come closer. As she did so, the person walked down the slope, evidently expecting her to follow. Hesitantly, she pursued the mysterious stranger until they entered a cave on the side of the mountain.

Once Jordan entered its narrow mouth, she saw the flickering glow of torchlight from around a winding passage. That path emptied into a much larger cavern, its ceiling several stories high and its circumference the size of a city block on Earth. In the center of this space was an eight-foot wide column made of crystal that stretched to the ceiling. In front of the column was simple burgundy-colored rug twenty feet long by ten feet wide. Standing in the middle of the rug was the person Jordan had followed.

The figure pulled back the hood and revealed deep blue hair, a piercing gaze, and pointed ears. It had to be SnowFire.

Exuding confidence and a leashed rage, SnowFire's eyes were ice-blue. Jordan stared in awe and terror, being so close to the personification of a Mokta legend. She remembered her hazily from the night she almost died, standing between herself and Queen Amstar. There was no question this was the same woman. Even as Jordan fought the urge to run away screaming, she backed away a few steps at a time, starting and stopping.

"Do you wish to gain answers to your questions?" SnowFire said in Mokta, halting Jordan's slow retreat.

"Yes," she replied, also in Mokta.

Jordan was still frightened of SnowFire but at the same time, a part of her was impressed by this fabled woman's confidence.

"Then ask me, Jordan of Earth, daughter of Janice."

"You saved my life and I am grateful, but why did you do this to me?" Jordan asked, pointing her hands at her head.

SnowFire's anger simmered just beneath the surface. Statuesque, the mythical figure stood there with her arms crossed at near-waist level. Jordan could tell that the other woman wanted to be there and how important this moment was. But she also knew SnowFire wanted something from her, she just couldn't tell what.

"You lost a lot of blood to that Obscenity of the Mokta. I gave you some of my own to replenish yours."

"But you are a spirit. How can you have a body with blood and everything?"

Jordan watched as SnowFire's anger momentarily abated and was replaced by amusement.

"I have many forms," SnowFire replied. "Right now, you could touch this body. It functions much the same as yours. With it, I can breathe the air, eat food, or even bear a child, as I have done in times past. Sharing its blood with you was not difficult."

"Why me?"

"Why not? I decided to let you live. Is that not what matters?"

Jordan's temper started to flare, but she kept her emotions in check. She wanted more information.

"I suppose so. Thank you. But what happens now?"

"That is up to you."

Jordan closed her eyes in frustration and took in a calming breath. One question persisted in her mind and had to be asked.

"How did you even know about me?"

SnowFire's glare narrowed as she appraised Jordan's words. A hint of a smile crossed her lips before falling back into the scowl of a woman losing her own patience.

"I became aware of you when the Qui Tol brought you and your gemta to Algoran. I followed you both with some interest, as I have all who were brought from your Earth."

"Do you have the power to send us home?"

"No. But even if I did, I doubt I would do it," SnowFire shared, even as she folded her arms once more and raised an eyebrow. "You intrigue me, child of another world."

Jordan stepped forward, wanting to understand.

"Me? Why?"

"You survived the *mosdon*. In my entire existence, no one has ever lived, once injected with its poison."

She does not know that it was God that saved my life. But I do not think it would be smart to tell her that. I do not fully understand it myself right now.

"It is true. I was dying from the poison, yet I live."

"Long before I chose to mate with a Mokta, I had been alone, watching over the mountain region where your tribe now lives. My mate fascinated me and stirred feelings within me which I had not known I possessed. I was happy to be with him and to have his children. But I also watched him grow older, along with our children. And one-by-one, I saw them die."

For a moment, SnowFire's anger was replaced by the purest sadness and grief. Her shoulders slumped, and her eyes showed Jordan how ancient SnowFire really was. In that moment, Jordan felt sympathy for her.

"I did not know the Mokta had such short existences," SnowFire continued. "My children lived longer than my mate but when they left the mountain, traveling until they met and mated with other Mokta, their offspring lived even shorter existences. The cycle continued until, less than ten generations later, they lived no longer than my mate had. My blood in them had diminished to almost nothing.

"Every so often, I would find a dying Mokta and save them like I did you. Some did not live long with the new blood. Others were hunted down and killed because their changed appearances raised fears from the legends about me. About two hundred cycles ago, I stopped trying. I kept myself hidden within the Mokta Mountain and observed the world from there until your amazing recovery."

With those words, SnowFire's morose contemplation ended and she gazed straight at Jordan hungrily. Jordan had seen that look in zala beasts right before they struck. It made her automatically defensive.

"I realized there was something different about you. And if you could survive the mosdon, I felt you could survive my blood. I wondered if it might even make you immortal or at least much longer lived than your own people."

Jordan didn't like what she was hearing. She clenched her fists as her anger grew.

"The Obscenity of the Mokta greatly offended me, attacking all of you, trying to take your blood. That is why I killed her and made an example of her people," SnowFire continued. "But one good thing came of her treachery, it gave me the opportunity to share *what I am* with you. And you will have it with you always, as will your descendants."

Jordan was beginning to feel overwhelmed. She looked at the gems in her palms and then at SnowFire.

"Why? What is it you really want?"

"I have stated my reasons, Jordan SnowFire. I want to extend your life and by extension, the lives of all your descendants. I refuse to see my children taken from me any longer! I refuse to exist alone!"

SnowFire rushed towards Jordan, looking desperate, her eyes ablaze with energy. She clasped Jordan's shoulders, inhaling sharply. "I refuse!"

Jordan woke suddenly with a quick gasp, her heart pounding furiously in her chest. Beads of cold sweat dotted her forehead, arms and upper back. She had to work to calm herself, taking slow and deep breaths. As her adrenaline rush faded, she became aware of the last drippings of rain falling from nearby trees and the pleasant coos and twitterings of birds. Coherent once more, she looked to the left and right and verified she was still in her tent.

It was a dream? Being on the mountain, the cave, that conversation? All of it was just in my mind? Or was it?

A snort to her right grabbed her attention. She smiled to see Bopol still lying at her side. Trying not to disturb his sleep, she was surprised that her rude awakening hadn't done so already. She reached over to grab a drying towel from one of the bags to dry her sweat-dampened forehead and neck.

Jordan quietly emerged from the tent and walked to the nearby stream. She bathed in the refreshingly cold waters and cleaned her hair with an herbal shampoo she had learned how to make in the last year. The scents of local flowers in the shampoo and soap she was using were mild but pleasant enough to make her smile. After rinsing the mixture out of her hair and taking one more plunge beneath the waters, she waded back to the shore.

22

CHANGING ROLES

ZOSKA APPROACHED JORR-DON, WHO SAT on a large rock looking at the stars in the darkening sky. Now that Zoska was further along in her pregnancy, it was somewhat awkward for her to sit down on the ground next to Jordan, but she managed.

"Not quite huntress accuracy," Zoska joked.

"No, but you did fine, for a gemta-to-be," Jorr-Don said, grinning as she looked at her.

Zoska was afraid Jorr-Don might start laughing at any time. "You are enjoying watching me grow with child and the trouble it causes me, are you not?"

As she had predicted, Jorr-Don could no longer hold back her giggles. Zoska sneered in response.

"Oh, do not be angry!" Jorr-Don answered. "Would you not have fun at my expense, if our positions were reversed?"

"Oh, I look forward to the day you conceive, to see life bloom within you," Zoska said, winking.

Zoska was pleased as Jorr-Don blushed, the jab hitting its intended target.

"Oh, you do, do you?" Jorr-Don quipped.

"I sincerely hope you have twins—or more—and become very heavy with child," Zoska savored. "I would enjoy that!"

"Yes, I am sure you would," Jorr-Don replied with a sigh. "But you cannot fool me. I know you love having this baby."

Zoska smiled, shifting once again to attain a semblance of comfort. She noted that Jorr-Don had her hands out, ready to help her. It was a kindness she appreciated, even if it wasn't necessary this time.

"I do," Zoska replied. "But between you and me, I am worried that I will not be much use to you for the rest of this mission."

"Your skills will never dull, Zoska. But protecting your baby—protecting yourself—should be your highest priority. And you need to let us see to your safety now."

Now it was Zoska's turn to blush.

"I know you are correct, but it does not please me to hear it," Zoska admitted. "I crave the hunt and the excitement, even the fear!"

Lifting her arms in excitement during her last words threw Zoska off-balance. She started falling backwards, but Jorr-Don caught her and gently returned her to a stable position.

"You are not done being a huntress," Jorr-Don stated reassuredly.

"You think so? I am not so sure. I may not be Hosp but I do want to have more children after this one. By the time we have weaned our last, I will have to choose another profession. Remember, I told you hunting is left to the young."

"Even if you had a child once a cycle for the next four cycles, you would still be under thirty. That is still young!"

Zoska still could not find a comfortable position. She reached out to Jorr-Don, who helped her stand up again.

"You still do not understand. You were not raised with the teachings we all received as children," Zoska said patiently. "Chieftess told us, we are hunters when we are young because we have no distractions, only the hunt and our packmates. But once we start having and raising children, our bodies change. More importantly, what matters to us changes, too. The hunt would take us far from our new families. That is dangerous because our thoughts would always be with them. That would make us hesitate and second-guess ourselves in a profession where mistakes mean death. And if we die, what happens to our children?"

"Hm! I never thought about it like that. Chieftess is wise."

Zoska turn ded and slowly stretched her back from side to side. "She is just passing down wisdom that comes from the time of the First Chief.".

"So, you are saying this is the last time we will be hunting together as a pack?"

"Yes, Jorr-Don. I feel honored to be here doing this."

Zoska clasped Jorr-Don's hands in her own and looked confidently in the other woman's eyes. "I will protect my unborn child, but I will not turn back. I will support you."

Jorr-Don smiled. "It would probably be more dangerous for you and Reiban to go back now anyway."

Zoska released her grip and patted Jorr-Don on the back.

"Probably. And Chieftess said there is more safety in numbers."

"She did say that, did she not?"

Zoska nodded. Then she grinned with pure delight. "Besides, you will need me if you find you are with child, too."

Knowing that would unnerve Jorr-Don, Zoska wondered what her reaction would be. She didn't have to wait long.

"What is this obsession you have with me being pregnant, Zoska?"

"I have eyes and ears, my friend. The longer you and your mate are together, the better your chances of conceiving."

Jorr-Don blushed brighter than before. "M-maybe so. But until I show signs, just treat me normally, okay?"

"Let me ask you this, Jorr-Don, if you showed signs of being pregnant tomorrow, do you know what would you do? Would you follow your own advice, put your child first and turn back or would you push forward and complete the mission?"

A powerful silence hung over the two of them for a few minutes. But when Jorr-Don looked at her and nodded, Zoska relaxed and returned the gesture.

"I have already assured my mate that our own family comes before the mission," Jorr-Don answered.

"Then I am proud of you," Zoska replied. "That is the right decision."

"Thanks."

Zoska watched Jorr-Don grab her bag from the ground and pull out a small loaf of sweetbread for a snack. When Jorr-Don handed it to her, she tore off a small portion for Jordan and kept the majority for herself. Looking at Jorr-Don's confused expression, Zoska made her position clear by taking a huge bite out of the part she claimed as hers.

"What is wrong with you, Zoska? You did not need to do that. I was sharing with you."

Zoska looked at her with mock innocence.

"What? It is for my child."

Zoska maintained the façade as Jorr-Don put her hands on her hips and stared accusingly.

"That was my last sweetbread," Jorr-Don said in a low growl.

"My child thanks you."

"Not from where I am standing. That was all you, my friend."

Zoska jammed the rest of the sweetbread into her mouth and chewed it up until she could swallow it all. Then she belched and patted her belly, looking satisfied.

"No. Now it is all me," Zoska gloated. "The snack, that is."

She could see that Jorr-Don was not amused.

"I hope it all goes to your hips," Jorr-Don said under her breath.

"What?"

"Nevermind," Jorr-Don sighed.

Zoska realized that it was time for a change of topic.

"What is our next move as a hunting pack? Will your changes affect our goal in any way? Or is the same as before?"

"It is the same as before. The difference in my appearance does not change our goals. When we leave in the morning, we will keep heading towards the Southlands. I just wish we did not have more questions than answers for all of our efforts."

"How do you mean?"

"I . . . dreamed of SnowFire."

That intrigued Zoska. It also scared her. "You mean, once you fell asleep today?"

"Yes."

"What happened? Did you talk to her?"

Zoska watched as Jorr-Don crouched down and picked up a small stone. Her friend angled the stone between her thumb and index finger, balancing it before she hurled it towards the stream. The stone bounced four times before sinking into the waters.

"She was intense," Jorr-Don shared. "I would like to think it was just my mind trying to figure things out, but it felt so real!"

Zoska leaned against a nearby tree. "What did she tell you in the dream?"

"She told me the Onchei Queen nearly killed me. She saved my life by giving me some of her blood. That is why I have changed."

Zoska put her hand over her mouth, unable to repress a gasp. "SnowFire's blood runs through your veins?"

Zoska was glad for the tree's support. She had not realized she was breathing faster, her concern escalating in a few seconds to near-terror.

"I do not want you and the others to fear me, Zoska."

The sad and burdened look in Jorr-Don's eyes snapped Zoska out of her panicked state. She started breathing normally again. After a moment, she was able to think clearly, less emotionally.

"Bopol does not, not really," Zoska considered.

"No," Jorr-Don concurred. "He knows the legends of SnowFire, but he only has eyes for me."

"Treasure him, my friend. He will follow you anywhere."

Jorr-Don managed to smile again. "I do. Believe me, I do!"

Zoska wanted to be happy for Jorr-Don and Bopol but one concern lingered in her mind. "Understand this as well, Jorr-Don: He will follow you, even if it leads to his death. That is especially true now."

"Why . . . why do you say especially now?"

Zoska pushed off from the tree and walked towards Jorr-Don. She rested her hand on the other woman's shoulder. Her terror was gone but a warning remained, one she conveyed with her eyes to Jorr-Don.

"Even I know some of the legends of SnowFire. We may call her The Spirit of the Mountain in reverence, but it is also spoken in fear."

"I do not understand. She is your—*our* ancestor, right? I know there are several tribes of Mokta on Algoran and we are the Mountain Mokta, that SnowFire and the First Chief created what we now know."

Zoska nodded. "That is what the stories say, yes. One of First Chief and Snowfire's sons became the Second Chief. And his nine siblings left to form the other Mokta tribes, spread across the lands."

She understood Jorr-Don's confused expression. But her friend's ice-colored eyes continued to unnerve her.

"So, SnowFire is The Mother of All Mokta?" Jorr-Don asked.

"There were supposedly one or more tribes in existence before the First Chief's time. But our tales vaguely reference something happening to them. Regardless of that, if members of the other tribes traveled the world, they would have mated with descendants of SnowFire eventually."

Jorr-Don stumbled backwards, stunned by this revelation. "That is incredible," she whispered.

"What the old stories are very detailed about are SnowFire's extreme moods. Her ferocity in battle and the terror of her wrath, whether in politics or jealousy. She loved her mate and all her children. She declared war because of them and she was powerful enough to wipe other tribes from existence, just because they posed a threat to the Mokta."

Zoska sympathized as she saw Jorr-Don looking down and stroking her azure hair silently for self-reassurance.

"This is a lot to comprehend," Jorr-Don pondered. "I am just a huntress, a girl from another world who was adopted by the Mokta. I am nobody."

"You are someone important to Bopol. And you and your gemta are special to the Mokta."

Jorr-Don stopped fidgeting with her hair and looked at Zoska. "Why? Why is that?" she asked.

"You know that you and your gemta are not the first to be taken from Errrth and brought here," Zoska answered. "But with what the two of you endured and overcame just to survive here, many of us from the village took you into our hearts. We not only feel for you, but we care what happens to you. That has been especially true for Chieftess and then Bopol as well. Reiban and I consider you family."

Jorr-Don smiled. "You honor me and my gemta. Thank you."

She kept silent as Jorr-Don paced for a moment. She knew it wasn't her choice to become like this, Jorr-Don hadn't asked SnowFire to save her. Zoska could tell that her friend only wanted to be normal . . . and that wasn't possible anymore. She could only imagine how that must feel.

"Will the village accept me now? I cannot change my biology back, no one can. Somehow, I have to accept what is happening to me, so I can move forward. But nothing is going to be the same anymore."

Zoska tried to find something positive to say. "It is not all bad. Like you said, she prevented your death."

She was glad that made Jorr-Don smile again.

"Yes. And I want to have more time with you, my loved ones."

Zoska wanted to keep cheering up Jorr-Don. "*Especially* your mate," she added.

"Especially my mate," Jorr-Don repeated with a chuckle.

"So, you can make babies!"

Zoska couldn't hold back a grin as Jorr-Don turned to her in amused exasperation.

"Again, with me having babies!" Jorr-Don griped.

"Maybe if I say it enough times, it will happen."

Zoska put her arm around Jorr-Don's waist and pulled her close as they began slowly walking back towards their temporary camp. Jorr-Don placed her hand on Zoska's belly.

"Do you think you will have a male or a female child?" Jorr-Don asked.

"A girl. Definitely a girl."

She could see that surprised Jorr-Don.

"Why do you think so?" Jorr-Don asked.

"Because Reiban wants it so much. He has charmed me so, like he did with the daughter of the ruler in his story."

"You mean the story with the ruler who wasn't really a ruler, who offered his daughter who was not really his daughter?"

Zoska cleared her throat, not wanting to get sidetracked by the story's specifics. "Yes. But I was only referring to my mate's ability to compel others. The story itself is—"

"It is a mysterious story," Jorr-Don interrupted. "I think that is why I like it!"

Zoska raised an eyebrow in warning. "Do not make me think you are stupid, too, Jorr-Don."

"Why not add it to the list? You already think I am pregnant."

That made Zoska smile. She had finally gotten Jorr-Don to bring up the subject on her own.

"You *could* be pregnant!" Zoska teased.

"I do not have any symptoms, remember?"

"At first, there are no symptoms."

"I do not know whether you're a hopeless romantic or just a madwoman."

Zoska stopped and put her hand on Jorr-Don's arm. Then she grinned. "Is there some reason I cannot be both?"

Jorr-Don laughed at that. "I hope your children are just like you, Zoska."

"Many thanks. And I hope our children grow up the best of friends like us."

The two resumed walking side-by-side down the winding dirt path.

"I do, too," Jorr-Don added.

"Sooner than later."

"Zoska . . . "

23

GRIEF AND ANSWERS

THE ABDUCTOR EMERGED FROM THE light portal onto a stone pathway which ran through the center of the community within the Southlands. Normally, she would see green fields rolled just outside the well-trodden trails that weaved between the single or dual-level houses and storage buildings made of clay and stone. She would hear the sounds of people repairing existing technology or see demonstrations of new technology to young minds, friends, and relatives sharing a meal or simply having a conversation with one another. Birds and insects were always somewhere nearby.

Instead of that oasis, what she experienced petrified her. All of the buildings and technology were still in place, precisely as they should be, but the town was still, silent. Not even the animals or insects were present. Were the creatures dead or had they merely fled whatever happened here?

The fields were burned, smoke still rising from what was left. Every single one of the people, from the oldest to the youngest, lay dead in the streets. No, not just dead— they had been slaughtered!

Zeetra unfastened her helmet and dropped it to the ground. The young Onchei woman ran a hand through her short white hair.

She slowly turned and tried to understand the scope of what had happened. As far as her eyes could see in the waning daylight, limbs were literally torn or cut off from many of their bodies. Some of the dead were decapitated while others had burn marks from Onchei guns and energy rifles that had been used against them. And still more were burned skeletal remains. Unliving faces were frozen in mismatched expressions of terror, pain, or disbelief adorning the scattered corpses, which were spread across the landscape.

There was no question about it: she was the only survivor in the entire city. Her parents, siblings, friends, co-workers and, very likely, even her Closest One were all lost, the victims of a battle so one-sided that it defied description.

Before the light portal closed behind her, the sound of a dropped javelin reached her. She slowly turned her head, hoping against hope to view a surviving Onchei. Instead, it was only a Mokta warrior, who stood motionless as she viewed the desolation.

The stench of death was everywhere. It invaded her nose. Ignoring the Mokta, she doubled over and vacated the contents of her stomach onto the ground, heaving and gasping in despair. Tears of grief coursed down her face. She heard the Mokta's footsteps approaching her.

"I was expecting to find myself hopelessly outnumbered, possibly killed on arrival," the warrior said. "But not this."

Zeetra turned her head to face the warrior, but her limbs were too weak from the shock for her to stand again.

"Pick up your weapon and kill me, Mokta," she demanded in the Mokta language. "I do not deserve to live."

"I cannot do that, Qui Tol," the woman answered. "I am sympathetic to your tremendous loss but I have too many questions, both for myself and two of the Qui Tol's victims."

"Victims?" Zeetra scowled.

"The two females your people took from Errrth."

She fumed at the arrogance of this Mokta warrior. Who was she to cast judgment on a whole people? She looked like a Chieftess and as such would be trying to safeguard her people. *As part of the military, it is what I would have done for my own people, if I could have.*

"I took the older female back to that world," Zeetra said wearily. "And I was sent to return the other one but I could not find her."

"I see. That mission appears to have saved your life." The Chieftess looked along the ground.

"You make that sound like a kindness," Zeetra replied bitterly.

She watched as this Mokta walked closer to some sparkling substance that looked like dust. The warrior gasped as she bent and prodded at a larger piece.

"Do the SnowFire gems exist here, too?" the Mokta said, thinking out loud.

"What are you talking about?" Zeetra peered at her.

"Gems like this one," she held up a fragment of the shiny, deep blue jewel between her thumb and index finger.

Zeetra viewed the jewel briefly and returned her gaze groundward. The blue stone was similar in shine and texture to the red *emla* jewel embedded in the betrothal ring of her mother. She used to be so proud of it, showing it off and telling its story to anyone who would listen.

"I have never seen that particular gem before," she replied.

"Then what has happened here—this calamity—should not be possible."

"We are in agreement about that."

"No, let me explain what I mean," the Mokta continued. "This substance is part of an ancient history. It is said to be what remains of our

Spirit of the Mountain, a being of great power who is a legend among my people. The Mokta are said to be her descendants. At least, that is how the story goes."

Zeetra wiped her mouth with her sleeve as she sat on the ground listening to this warrior. A chill ran down her spine and resentment rose from within. Zeetra, a trusted operative for the Onchei Science Directive, was crushed upon witnessing the massacred populace of her home town. Her grief-stricken heart was not ready to hear what sounded like Mokta fairy tales.

"I do not believe old Mokta legends could have foretold what happened here," Zeetra replied through clenched teeth.

"I understand that but listen to me. As far as I know, this jewel is not found anywhere else but on the mountain, where our village is. Yet it is also here, at the site of a terrible battle," the woman said. "I am saying, as unbelievable as this may sound, that this is the work of SnowFire, the Spirit of the Mountain!"

That drew ire and disbelief from Zeetra. She suddenly stood. "You think *one* warrior did all this??"

The Chieftess fell back into a protective stance before somewhat relaxing. "If it was SnowFire, then it is possible," she said gently.

"Is she some kind of celestial avatar then? A host for the twin stars?" Zeetra snorted and turned away.

"No, nothing like that. But according to our tales, she is extremely powerful."

As a slight wind picked up, it blew the death stench towards them even more strongly, causing both women to gag and cover their mouths and noses with their clothing.

"Let's continue our conversation away from . . ."

"Does it make you uncomfortable?" Zeetra asked. She scowled and looked at the warrior mockingly.

"Breathing in all of this will shorten *our* lives if we stay too long."

"Why should that matter to me?"

The Mokta carefully grabbed Zeetra's arm and tugged at it in the direction she wanted to go. Zeetra yanked it away, aggravated. The Mokta seemed to be exercising patience with her.

"If you don't care what happens, then there is no harm in you leaving this place, either," she extended her hand more gracefully in a beckoning motion. "Will you come with me?"

Zeetra offered no resistance this time. It took almost twenty minutes but she and Kitranor eventually walked beyond the town gates, where the miasma was considerably reduced if not eliminated. The Chieftess had remained silent all the while.

"What is your name, Qui Tol? I am Kitranor, Chieftess of the Mountain Mokta," the warrior woman asked as she shifted attention from the dead to the living.

"I suppose it does not matter whether I tell you now. I am Zeetra," she said with a sigh. "I have no one and nothing."

"That is not true."

"Insanity! We've just left the bodies of everyone I have ever known back in the city!"

"Forgive, Zeetra," Kitranor said, cautiously. "I simply meant that you do not have to be alone. I believe I can help you."

"Why would you do that?"

"You have not harmed me. You were only following your orders and it sounds like you were trying to set things right with two who are close to me."

"I never meant to harm anyone."

"I do not know that I can believe you, although I would like to," Kitranor said.

Zeetra scoffed, kicking some pebbles on the ground. She tried to contain a sob but failed.

"You do not have to believe me," she said. "Return to your people and claim victory over the Qui Tol if that is what you wish!"

"My only wish was to have answers to my questions, though I was ready to fight and give my life."

"As you can see, there is no one to fight. Leave me," Zeetra said, pulling out a short, thick blade from her belt. "I will join my people soon."

Without hesitation, Kitranor grabbed the Zeetra's arm at the wrist below the knife. As their eyes met, Zeetra was surprised at the compassion and strength of personality that she witnessed in the Mokta Chieftess.

"There is another way. You need not die this day," Kitranor said calmly.

"I cannot live like this, without my family!" Zeetra replied.

"You can have a new family."

"What?"

"There could be survivors somewhere in this area. But if there are none, leave all this—your land, your strange clothes that let you walk between worlds, your former mission—and join the Mokta."

"Your people call us Qui Tol, you fear us. Why would you offer this to me?"

"I am not saying this would be an easy path. My people do fear your people. They may even distrust and hate you. But I am Chieftess of the Mountain Mokta. I can speak to them, convince them to give you a chance."

"I sense you mean well, Chieftess, but your people will want me dead. And I no longer wish to live," Zeetra said, yanking her hand away from Kitranor's and eyeing her blade.

Kitranor narrowed her gaze, studying Zeetra. "You seek an end to your loss and suffering, do you?"

"Would you not?"

"Perhaps. Maybe I would feel as you do. But the Mokta often say: 'Do not run from pain and sadness. Defeat them and make them serve you.'"

Zeetra tilted her head in confusion. "What? I do not understand?"

Kitranor stood pondering for a few moments.

"I believe it is within you to survive this and I am offering to help you," Kitranor said at last.

"Why? What do you want in return?" Zeetra narrowed her eyes.

"Right now, all I want is for you to put that knife away."

Zeetra looked down at the weapon for several seconds. Then she took the blade end with her other hand and gave the knife to Kitranor. Emotionally spent, she dropped to her knees, her head lowered.

"My life is yours, Mokta Chieftess. All that I was died with my people, even my name. Do with me what you will."

"I do not need a slave," Kitranor said. "And I need to call you *something*, so you can keep your name, Zeetra."

"As you wish."

"I want information. Why did you and your people go to Errrth and bring its people to us? Why did you take the blind female back? Why were you going to take her daughter back?"

"My people used to be tribal like yours. Over our history, we grew in number, took lands for ourselves and made kings, queens, and armies,"

Zeetra said. "We are a long-lived people who can be very patient and always seek to improve ourselves. We used to occupy most of this region at one time.

"As time passed, we invented things, made machines—tools to help us do many things. Eventually, we developed the tunnels. It took us generations to find other worlds like this one," Zeetra motioned wearily towards the sky. "But we did."

Kitranor raised an eyebrow. "Worlds like Errrth."

"Yes, Earth."

"What were your people's long-term plans? Why were they doing all this?"

"I was not told that, so I do not know. I guess we will never know," Zeetra said wistfully.

The two women stood in silence, the gravity of the dead's presence nearby. Zeetra rested her hands on her thighs and began to cry, once more unable to contain her grief. Kitranor got on her knees and did her best to comfort Zeetra.

"What will I do now?" Zeetra said after some time, her voice near-hoarse. "Go with you to your village?"

"Not yet. Four of my people are on their way here, including the girl you wanted to take back to Errrth. We will wait for them."

"Here? Among the dead?"

Kitranor and Zeetra looked around them. It was obvious that they couldn't leave things as they were. Predators would come, it wouldn't be safe for them. Nor was it healthy to continue breathing in the charnel air.

"What are your people called?

"My people, if there are any left besides myself, are called Onchei."

"Onchei. I see," Kitranor said. "Do the Onchei bury their dead?"

"No," Zeetra's mind flashed to standing next to her parents in front of her grandmother's funeral pyre a cycle ago. "We burn the dead in a very hot fire until they are ashes. Then we let the wind carry their ashes away."

The Chieftess seemed to weigh options in her mind. After a bit she nodded, stood up, and offered Zeetra her hand once more, to help her up.

"We will observe your custom," Kitranor said. "As difficult as it will be, we will make a clearing, gather all of the dead and burn them until they are ashes. If your customs require any ceremonies to honor them, I will act as a witness."

"Why would you help with the cremations and observe the rites?" Zeetra asked.

"The dead here were your people and now they are gone," Kitranor said somberly. "I will do what I can do."

Zeetra didn't know how to express her gratitude. Kitranor put her right hand to Zeetra's face.

"Right now, you feel like your world has ended. And in a way, it has," Kitranor said. "But another world is opening for you. I cannot give you back what SnowFire probably took—your loved ones, the life you knew. It will take time, but someday you will feel you belong again."

"You say that like you have experienced it yourself."

"No, not me. Someone I know, who I think of as a daughter. She went through this but she survived. And you will, too."

24

PASSAGE TO ONTHOR

REIBAN APPROACHED THE HARBOR WITH practiced confidence, carrying two bagfuls of recently butchered meat ready for sale. He approached one of the ship captains, an experienced and weathered Hektolo man who took immediate notice of Reiban's offerings and walked forward to meet him. The captain's wide and short body demonstrated that, despite his years, he was sturdy enough to man ships until his dying day. He had scars on his forehead and neck, a burn on his left hand and walked with a limp. The captain had seen his share of fighting over the course of his career.

"Looking to book passage somewhere?" the older man asked, his expression neutral.

"Yes. My three companions and I are heading to Onthor, on the other side of this sea," Reiban said. "Do you barter in fresh meats?"

"I think we can do business," the older man replied, smiling as he inspected what Reiban had to offer, in terms of the quality of the meats. "I am Mej, captain of the *Gisda*. For what you have here, I can take you and your people to Onthor."

"Excellent! When will we leave?"

"How soon can your people be here? The *Gisda* is ready now."

"I will retrieve them now, Captain Mej. We will return shortly with an additional bag of our meats, as a gift to you for your generosity."

"The *Gisda* and I will be here," the captain added gruffly.

Reiban walked away from the harbor, but once he was out of the captain's sight, he broke into a run to meet up with the rest of his pack. They were on the edge of a forest, almost a mile from the harbor. As soon as he returned, Zoska stepped forward, embracing and kissing him.

"From the way you were running, I knew you either succeeded in booking passage or there was an angry group of people chasing you," Zoska said with a knowing smile.

"It is the former, I assure you," Reiban quipped.

"They accepted the meat? Do you need more?" Bopol asked.

"The captain was quite pleased with what I had, but I offered one more bag to assure he would wait for us all."

"Smart thinking," Jordan added.

Jorr-Don was dressed differently than the rest of them. Zoska had bought a hooded cloak to hide Jorr-Don's hair, which was tied in a tight bun, and gloves for her in the town that neighbored the harbor. Over several days, their group had noticed people's strong reactions, both fellow travelers and the local townspeople, to Jorr-Don's deep blue hair, tan skin and ice blue eyes. While few said anything, most expressed fear and distrust. Some clearly knew the hunting pack were Mokta, being familiar with the SnowFire gems and fewer still knew the legends of SnowFire. But increasingly, people were choosing not do business with them because of Jorr-Don, so the group had to change tactics and hide the young woman's appearance.

"We need to go to the harbor now," Reiban said. "The Captain said the ship is ready and he will take all of us to Onthor."

"I prepared an extra bag from our meat stores, just in case we needed it," Bopol said.

"Good," Reiban replied.

"I will help Zoska along. You two get started," Jorr-Don said.

"Jorr-Don! You make me sound—" Zoska protested.

"—like a woman sixty moonturns from delivering a child?" Jorr-Don interjected.

"Helpless. I was going to say helpless," Zoska said.

Zoska grudgingly allowed her best friend to aid her. Just over an hour later, the quartet arrived at the harbor. Reiban took over for Jordan and guided his mate up onto the ship. Bopol presented the captain with the final bag of fresh meat, then the captain showed the four of them where they would be sleeping/staying during the voyage.

"It will take anywhere from four to six days to reach Onthor, depending on the state of the sea and the weather," Captain Mej said.

"Our thanks, Captain," Reiban replied.

"Will your mate be a problem? I will not be delivering any newborns this trip."

"She is several months from her time. It will not be a problem."

"See that it is not."

———

Two days passed uneventfully, aside from Zoska's sea sickness. Jordan and Reiban did their best to comfort and keep her hydrated, but she didn't eat well those days. By the third day, she was better and able to rest and on the fourth day, she seemed acclimated to the environment and was able to eat more normally.

On the fifth day, the captain approached Jordan. She responded pleasantly but was guarded nonetheless.

"I heard them call you Jorr-Don?" Captain Mej said.

"Yes," she replied.

"That is not a Mokta name I am familiar with."

Jordan didn't respond to that.

"Young woman, on this ship, you are my passenger and guest, but my word is like law here. Do you understand me?"

Jordan nodded.

"Then take off that hood and let me see you plainly."

Jordan complied, slowly pulling her hood back as she looked at the captain. His eyes widened, and he gasped, letting out a curse in his own language. Jordan was worried that the captain would get angry or worse.

"I have not seen this condition so extensive before," he said, sounding sympathetic.

"Condition?" Jordan asked, confused.

"Most people do not know the power the SnowFire gems contain," he whispered. "You held onto one for too long, did you not? And it changed you?"

Not sure how to respond, Jordan nodded again.

"My mate made SnowFire earrings for me as a gift," she said. "You have seen this before?"

"I thought as much," Captain Mej said. "Only once before in my lifetime. But other shipmasters have shared their tales. People like you have their own legend."

"Really?"

"Mokta visited by SnowFire herself, always females," he said. "You were wise to cover yourself. Others have been attacked, many killed."

"Why?"

"Those who know the stories of Snow and Fire rightly fear her. Outside the Mokta, some call her a powerful evil creature while others say she is a sorceress or even a celestial being. She can lay waste to the entire world and she cannot die."

Jordan sat down with a sinking feeling in her stomach, fearing she was about to become nauseous. The choppy waves would periodically lift the boat up gently and then drop it down suddenly. This caused the vessel to shake and rattle against the water's surface each time, which did nothing to help Jordan's insides feel any better. The captain put his hand on her shoulder reassuringly.

"But those are only people's opinions. I do not share them."

Jordan nodded as she heard his words. Her eyes showed her gratitude as she respectfully kept silent. The Captain gave a good-humored nod in response, pleased but not quite allowing a smile to cross his lips.

"I have had many passengers on this ship over the years. And as a practice, I keep an eye on everyone at all times. It keeps me breathing and still owning this vessel," he stated. "As I have watched your little group, I have been impressed. You all act like kin to each other. You are respectful and based on the meat we have shared over the last few days, you are good hunters. If you were some evil creature looking to bring mischief and death, we would not be having this little chat. I would have killed you in your sleep."

That thought sent chills through Jordan.

"But you seem a kind person. No harm will befall you as long as you are on my ship."

"Thank you, Captain."

"Now cover yourself again. We will be reaching Onthor's port in a few hours and you never know what fools are waiting around at the docks."

"Yes, Captain. Thank you."

Jordan pulled her hood back over her head. She saw the captain wink and smile as she turned to walk back below deck to check on Zoska and the others.

25

BOUNTY

BOPOL AND JORDAN FORMED A protective circle as best they could around Reiban, who was guarding Zoska. It had been a week since they had arrived in Onthor. Blocking their path through the thick wooded area, they faced ten aggressors from a people they had not seen before. The daylight shining through the breaks in the trees let the hunting pack see that both the males and females facing them were slightly taller and had a paler skin tone than Jordan but looked easily as strong as any Mokta. They all had tattoos on their foreheads, cheeks, and forearms. They also wore metal piercings through their chins. So far, they had refused to identify themselves.

"What is it you want?" Jordan demanded, her own face and hair mostly hidden by her hood.

"We have heard there is a Mokta with blue hair in this area," one of the younger males said in the Mokta language. "Give her to us and we will let the rest of you go."

"You do not want to do this," Jordan said.

"Is it you, woman?" the young man asked. "Why do you hide yourself?"

"You want to *see* me?" Jordan replied, the warning in her voice clear. "Are you sure about that?"

"Jorr-Don, do not do this! You do not have to!" Bopol exclaimed.

Jordan kept her javelin close with one hand and pulled down her hood with the other. Inwardly, she was terrified, but she refused to let that show on her face or in her voice.

"Do you want to know what happened to the last person who threatened my life? She had to face the Spirit of the Mountain," Jordan added.

"The Spirit of the Mountain is just a myth! Your people are story-tellers," the young man mocked.

"Oh, but am I like any Mokta you have ever seen? I come from a faraway place called Earth. And I was changed by the SnowFire gems and the Spirit of the Mountain," Jordan said. Seeing a hint of doubt in the young man's eyes, she continued. "Now she protects me. The one who attacked me before died a horrible death, pierced through by the sword and burned with fire. And not only that, all of her people died in like manner!"

The uncertainty in his eyes was quickly turning to fear, such that his countrymen compelled him to explain what Jordan had said to him in their language, which he did. The aggressors looked at each other with confusion, some clearly not believing and others very fear-ful. They all looked at Jordan, who was projecting an air of confident ruthlessness even as she fought to keep her legs and arms from shaking.

The clouds above were gathering together and darkening. The smell of ozone filled the air and distant thunder could be heard. At first one-by-one, then collectively, the rest of the assailants sheathed their weapons and ran for their lives.

The clouds' darkness dulled to a mere gray and the thunder ceased. The impending storm turned into a simple rainshower.

Bopol was the first to approach Jordan to offer comfort.

"Jorr-Don, are you all right?!" he said, holding her in his arms as she trembled.

"I could *feel* her. SnowFire! She was so close," Jordan said. "Another minute and— at least they had the sense to run. It saved their lives."

Bopol continued to hold Jordan tenderly. And she showed him all the fears and tears she had been holding back, grateful for his silent understanding and strength. Several minutes later, she comported herself and gave him a quick kiss, turning to face her closest friends.

"I am all right. But it is clear to me that we need to get through these last lands quickly and find The Abductors," Jordan said. "The people in these lands already know about us, about me. That increases the danger to all of us."

"Someone is offering payment for your capture," Zoska said, angrily. "And you were stupid enough to show your face to them. Now they know where we are and can tell others. Next time, they may not be so fearful."

"Zoska—" Reiban warned.

"She placed us all in peril! Am I wrong?" Zoska added. "And if that bunch was any indication, they do not seem too picky whether you are brought in alive or dead. So, we would just be target practice for them."

"If that is true, they are setting bounties on their own heads," Jordan said, attempting to ignore Zoska's verbal jabs. "We already know SnowFire will not spare them if they attack me."

"Let us look at this in regard to the mission," Reiban said. "We have about one or two more weeks before we reach the Tavaa region, where Chieftess said The Abductors have been seen in times past. I do not know if we can avoid contact with the locals, especially if they are making bounties."

"Perhaps I can better disguise you, Jorr-Don," Zoska offered, attempting to calm down and seek a solution to their problems.

"We know dyes do not work on my hair," Jordan replied.

"No, but we saw some white-haired riding beasts yesterday," Zoska said. "I think I could make a wig for you from one of their manes. And I could add some red tint to your skin, make you look more Mokta. Perhaps the kuvu root we use for painting on crafts might work on your skin. I cannot do anything for your eyes, though."

"From a distance, that should not matter," Jordan said, sounding encouraged. "Let us give it a try."

———————

When the hunting pack started traveling the next morning, they appeared to be four ordinary Mokta again. Jordan felt a bit awkward wearing the improvised wig of white hair which had an odd smell but was far preferable to being targeted by strangers. The makeup Zoska had used also had a unique odor to it and caused her skin to tingle some. When Jordan had looked at herself in a pond's reflection, she didn't recognize herself.

The terrain ahead of them was unremarkable compared to the mountains and valleys they had traveled through to make it thus far. There were fields of orange flowers and rolling grassy hills. All in all, it looked like these lands might make for a pleasant remainder of their journey.

That was good news for Zoska, who was growing heavier with child by the day. Reiban and Jordan took turns watching out for her, guiding her along and making sure she took time to rest and have small meals throughout the day. It added time to their adventure, but the entire pack felt the well-being of mother and child was worth it.

Looking off in the distance, Jordan watched as the sun began to set. A melancholy mood started to overtake her. Jordan noticed Zoska lumbering in her direction, looking sympathetic.

"Whose death do you see over that ridge?" Zoska said with somberness and concern.

"Wh-what?"

Finally reaching Jordan, Zoska put her arm around her in almost a side-hug and sighed.

"You carry a burden none of us can understand," Zoska continued. "It must be hard for you."

"I am not sure I understand it myself. I never thought I would have a connection with a legend like SnowFire."

"She is no longer just a legend."

Jordan looked away from Zoska into the distance.

"She frightens me," Jordan admitted.

"And me. But I understand her, in a way."

"Really?"

"We are her children, Jorr-Don. Her descendants, even you."

Jordan nodded in response. "I suppose."

"She is the unspoken Queen of the Mokta. She is responsible for all of us."

"Okay, I can understand that."

"And a queen will protect her subjects at any cost. She will become as terrible as she must to do whatever needs to be done. Because by the moons' rising each night, her kingdom must be safe and free from threats. She can never relax her guard and must be consistent."

Jordan's eyes widened in understanding. "You are describing Chieftess now."

"The role is the same. We are a village, not a kingdom. But our village may as well be one to us . . . and her."

Jordan nodded again.

"So, whose death do you see over that ridge?" Zoska repeated.

"I do not want to see *anyone* die! I am afraid for us and whoever we encounter."

Jordan was glad when Zoska pulled her into a full hug. She hadn't known just how much she needed the reassurance and support.

"Then it is your burden, too," Zoska added. "The burden of the queen."

"SnowFire is the queen, not me."

"And who is the one representing SnowFire right now, hm?"

Jordan didn't respond but they both knew the answer to that question.

26

REUNION

TEN MORE DAYS PASSED FOR the hunting pack. Jordan and Bopol had chosen to take the lead, acting as scouts and first defense against any threats. So, they were the first to see the Abductor buildings from afar. They returned to discuss their discovery with Reiban and Zoska.

"These must be the lands Chieftess spoke of," Bopol said. "This place is built like none we have seen in all our travels. We dare not underestimate The Abductors. They may have hidden defenses or the capability to shoot across great distances."

"I agree with Bopol, but I was a little surprised," Jordan said. "If the devices they have built are as advanced as I believe, should they not have detected our movement near their village and raised some kind of alarm?"

Zoska lifted her head towards the sky and inhaled a whiff of air. She recoiled suddenly, looking confused.

"I only smell death here!" Zoska said.

"You can tell from this distance?" Jordan said.

"Yes. My senses are very strong right now. This tang is like the Onchei fortress when we woke, after the queen attacked you."

"I wonder . . . did the Abductors meet a similar fate?" Bopol asked.

That sent a chill through Jordan. "Did we travel all this way for *nothing?*"

"We must confirm with our own eyes," Bopol said. "We should go to their village."

Jordan and the others nodded in agreement and they continued, entering past a tall stone gate into a township that stretched for a mile or more. The structures were made mostly of uniform gray stone, although some were wooden and a few with something like large bricks, standing one to two stories tall with glass-like windows and wooden doors. Jordan recognized networks of electronic poles towering above the neighborhoods, reminding her of telephone lines from Earth. The buildings hummed with power.

But Zoska had been right. There were bodies on every street and in every building, skeletal forms and corpses torn apart, the strong, lingering stench of demise looming menacingly over the whole area. The odor was so strong that they had to cover their noses and mouths. And even that wasn't truly sufficient. They had to stop and go around the city-wide open grave, which lessened but didn't eliminate the presence of the decay. Even animals were avoiding the area, as if it was cursed.

Once the group put some distance between themselves and the necropolis, they saw smoke from a small fire in what appeared to be a neighboring township only a couple of miles away.

"Perhaps someone is cooking a meal?" Reiban suggested.

"Either that or it is the final fires of a battle," Bopol added grimly.

"We should go and see. There is nothing else we can do here," Jordan said.

Zoska nodded, covering her face with her furs. She was doing her best to contain her nausea from the still-strong carnal fumes.

It took about an hour to enter the neighboring community. Once there, they found that at least the bodies had been removed. There was a certain hazy scent of fatality, but it was tolerable and fading. The empty buildings, constructed in the same manner as its sister city, were the primary reminder that this place had suffered a similar fate.

As they grew closer to the source of the smoke, they were extremely surprised to find Mokta Chieftess Kitranor cooking soup outside one of the buildings. She looked deep in thought.

"Chieftess!" Bopol cried out with a loud voice.

She smiled when she looked up and saw her son and the others. "*There* you are! I was wondering when you would get here!"

Kitranor ran to meet them. She was delighted to see how pregnant Zoska was and to have the company of Reiban and Bopol. Then she saw Jordan.

"Greetings, Chieftess," Jordan said, smiling somewhat uneasily. "How did you make it here before us?"

"I will tell you. But first, did you accept Bopol as your mate?"

"Yes, Chieftess. I accepted him gladly!"

That made Kitranor smile with pride. "Very good."

Kitranor put her hands on her hips and looked at Jordan askance. "Now, you must tell me why you are wearing paint on your skin and that ridiculous false hair? Is there some reason you need to look more like your brethren and not like yourself?"

Jordan laughed. "I am afraid so. The people of this land have offered reward for my capture."

"For what reason?" Kitranor asked, bewildered by the statement.

Then the Chieftess looked closely at Jordan, almost squinting.

"Your eyes, they are a different color than before?" Kitranor said.

"Yes . . . and that is not all," Jordan replied, removing her white wig and revealing her deep blue hair.

She had never seen the Chieftess show fear until now. Kitranor almost lost her balance as she stepped backward, her eyes wide and never leaving Jordan. The others abruptly stopped their laughing and conversing. All eyes were on the Chieftess.

The Chieftess closed her eyes, took in a deep breath and released it, managing through sheer effort to calm herself. Kitranor slowly nodded at Jordan.

"You have encountered the one who calls herself Snow and Fire," Kitranor said.

"Yes," Jordan said. "She saved our lives. She healed me from near-death."

"Where is the gem I sent with my blessing, along with my son?" Kitranor said. "You must have had it with you."

"I did."

"And where is it now?"

Jordan lifted her hands to waist level and turned them over so the Chieftess could see the gems fused into her palms. Kitranor's eyes widened again, this time in fearful amazement. Then she lowered her eyes respectfully.

"You do not know the honor—and burden—of what SnowFire has passed on to you, Jorr-Don," Kitranor said in a soft voice, her eyes still looking downward.

"What do you mean?" Jordan replied.

"If the stories are true, SnowFire's power will *continue* to change you," Kitranor continued. "Someday, you may become the living embodiment of all that she is."

"I do not understand," Jordan replied, genuinely perplexed.

"According to our legends, this has happened before, though not in recent times. The tales say that SnowFire judges a person in possession of the gem to see whether they are worthy of life or death. Often, she lets them die. But if she does save them, it is with a small spark of her own power, which continues to exist within them. That is why they change, as a living resemblance in her honor. You may already be immortal. I do not know."

Dread seized Jordan. She couldn't speak or move. Kitranor had unwittingly reminded Jordan of her SnowFire dream, where that powerful being had made the same claim.

She felt a spark of dread as, mere feet away, Bopol was visibly startled at his mother's revelation that Jordan might be immortal. She could only imagine what thoughts, fears and even doubts might be running through his mind. Were they anything like the ones she already harbored? Would the alterations SnowFire made to her change who she was? Would it affect their relationship? If they had children someday, would they be impacted by this?

Jordan made eye contact with Kitranor. She realized her mother-in-law must have picked up on her distress because she put her hands on the younger woman's shoulders and began to speak confidently.

"Do not be afraid, Jorr-Don. I spoke of legend, not fact," Kitranor insisted. "All we know is that you have been touched and healed by SnowFire's power. And that it has altered your appearance."

"Yes, Chieftess," Jordan replied respectfully.

"There is one other fact to discuss. Being chosen in such a manner by SnowFire, it makes *you* Chieftess of the Mokta."

"What? No! I don't want—it's *too soon!*"

"It is not a matter of what you want, Jorr-Don," Kitranor answered sternly. "SnowFire's actions, whether in legend of old or in reality today, will not be taken lightly by our people."

"Chieftess, please . . . I—I beg you! Take time to teach me what I need to know," Jordan said. "But *remain* Chieftess until I am ready!"

Jordan felt a glimmer of hope as Kitranor lifted her eyes and smiled.

"There is wisdom in your words. A chieftess cannot rule without being taught. One of the Mokta elders guided our tribe while I received my instruction. Very well. I will remain Chieftess and impart all that I know to you for now," Kitranor said. "That will give you and my son time to enjoy being mates and start a family."

Inside, Jordan was reeling. Her mind was forced to contemplate becoming ruler of the entire Mokta village soon as well as the changes SnowFire had made to her body and the more-real-than-ever prospect of having children with Bopol. Individually, each of those would be daunting—but all at once, they were almost too much to bear.

Jordan took a deep breath. Out of the corner of her eye, she saw Bopol approaching, clearly concerned. When he was close enough, she latched onto him and buried her head in his chest.

"Chieftess, Jorr-Don has been through much," Bopol said to his mother. "She will need time to adjust."

"Yes, I can see that," Kitranor replied.

Just then, a young Onchei woman walked out of the building.

"Chieftess, did you forget about the meal?" she asked. "It's been cooking for a while—"

"Ah, Zeetra!" Kitranor brightened. "Come. I want you to meet—"

"A survivor?" Jordan tensed and pulled away from Bopol. "And she is Onchei!"

Zeetra bristled at underlying hostility in Jordan's voice.

"How do you know I am Onchei?" Zeetra asked.

"We met some of your people," Jordan said bitterly, stung by the still-recent memory. "One of them nearly killed me and had evil plans for the rest of my pack."

"Where did you encounter these Onchei?" Zeetra asked.

Reiban stepped forward to answer. "It was in a terrible, storm-plagued kingdom about forty moons from here."

"A kingdom?" Zeetra said.

"Yes."

"The Onchei stopped being a monarchy nearly four hundred cycles ago!"

"They had a queen who was half-Onchei and half-Mokta," Reiban replied. "Her father said he used to be king over all Onchei. His name was Yami."

Zeetra's eyes widened in astonishment.

"That can't be! Yami and Amstar? Our history states that they were driven out of the kingdom and killed. That was many generations before my birth but every young one learns—" Zeetra abruptly halted, her eyes squinting and becoming teary at yet another sorrowful reminder of the loss of her people. She sighed and closed her eyes, composing herself once more before resuming. "We *learned* the fable of King Yami and his daughter during our early teachings."

Jordan stepped forward, curious. "Then, there's an Onchei culture that branched away from what we saw?"

"These people are the Qui Tol," Kitranor said. "Or they were. She is all that is left."

Jordan's eyes narrowed at Zeetra and her breathing quickened.

"You are an Abductor?!" Jordan shouted, furious. She gripped her weapon tighter, as if ready to use it. "The Onchei were the Abductors all along? Why? *Why* did you take me and my gemta from Earth? Why did you bring us here??"

"Wait, *you* are the younger one?" Zeetra gasped.

Impatient and filled with growing rage, Jordan stepped towards Zeetra. She held her weapon with both hands, horizontally at waist level. One swift motion would be enough to kill.

"You get one more chance to answer me before I gut you with my javelin!"

Zeetra seemed oddly calm. She relaxed her body, lifted her chin and closed her eyes, allowing herself a satisfied smile.

Jordan didn't understand fully why this Onchei— this Abductor— wanted to die, but the way she was feeling, she almost didn't care. If the Abductors hadn't brought her and her gemta here, Jordan's gemta wouldn't be blind, Jordan wouldn't have met SnowFire and been changed, she wouldn't have to contemplate becoming Chieftess yet. Everything would have been so much simpler if the Abductors had just left her family alone! So, Jordan pulled back her javelin and prepared to grant this Onchei's unspoken wish.

"Jorr-Don, stop!" Kitranor shouted, holding her hand between them. "She is under my protection now."

"*Your* protection? Why does she even get protection?"

"She has left behind her former missions and accepted my invitation to join our tribe," Kitranor said. "She has also agreed to do right by you, as she did in returning your gemta to Errrth."

"Gemta is on Earth?" Jordan said, dropping her weapon and backing up, her mood now conflicted.

"Yes," Kitranor added, nodding.

"When was my gemta taken back to Earth, Chieftess?"

"Januss was taken fifteen moons after your pack left."

She is home! She has been home for months. And now, the Abductor is offering to take me back to Earth, too?

Jordan had to sit down to center herself. Bopol started to move towards her but the Chieftess stopped him with a blocking motion of her hand. Her eyes were sad but resolute as she shook her head slowly. Bopol reluctantly obeyed.

Jordan's mind was in a kind of mental vertigo, so many thoughts and ideas flashing by rapidly. She was torn in so many ways over these newest revelations. She put her head in her hands and opened her mouth to scream but made no sounds, only panting breaths.

We came all this way to see if there was a way to go home! But now that there is, do I still want to go? Mom is home. She is probably with Dad and Mark, she will be okay. I will miss her but . . . as messed up as my life is, is it not supposed to be here—on Algoran—now?

Jordan could almost picture her brother's face as well as her father's. In her mind's eye, she could see their sadness. They were reaching out to her. She felt a longing to go to them, comfort them and explain everything.

But, standing near her, Jordan also saw Bopol's strong and loving face, felt her growing love for him, her need to be with him. She also saw the friendly, if worried, faces of Zoska, Reiban and the Chieftess. Jordan could envision the Mountain and the Mokta village which she was a part of now, the people who would depend on her, when she became their Chieftess. And lastly, Jordan saw the haunting form of SnowFire. All of it required answers to questions brimming within her.

"You can send me back to Earth, the planet I was born on?" Jordan asked, looking up at Zeetra.

"I can give you a machine to send you where I sent her, your gemta," Zeetra answered. "I have no more use for the machine. There will be no more abductions."

"You swear that?" Jordan roared, standing up and grabbing the Onchei by the back of the hair in one swift motion. She held her javelin to the Onchei's throat with the other hand. Her friends were stunned by Jordan's savagery, not having time to intervene. "I will slice you open and kill you slowly if you are lying to me!"

"I—I swear it," Zeetra replied in a pained whisper. "I have no more reason to take your people than I do to live."

That response surprised Jordan. She pressed her javelin blade up against Zeetra's throat, the blade so sharp it caused a small slicing cut. Zeetra stayed motionless, almost mesmerized by Jordan's ice-colored eyes.

"I wonder if *this* was the last thing my people saw?" Zeetra whispered.

"Jorr-Don!" Kitranor cried before Jordan could react to Zeetra's question.

Jordan was not used to hearing so much fear in the Chieftess' voice. Jordan dropped her javelin but continued to grip the Onchei by the hair, holding her close still.

"If Chieftess has added you to the tribe, then you are Mokta," Jordan said with cold fury. "Your oath has meaning. But if you *ever* break that oath, I will finish you myself."

"I understand."

"Show me this machine and how to use it," Jordan commanded, roughly letting go of Zeetra.

Jordan hadn't expected to feel this way when she finally encountered an Abductor. Her own rage made her feel so strong, so in-control, when she had felt mostly helpless since being been brought to Algoran. It was almost intoxicating. Then Jordan turned her attention from herself to her loved ones and was amazed to see the silent but clearly shocked reactions from each of them, even the Chieftess. Jordan moved towards them and started to speak, hoping to reassure them, but the looks of hesitation and discomfort in their eyes changed her mind. Wordlessly, her eyes pleaded with Bopol to come to her, she needed him. A few seconds later, he responded in kind.

From the corner of her eye, she watched as Zeetra walked to a nearby building. A minute later, she returned with a square box. Zeetra pressed a red jewel on the top of the device that caused it to light up and she checked its settings. Then she turned to Jordan.

"This is still focused on the location I sent your mother to, back on Earth. Press this symbol," Zeetra said, pointing to an amber-colored jewel carved into a half-circle. "A portal will open to take you there. The portal will close after about thirty bils—er, half a minute in your English language. If you decide to come back, press this symbol. That will open a portal for your return."

Jordan studied Zeetra's actions as the Onchei turned the cube-shaped device to show Jordan its other side, which displayed greenish-blue jewels forming a triangle with a line through their center. Zeetra handed the cube to her.

"I understand. And I believe you," Jordan said, taking the device.

Jordan walked up to her mate. Bopol looked pleased for her but she could tell by his body language, the way he was standing as well as the tenseness in his muscles, that he was still troubled. She put her hand on his cheek and smiled.

"You know I have to do this, right?" she said.

"I suppose so, yes."

"And you know where my heart is."

"Yes."

"Then relax. You have nothing to fear."

"All right, Jorr-Don."

"I love you."

"And I love you."

They kissed, embracing one another. Her affection was sincere and tender.

"I know that you have to do this, but I do not want you to go," Bopol implored.

"This is not like you. Where is my brave warrior?"

His eyes were as stoic as ever but Jordan felt a sadness from him.

"He is here," Bopol said. "He has not changed."

For a moment, Jordan wondered what Bopol was trying to tell her. But at the same time, the opportunity to go back to Earth was strongly beckoning. She looked into her mate's eyes and tried to convey her love and commitment to him. She slowly backed away from him, never losing her smile. She pointed the device to her right and pressed the yellow-orange symbol, causing a portal to open.

Jordan waited a few seconds, almost surprised that her actions had caused this portal to open, instead of one of the Abductors. This was her choice and she was committed to it.

She took one more moment to take in the sight of Bopol and the others. This was her family every bit as much as the one she had on Earth.

"I will see you all soon!" Jordan said to them pleasantly as she ran through the portal.

27

SIBLINGS

WHEN JORDAN WAS TWELVE AND Mark was seven, she truly enjoyed spending time with him. Whether they were watching movies, playing video games, real-life ones like Hide and Seek or just sitting around and talking, there was always a certain excitement they both shared with each other. Jordan felt protective of Mark and although he never told her, Mark felt the same way towards Jordan. She was his best friend. Even when she tried to act distant to look cool to her middle school friends, he could see through it. She was aware that he knew it, too. They always sensed what the other was feeling and going through, since they had always been there for one another.

Now, Mark's fingers hovered above the keyboard and he stared hesitantly at his laptop's screen. He clicked a button to begin streaming some instrumental guitar music, an attempt to help him relax before he began typing a journal entry for the first time. His reluctance stemmed from how difficult he knew it would be to write out his memories in this manner. But his therapist had insisted he was ready and needed to do this. He could feel tears welling in his eyes as he created the title of the entry:

"The Day Everything Changed"

By Mark Lewis

When I was twelve years old, someone broke into my house and kidnapped my mother and my sister, Jordan. I was sleeping in the room next to Jordan, but I didn't wake up, so I couldn't stop whoever took them. They were just gone, taken from me—ripped out of my life. I didn't know how to handle any of it, I was still a kid. I was mad at Dad for divorcing Mom, so I didn't want to live with him. I didn't speak or even leave my room for weeks. I didn't want to leave the only home I'd known, and I kind of lost it. Dad had to call an ambulance and they medicated me until some doctors could figure out what was going on. They said I had severe depression, anxiety and anger issues. They were right. I'd lost everything I'd ever known except for Dad and I didn't want him around me at the time.

It took most of a year for me to make peace with my mother and sister being gone. For a long time, I told myself if Dad had been there, he could have saved them but that wasn't fair. Mom had wanted the divorce, not him, but it was easier to be angry with Dad than Mom. For me to move on, I had to forgive everyone, even myself. And that was the hardest thing of all. I'm not sure I have yet but I'm trying.

During my therapy, I had to be taught how to acknowledge my feelings again. I was hurt so badly that I didn't want anything else to hurt me. I didn't really know who *I* was anymore and it took most of that year to work past the fear, anger and pain inside me. I had to learn to trust again—that people wouldn't abandon me, that I was someone worth loving and being friends with. Somehow, I forced myself to attend the dual-funeral for my Mom and sister. If they were really gone, I needed to say goodbye.

Not long after that, I started attending high school, even though I was a year behind. Late in my freshman year, knowing how much I liked music, Dad took a chance and bought me an acoustic guitar. I loved it so much, I taught myself to play. And before long, I found myself writing and even performing those songs in public, either in parks or at school. I guess that's when I started making friends, too, like Kayla Montgomery.

Kayla's kind of blunt and easy to read, her feelings are always close to the surface. She's a flute player and an artist who likes making pencil sketches. She understands what I've been through. Her father died in a car accident when she was nine. She's an only child and her mother didn't remarry. Kayla used art to find her way out of her own darkness after her dad died. She's the only one who can make me laugh. It took being around Kayla to make me realize that I hadn't laughed since I lost Jordan and Mom. And it feels good to laugh again. I guess that shows I'm still making progress.

Mark made that the end of his journal entry and saved it. Still listening to the music, he was looking forward to seeing Kayla again.

———————

"I'm thinking of cutting my hair," Kayla said as they sat in the cafeteria, enjoying their meals.

"Why?" Mark replied.

"I've had the same hairstyle forever, at least since last year! Don't you think it's time for a change?"

"Maybe but not the length . . . not by much anyway. How about another color? And I suppose you could wear it differently."

"What color? How should I wear it?"

"How about red?"

 Kayla made a yuck face.

"Ohhhh-kay, how about blonde?" Mark asked.

"You think I could be a blonde? Really?" Kayla replied.

"Why not?"

"Hm! Okay, I'll consider it. And the style?"

"You could always try dreads."

"Mark Lewis, I'm going to pour this milk on your head!"

"What? You'd look good in dreads."

 Kayla peered at him suspiciously for several seconds as he tried to keep a straight face. Then they both snickered in amusement.

Mark worked part-time at a music repair shop not far from home, which gave him what every teen craved: disposable income. Today, he had used some of his cash to take Kayla out to eat at a local burger restaurant. They took the bus to get there but were planning to take the scenic route back home. It was a clear and cool October Saturday. A moderate breeze was blowing outside, with strong gusts at times. Mark didn't mind; it would give him and Kayla reason to huddle together to stay warm. He left a reasonable tip for the waitress on the table, stood up and offered his hand to his girlfriend like a perfect gentleman.

They strolled arm-in-arm to the door, which Mark held open for her. The strong draft made walking forward a challenge, but they persisted till the gust dissipated. Stopping to talk under the large tree in the parking lot, whose powerful limbs and abundant leaves struggled against the streaming air currents, Mark and Kayla stood close to the trunk. It helped deflect some of the wind and allowed them to hear each other better.

"What do you think about collaborating on music?" Mark asked.

"Your guitar and my flute?"

"Yeah! And I'd sing, if you want."

"I wish I could sing."

"Maybe I could teach you? I mean, I'm not great or anything, but—"

"Are you kidding, Mark? You have an incredible voice, I love it! It's just . . . I've never really had more than a sing-in-the-shower voice."

"You're being modest."

"No! You really don't want to hear me sing!"

"Kay-la!"

"I'm telling you, I'm tone deaf! I couldn't sing my way out of a paper ba—"

A sudden shrill humming began about ten feet away from them, capturing their full attention. The air itself began to shimmer and swirl into a circular pattern before them, defying the near-tempest winds surrounding them. A charge of electricity and the smell of ozone tinged the air right before the strange vortex sparked and surged into a spinning portal of light right before Mark and Kayla. The gateway grew wider and taller, thrumming with power, a bright hole like nothing they had ever seen.

Other people close enough to see this phenomenon ran away in panic. But Mark was enraptured as much as terrified.

After several seconds, a woman ran through the maelstrom, emerging from the light to solid ground. Her momentum continued to shove her forward until she ran into the tree, causing her to drop her javelin and grunt in discomfort. The brilliant light from the opening in the air obscured her features from Mark but the sound of her voice was unmistakable and instinctively, he knew it was his sister, Jordan. Too stunned to speak, he just kept his eyes on her, despite the sharp glare. Kayla watched over his shoulder as best she could.

After half a minute, the aperture closed, and Jordan slowly lifted her head, turning to face them. The situation was cruel, in its own way. Mark worried he was hallucinating, that this was some kind of dream.

"Mark?" Jordan stared at him, wide-eyed.

He nodded vigorously before hugging her tightly. Pulling her close, he sobbed and laughed at the same time, relieved and filled with delight. The part of him that had been metaphorically holding his breath for nearly five years finally released everything he had been burying. Beyond being cathartic, he felt like he'd regained a piece of himself that had been stolen. In his embrace, Jordan and her furs reeked of sweat, blood and smoke, but that wasn't important to Mark. All that mattered was that his sister was alive and home again.

Tears streamed down Jordan's cheeks. Her voice made incoherent ramblings as she held her brother tightly and ran her hands through his hair. To say she was overjoyed was an understatement. It wasn't just that Jordan had missed Mark, she regretted that she hadn't gotten to say goodbye. She knew Mark and her father must have assumed that she and her mother had been killed. All this time, she'd been haunted by how that must have devastated them. Also, having been denied the opportunity to sit and talk with Mark over the years, to ask his opinions and witness his accomplishments or help him through his failures, Jordan had struggled with her dereliction of sisterhood, a personal deficiency. Now, she felt like she finally had a chance to set things right.

She saw that Mark had lost his middle school pudginess and grown over a foot taller, exceeding her height. He had also become stronger and very handsome. His brown hair had lightened some and was longer than she'd ever seen it, even though it wasn't quite shoulder-length yet. She observed the young woman with long brown hair who was standing very close to Mark in an almost protective stance. She was glad he had a close friend like that. Or was she more than a friend, Jordan wondered.

Mark stared curiously at her, particularly her face.

"Have I changed so much?" Jordan asked, slightly embarrassed. "Is it the hair?"

"No . . . not the hair," he replied, his eyes fixated. His deep voice further surprised her. "But you have changed."

"How do you mean?"

She waited patiently as Mark looked down for a second. He looked like he was trying to choose his words. A few seconds later, he returned her gaze again.

"There was a time when any imperfection would have really bothered you, especially on your face," he said with a reminiscent smile.

Jordan nodded in understanding. "And now you see my scars from the hunt."

"Yes. You're okay with them?"

Jordan smiled and spoke proudly. "Of course. I earned them!"

Mark seemed to relax some. "This may sound ironic, but you're a lot more down-to-Earth than you used to be."

Jordan laughed. "'Down to Earth?' That is funny, Mark!"

Several seconds passed as the siblings looked at one another in wonder.

"Mom told me and Dad where you were," Mark continued.

"Mom is okay?" Jordan inquired, obviously worried.

"She is doing well. She is at home," Mark answered in the Mokta language.

"She taught you Mokta? I am impressed!" Jordan replied, also in Mokta.

Kayla fidgeted in place, clearly uncomfortable with Jordan and Mark beginning to speak in another language.

"Who *is* she, Mark?"

"Kayla, this is my sister, Jordan," Mark said, turning to look at his girlfriend with tears still in his eyes. "She's finally back home!"

Jordan could see the apprehension in Kayla's body language, the way the teen kept one hand touching the tree behind her and the other balled into a fist in front of her. Kayla's eyes were afraid but shifting between Jordan and Mark, her posture aggressive, as if figuring out how to attack if there was need.

Lifting both arms in a surrender gesture, Jordan slowly and calmly moved towards Kayla, never breaking eye contact.

"Hello. I can already see that you are a good friend to my brother. You are watching out for him," Jordan said in a measured voice. "I am glad he has someone who cares about him like that. I want you to know that I could never harm him—or you."

"How can I believe you? You appeared from some kind of—I don't know *what* that was!"

"Kay, wh-what—" Mark sputtered.

Jordan could feel a wave of anger wash over her, furrowing her brow. Trying not to give in to it, she gritted her teeth, closed her eyes and turned her neck from side to side, releasing tension with the small cricks and cracks that emitted from her neck.

"I have come a long way to see my brother and family. I would . . . like to get to know the ones close to him, too," Jordan said, extending a hand.

When she opened her hand up, both Kayla and Mark could see the embedded gemstone. Kayla gasped, and Mark took in a sharp, sudden breath and held it.

"Is that some kind of art thing? Like a tattoo but with jewelry?" Kayla said. "It looks painful."

"It does not hurt. And it is not art," Jordan said, briefly looking at her hands. "As far as I know, I am one of a kind. This happened a few months ago."

"Are you all right?" Mark asked, concerned. "How did that happen to you?"

"Basically, yes, I am fine. As for how it happened, I am not sure I can explain in a way that makes sense," Jordan said, looking around, even skyward, trying to get her bearings. Being back on Earth was even more disorienting than Jordan had expected.

Mark gently put his hand on Jordan's shoulder. "I can only imagine. But look, we should probably get going. You're drawing a crowd."

Jordan looked over her shoulder and saw people standing outside the restaurant pointing at her or taking pictures with their cell phones. Others nearby had stopped and were staring. When her attention turned to Kayla again, she could see that the young woman had not shifted opinions about her. She was still defensive and standoff-ish.

"Yes, I agree. Which way?" Jordan asked.

"Home. Dad bought a house a couple of miles from here."

"Lead the way," Jordan said, picking her javelin up off the ground.

"If anyone asks, you're a cosplayer, Jordan," he said.

Jordan searched her memory for what that meant. When her recall kicked in, she laughed a little harder than she meant to.

As they walked along, Jordan realized something.

"You did not tell her anything?" Jordan asked Mark.

"Mom told me not to talk about it with anyone but her and Dad."

"Can you tell me now?" Kayla asked, clearly irritated.

"It is going to sound insane," Jordan said, as much to herself as her brother.

"Yes, I can tell you, Kay. I'm sorry I didn't before," Mark said. "And my sister is right, this may sound pretty out there."

"I can handle it!" Kayla said abruptly with a huff and shrug.

"Okay. Well . . . Jordan was on another world," Mark said slowly and deliberately. "They call it Algoran."

"Another . . . planet?" Kayla said.

"Yeah," Mark replied.

"How could she breathe or—"

"It is a lot like Earth, only colder," Jordan interrupted

"Another planet?" Kayla repeated, horrified. "That light portal, it brought you here from there?"

"That is correct," Jordan replied.

"Are you still, um, human?" Kayla asked.

"Kayla!" Mark interjected.

"Aliens creep me out! At least, the ones in the movies do."

"I am pretty sure I am still human," Jordan answered honestly.

"Whew!" Kayla said, relieved.

"At least mostly," Jordan said under her breath.

"Mark?" Kayla said, looking at her boyfriend alarmed.

"My sister always did have a quirky sense of humor," he said.

"Once you survive the first moon with me, I am sure we will get along fine," Jordan said.

"First moon?" Kayla asked.

Jordan sighed in frustration. "Sorry, the first day. I have been speaking Mokta for years and the Mokta people count days by the number of moons that have passed. Years are cycles. It is just a different way of telling time."

"Oh," Kayla said.

As they walked through the neighborhood, a dog began barking aggressively at them in a yard behind a chain fence. Mildly annoyed, Jordan turned towards it and exhaled through her nostrils loudly in a huff, showing the canine a fierce look. And while the animal didn't lose its defensive posture, it stopped its bluster and let them pass in peace.

To Jordan, Mark seemed intrigued by this. Kayla was further unsettled but said nothing.

The rest of the walk to the house was without any words.

28

THE WAY FORWARD

THE LACK OF CONVERSATION WAS surprisingly peaceful as they continued their walk towards the Lewis residence. It gave Jordan time to think as she looked around at the neighborhood and the metropolis in general, feeling both wonder and disappointment. She recognized her hometown but, in what seemed an irony, the city of Chase Creek, Colorado seemed distant and foreign to her now. The once-suburban sprawl had developed into something else over the last five years. More people had moved to Chase Creek. This had led to the construction of more homes, apartment complexes and schools. Additional buses were running, and Jordan saw a metro rail as it crossed over a bridge in the distance.

However, to Jordan, it wasn't just the construction that had changed this place. Earth itself was strange to her now. The sounds of nature were mostly drowned out by vehicles or planes. The scent of fresh air had been replaced with that of fuel, exhaust and other chemicals. There were so many unnatural sounds and to such a degree that it was distracting, almost deafening at times.

This is the world I was born into. It was my whole life until I was seventeen, Jordan thought. *But it does not feel like home anymore.*

She looked at her brother and his girlfriend, who were calm around each other, although Kayla kept some distance between herself and

Jordan. In one respect, Jordan envied their peace. And at the same time, she felt bad for them.

Does anyone around here even know how beautiful it is to live off the land, to appreciate nature and live in harmony with it? It seems like the majority of people have replaced their need for nature with technology. Before I left here, I guess I was the same way.

Jordan beheld the people walking by, many who seemed entranced with their mobile devices, only vaguely paying attention to where they were going. She observed a number of people in their cars watching LCD screens in the front or back seats while others talked on their phones as they drove. And still more walked along listening to various entertainment via wired or wireless earbuds.

Do as few people actually talk to each other in public as what I am seeing here? Is it like this across the city and beyond? I wanted to return here so badly, and it has driven me for so long. But now that I am here, and I see it for what it really is, I cannot relate to it anymore.

She put her hand to her chest, to her heart.

I have been here for less than an hour. And I already miss Bopol! I have gotten so used to him being by my side, talking with him. I wish he could be here with me now. It would make this so much easier.

"What's wrong?" Mark asked.

"I guess I am getting sentimental," Jordan said, smiling and looking embarrassed. "I miss my—oh, that is right. I have not told you that yet."

"Told us what?" Mark asked.

"I miss my husband," Jordan said.

Mark stopped and slowly swerved around to look at Jordan. He raised an eyebrow at her then grinned widely. "You got married?"

Jordan blushed. "Um, yes."

"Is it that guy from the Mokta—what was his name?"

"Bopol."

"Right! Bopol!"

"Do you have any kids?" Mark asked.

"No, no kids yet," she replied.

"Wait a second," Kayla interjected. "You married an alien??"

"Well, actually, on Algoran, *I* am the alien."

"Ah—wait, what?" Kayla said, flabbergasted.

Just then, a police car slowly rolled alongside them and stopped. Its lights were off and its sole occupant, a muscular African-American officer in his early forties with a trim mustache, lowered his window and made eye contact with them.

"Have any of you seen anything unusual in the area in the last half hour?" the officer said, looking concerned.

"What's going on, Officer?" Mark said, matching the policeman's mood.

"Someone reported some kind of disturbance, so I'm checking it out."

Just then, the Police dispatcher contacted the officer through his radio to report a domestic disturbance at another address. The officer acknowledged the information and committed to investigating it.

"I've got to check this out. The other was probably a false alarm. Take care."

Mark waved to the officer as he drove off. When the police car was out of sight, Jordan finally felt like she could relax.

Five minutes later, Mark led Jordan and Kayla into the house. Her mother was sitting at the dining room table, preparing a sandwich for herself. When she heard the door open, she stood up, curious.

"Mark? You are home early. Is Kayla with you? Mark?"

Jordan looked at her mother for seconds that stretched like minutes to her. She wasn't used to seeing her mother in Earth clothes, a pale-yellow blouse and blue jeans, with her hair pulled back into a bun. Her mom had on a silver necklace and earrings. Jordan put her fingers to her own lips, teary-eyed, happy to see her mom again. She cleared her throat.

"I am here, too, Mom," Jordan said, her smile evident in her voice.

"Jordan?" Mom said, abruptly turning her head in the direction of her daughter's voice.

Feeling her way along the wall and furniture, her mom crossed the room in record time and embraced Jordan. Then Mom sniffed into the air and pulled back cautiously.

"What has happened, Jordan? You smell . . . of death . . . and blood."

Jordan's enthusiasm waned, and she lowered her eyes. "You are right, Mom. A lot has changed since you left Algoran."

"Tell me," she said sternly and in Mokta.

"My quest was successful. We found an Abductor in the Southlands. She was of a race called the Onchei," Jordan said, replying in Mokta. "She may be the last of her kind. She was the one who returned you to Earth. She also gave me the technology to return as well."

"I do not understand. Only one Abductor?"

"The rest of her people were killed . . . massacred . . . by SnowFire."

Her mom gasped. "From the legends?"

"She is real, Mom . . . but it will take me some time to explain," Jordan said.

Jordan spent the next twenty minutes speaking in the Mokta language, telling her mother about the last few months. Mark and Kayla sat down, and he would whisper the bits and pieces he understood from their conversation. Sometimes he would have to pause to process the things he heard before relaying them to his girlfriend.

Her mom became the happiest when Jordan confirmed that she was now Bopol's mate. In contrast, she looked like she might get ill when Jordan shared her experience with Queen Amstar and what SnowFire did to the Onchei people. Slowly and with much difficulty, Jordan told her mother how SnowFire had changed her by giving her some of her blood. She let her mother touch the palms of her hands. Lastly, Jordan explained what she had learned about the Onchei people, including Zeetra.

"What did Chieftess tell you?" her mom asked finally. "She saw you and understood what happened. What did she say?"

Jordan considered what she was going to say for a moment.

"Someday, I will be Chieftess," Jordan said. "She is going to train me."

That got Mark's attention.

"Then you're not staying, are you?" Mark's head lowered.

"No. I am not," Jordan replied in English. "I cannot."

Just then, the front door opened, and her father walked in with a couple of plastic bags full of groceries. When he saw his daughter, he dropped the bags, causing the egg carton to crunch and spill its contents. He rushed forward.

"Jordan?" he seemed hesitant, as if she might be a mirage.

She hadn't known how she would feel when she saw Dad again. There was a giddiness within her that Jordan hadn't felt in years. Instantly, in her mind, she felt like the ten-year-old girl who loved riding roller coasters with her father, who ran to greet him when he came home from work just as she was leaving for school. Her feet moved by themselves and she ran to embrace him. She held him tightly, squinting her eyes and smiling.

"I can't believe it! My little girl is home! I couldn't be happier! You're—you're all right?" he asked.

"Yes."

Jordan adoringly looked at her father as he pulled back to view her more closely, tenderly touching her face. She could see his brow furrow as he viewed her scars. She knew he must have been surprised about her hair and eyes but she was glad he didn't talk about any of that.

"I love you, Jordan. I can't even tell you how much I missed you," he said. "Or how glad I am you were able to come home to us."

Jordan swallowed hard. "I cannot stay, Dad. I have to go back."

"W—What? Why?"

"Please . . . do not misunderstand. I have wanted nothing more than to be right here with my family again, ever since Mom and I were taken," Jordan said. "It feels like I am in a dream, a really happy dream. But I have changed so much, and I cannot stay. I do not belong here anymore."

"How can you say that, Jordan? Of course, you belong here," her dad insisted.

Jordan lifted up her hands and turned them over to reveal her palms and their gemstones.

"What in the world?" Dad exclaimed.

"Even if I could hide these, they are just one aspect of what is different about me, Dad," Jordan said. "I have a life waiting for me on Algoran, I would not be happy here. And I have chosen a mate, a man I love very much. I want to be with him."

"A husband?" her father said, his initial elation quickly overshadowed by reality.

"Your mother said you . . . might be marrying someone. You'll have to forgive your old man. I only want your happiness, Jordan . . . but I won't get to see any of it. I'll miss that, like I missed the chance for your husband to ask me for your hand in marriage or be at your wedding to give you away. Did you even have a ceremony? How do people on that world get married?"

After a moment's silence, Jordan looked at her father with a mixture of regret and joy. "We had a ceremony but it was just the two of us. My husband . . . his name is Bopol. And I believe my future is with him."

"Your future?" Dad repeated.

"Remember, Dad, how you used to tell me that someday, I would meet someone special, someone I would want to have for the rest of my life, make a family with and all that?"

Her father nodded warmly.

"So, this Bopol is The One, huh?"

"Yes."

Jordan tried to find words to dispel any lingering discomfort in the air. After a few seconds, she cleared her throat and changed the subject. "I will stay a few days. We have a lot of catching up to do."

"Yes, we do," Dad said.

"I will always be proud to be your daughter, wherever I am. I love you," Jordan hugged her father again. "You have to believe me, Dad."

"How could I not?" he said, tears flowing. "I see my little girl, who's a woman now, making all these mature choices. I am proud of you but it's hard for me, too. I just got you back . . . I guess I didn't think you would be leaving again so soon."

29

WITH TIME COMES HEALING

"WHAT'S GOT YOUR ATTENTION UP there in the clouds?" Kevin asked, walking into the back yard from the house.

He zipped up his brown leather jacket and stuffed his hands in its pockets, trying to warm up in the crisp winds. The twilight sky was a mixture of pinks, purples and deep blues. Jordan stood there with only her hideskin shirt and pants. He noted how she loosely gripped her arms, content while looking at the heavens.

"I had forgotten what a single moon looked like," Jordan answered. "The Algoran skies are not like this, especially at night. There is always kind of a green haze, but you get used to it."

"You've seen things I can't even imagine. Does it make this place seem boring now?"

"No," Jordan replied, looking back at him with a smile. "Just different."

They stood side by side for a minute, just peering skyward. Kevin shifted in place, lifting up on his heels nervously.

"I wish I could meet him," Kevin said. "Your husband, that is."

"I wish you could, too," Jordan replied thoughtfully. "You would like him. He is strong and rugged, a good hunter, but also gentle and kind, the son of our Chieftess. He is sweet and completely dedicated to me."

"That's good to hear," Kevin said, not sure how else to respond.

"He was a good friend to me long before he proposed. We are even better friends since becoming mates."

Kevin studied his daughter's face. It had been years, but he still could read between the proverbial lines of what she was saying versus what she actually meant. It was then he realized that when Jordan looked to the stars, it meant that her heart was back on Algoran with her husband. He sensed that was where she longed to be.

"You two share a special bond. You really do love him."

Jordan nodded pleasantly. "Yes, I do. I miss him very much right now."

"Is there some reason you can't bring him here?"

Jordan sighed. "I do not know how Earth's environment would affect someone from Algoran. With the pollution, germs, and viruses, I just do not think we can take that risk."

"Can—can we come visit you?" Kevin said earnestly, almost expectantly.

Jordan returned his gaze somberly and sympathetically. "Not unless you want to live there. I plan to destroy the transport device once I get back."

"What? Why? You won't be able to return here!"

"I know," Jordan said, her voice breaking on the last word. "But this machine is too dangerous, Dad. Ones just like it altered all of our lives and have broken up countless families over who knows how long. Not only that, I cannot risk someone from Earth getting ahold of this and learning how it works."

"I understand," Kevin said, teary-eyed. He let out a heavy sigh.

———

Janice had been listening just outside the door, intentionally keeping quiet until now. She cleared her throat loudly.

"Jordan, you must return to your mate. But I must . . . stay here," she said.

"Are you sure, Mom? You know you are Mokta, too."

Janice tried to smile reassuringly. "Yes, I know."

She followed along the outside of the house by touch until she reached the wooden fence. Then she leaned against it with one hand while feeling around in front of herself with the other until she closed in on Kevin and Jordan.

"You are need-ed on Algoran, but I am need-ed here," Janice said.

"What's going on? Is there something I should know about?" Jordan asked.

Janice smiled at that. "Yes. Your fath-er and I have rec—rec—we are *together* again."

"What? That is wonderful! Wow! Congratulations!"

Janice could tell her daughter was truly surprised by the elevated tone and volume in her voice. She also felt Kevin take her hand in his.

"Thank you," Janice responded.

"Thanks," Kevin added.

"What, um, what changed?" Jordan continued. "I am happy for both of you but I do not understand?"

"I don't think we ever stopped loving each other, Jordan," Kevin said. "But I let my job come between us. It kept me apart from her and you kids for too long. That's why your mom had . . . felt it best to separate at the time."

"But Jordan, when you and I were . . . taken, Kevin was a . . . good father to Mark," Janice said. "He made changes at his job. First, better hours, then work from home. Found a better job that . . . let him spend more time . . . with Mark. And when I came back, he . . . was good to me, took care of me."

"Without the distractions and fighting, our feelings for one another did the rest," Kevin said. "We had a small private ceremony last month."

"So, you have actually remarried?" Jordan asked.

"Yes," Kevin replied.

"It is true," Janice concurred.

Jordan hugged both of her parents at the same time.

———————

As the family enjoyed two large pepperoni pizzas, breadsticks, salads and sodas delivered from Loggie's Pizza, they also took advantage of the time to get to know one another better. Kayla was still edgy around Jordan but as the evening progressed, she attempted some conversation with her. By the time they finished the food and verbal exchanges, everyone was extremely full and a small treasure of memories had been shared.

Outside, the winds were blowing more fiercely than ever. The temperature was starting to plummet, and the sun had set a couple of hours earlier, so Jordan's dad offered to drive Kayla home.

As tactfully as she could, Janice recommended that Jordan shower and change clothes. She had already brought down one of her outfits to offer, since she and her daughter were close in size, and told Jordan where the nearest bathroom was.

Jordan recalled how to operate the shower, but it seemed odd. Taking a hot shower was relaxing and felt pleasant but there was no comparison to the icy springs of Algoran. Jordan preferred the feeling of submerging herself in the chilled waters, the intense shock to the senses that woke her from even the most exhausted states as well as the feeling of soil, grass and rocks beneath her feet upon emerging from the water. Alternately, as she stepped out of the shower, her wet foot slipped on the slick floor and she had to catch herself on the sink to prevent badly injuring herself. The resulting yellow and purple bruise just below her ribcage was an embarrassing reminder of just how out of place she was here.

After putting on the long-sleeved blouse and sweat pants, she took some extra time to dry her long hair. She styled it in various ways she remembered but no matter how cute, sophisticated or inspired, nothing could defy the significance of her cobalt-colored hair or haunting eyes.

No matter where I go, I will be an alien now—not human, not Mokta. Dread settled in her stomach. *I suppose technically I am* kinda *Mokta but not really. I am whatever SnowFire is except not exactly.*

She sighed, her eyes sore from all the crying she'd done recently.

She returned her hair to its natural style, hanging over her shoulders and draping down her back as she exited the bathroom. She heard music coming from her brother's room. Jordan knocked on the door and he told her to enter. As she did so, she was caught off-guard seeing Mark sitting in a chair by the window and playing his acoustic guitar.

"I did not know you played! When did this happen?" Jordan asked.

"About three years ago."

"Did you get lessons?"

"Taught myself."

"Huh! You are good."

Mark smiled at the compliment. "This is one I wrote for Kayla a few days ago. Wanna hear it from the top?"

"Yes!"

She sat on his bed, immediately captured by the rich yet subtle hook of the tune. He played lush and warm chords which rang out during the introduction. As she listened, Jordan espied the various posters on her brother's walls, black and white photos of guitars, both acoustic and electric. Then Mark opened his mouth and began to sing, switching to finger-picking for the verse. His beautiful tenor voice conveyed the simple joys of being young and in love with a pretty girl who understood him.

Jordan closed her eyes and could see the trees of Algoran, imagining herself and Bopol sitting beneath them, next to the flowering plants, just enjoying one another. She could feel herself smiling widely, emotionally touched in ways she hadn't expected. As the last chord rang out, she felt herself exhale and realized she'd been holding her breath. She opened her eyes, still happy.

"That was beautiful, Mark!"

"You really think so?"

"Yes. You have a gift. I am so impressed!"

"Thank you. Want to hear more?"

"Absolutely!"

He played her more of his songs, then some well-known tunes from their childhood, even guitar versions of television show themes they'd liked as kids. Jordan sat on the floor and enjoyed every moment of it, even singing along with some melodies and lyrics from the shows.

"You have a nice voice, Jordan. Do you sing?"

"You are being kind. The village has group songs for anyone to participate in, because when you have that many people singing, the ones who cannot sing do not sound so bad."

Mark laughed at that.

"Sometimes when we were out in the hunting pack and finished with the evening meal but not ready to go to sleep, we would sing those songs around the fire," Jordan said. "Zoska has the best voice. She would often start and encourage the rest of us to join in."

"That sounds fun. Is Zoska your friend?"

"My best friend, aside from Bopol. When Mom and I arrived there, Zoska made me feel welcome, like I belonged there. We did not know each other's languages yet, but she still tried. When Mom was sick that first winter, Zoska kept encouraging me each time I was sure Mom was not going to make it."

"Mom doesn't like to talk about that time."

"I cannot blame her, Mark, it was terrible. She had fever for weeks at a time. If Healer Latas was not so skilled, she would have died from the convulsions and dehydration, it was that bad."

"You both made it through. That's what matters."

It was then that Jordan realized that she was speaking a lot. And when her brother did reply to her, it was in Mokta.

"How long have you been talking to me in Mokta?"

"Almost an hour."

"Wow, you are good!"

"I did not understand everything, but I think I followed along okay."

Jordan laughed. "You pass."

"Tell me everything about your life on Algoran, Jordan. Not just the highlights, I want to know it all."

"Okay, you asked for it . . . "

She talked well into the early morning, describing her new home world, the moons and stars in the sky, life on the mountain in the Mokta village. And she told him about traveling across the world, the different people they encountered, how she earned the title of "Jorr-Don: Deathwing Rider" and many other stories. He leaned back on his bed and folded his arms behind his head and soaked in every word like a sponge until they both fell asleep just as the sun began to rise.

30

BREAKING THE ICE

SIX YEARS AGO, ERICA MELENDEZ had been Jordan Lewis' best friend. They had met in elementary school and been virtually inseparable since then, sharing a love for television and romance novels. When they weren't together in person, they spoke on the phone or via text or chat. They had strategies to go to the same college, get married around the same time and they had created tentative names for their future children.

All of those plans changed when Jordan disappeared, collapsing altogether when she was declared dead a year later. Erica also dropped out of college to address her own personal depressions and anxiety issues. It wasn't just Jordan's absence that affected Erica. Jordan had been the last shred of security in her troubled life.

Erica's parents' marriage had always been unstable at best and often volatile. Her father, Hector, had been unfaithful numerous times and her mother, Anna, had become increasingly angry and abusive towards him and Erica, their only child, in response. Erica spent less and less time at home and more with friends, especially Jordan. Less than a month after Jordan's abduction, Erica's mother discovered her husband having another affair. Outraged beyond reason, Anna attacked his lover and killed her in front of witnesses.

Even with the plea deal offered by the prosecution, it would be nearly two decades before Anna was eligible for parole. Given all she had endured from her mother, both verbally and physically, Erica had visited Anna in prison only once. And then only to tell the woman that she no longer considered herself her daughter. Erica never wanted to see her again.

Faced with the death of his mistress at the hands of his own wife, combined with his own increasing depression, Hector turned to alcohol for solace and became neglectful towards his daughter. He lost track of his work schedule, causing him to lose numerous jobs. He struggled to find new ones. Bills went unpaid, including the mortgage, so he lost their house, too. Erica had to significantly increase her work hours to move into and afford her own apartment. Between that and reeling from all she had endured, Erica couldn't focus her attention on college any longer.

While working full-time at a restaurant as an assistant manager, Erica met Hal Nowak. He was a law student who was interning with a firm in the neighborhood. The legal staff would often have meetings in the restaurant and he made up excuses to ask Erica questions, flirting with her and eventually asking her out. Their relationship was deeply healing to Erica and a year later, when Hal proposed, Erica gladly accepted. They planned to marry once Hal graduated and joined the firm as a junior partner. That job had been verbally offered but not officially extended to him yet. Once he started that position, Hal wanted to support Erica in finishing her own degree.

Everything was going extremely well for Erica until eight months ago, when the police contacted her with the grim news of her father's suicide. He had stopped contacting Erica over a year earlier and she'd worried that, because of his alcoholism and inability to keep a job or pay bills, he'd become homeless. However, not knowing where he was, she couldn't help him. With her mother incarcerated, it became her responsibility to inform the rest of the family and bury her father. For all his faults, Erica had loved her father and only wanted the best for him. Now he was gone, and she felt like an orphan.

While still recovering from that loss, Erica heard from friends that Jordan's mother had been found alive. Hoping for the best, she rushed over to where she learned Jordan's father and brother had moved, only to learn that Jordan hadn't returned with Janice. Worse still, Jordan's parents didn't know when or even if she would be back. They wouldn't even say where their daughter was.

The way she was feeling, Erica would have worked any number of hours and saved whatever money necessary to buy a ticket and at least try to save her best friend. But even this was denied her. Jordan wasn't dead, but she was so far away that she may as well be. Erica's aspiration to be reunited had been dashed and she felt adrift again and even worse than before.

The news about Jordan unlocked a flood of emotions and fears. Erica became unmotivated at work and despondent with her fiancé. She did the bare minimum to remain functional, health-wise. She could feel that she was withdrawing from everyone and everything, but she was in too much pain and despair to resist it.

Hal was patient with her but when she consistently refused to seek professional help for her depression, it led to arguments. Not wanting to further strain their relationship, Erica postponed their engagement. Hal reluctantly agreed but was clearly saddened by her decision. Within herself, Erica regretted driving him away because she genuinely cared for him.

Erica voluntarily began counseling and made renewed efforts to excel at her job and resuscitate her friendships and few remaining family relationships. One of the family members she stayed in touch with was with her cousin, Kayla Montgomery. Just last night, she had spoken on the phone with Kayla, who mentioned Jordan's name—in the present tense! When Erica pressed her about it, Kayla hesitantly admitted that Jordan had returned and was at her parents' house. That revelation had both lifted Erica's spirits and generated many questions. She couldn't sleep most of the night.

Now, it was seven-thirty in the morning on a frigid Saturday and Erica found herself standing at the front door of Jordan's parents' house knocking loudly and waiting for a response. She was armed with a large cup of double-strong hot coffee and longing to see her dear friend once more.

While everyone else slept soundly, choosing to ignore the inconvenient noise, Jordan's adrenaline kicked in and she shot to her feet as if responding to a charging Sasstonn. It took a few seconds to realize the situation was not dire and someone was merely thumping on the door.

Jordan's thoughts focused on something else that was much more significant and amazing. It was her second epiphany in less than a day.

SnowFire. I do not sense her presence here at all! And I do not think I have since I got back to Earth! She must not be able to leave Algoran!

Jordan looked at her palms and confirmed the presence of the gems and that her hair was still blue. She was becoming more accustomed to her appearance by the day.

The transformation is probably permanent. But this confirms what I thought: SnowFire is no god! Her reach is limited.

The pounding on the door persisted and whoever it was, they had begun ringing the doorbell. Still wearing her clothes from the night before, Jordan leapt over the stairway railing and landed in front of the door like a leopard. She looked through the door's peephole but the figure standing there was unfamiliar.

She thought it was likely one of Mark's friends.

It took her a moment to figure out how to undo the various locks and chains before swinging the door wide, startling the woman on the other side. Jordan narrowed her eyes, knowing she recognized the woman's face but not who she was.

"Jordan?" the woman asked, almost disbelievingly.

Jordan thought she recognized the woman's voice. "Erica?"

"Yes! I—" Erica began to say as she reached forward to offer a hug.

Jordan raised a hand to block Erica and shook her head slowly, a stern expression on her face.

"I am sorry," Jordan replied. "Can we just talk first?"

"Are you all right? Everyone thought you were dead! What happened to you?"

"You probably would not believe me."

Jordan wasn't sure why she felt defensive around her old friend. Something about her was offsetting in a way it never had been before. She could see that Erica was hurt by her initial rejection. As the other woman stepped back, Jordan got a full view of her. In the last five years, Erica had become more fragile somehow, both physically and emotionally.

"Want to go for a walk? I will . . . explain what I can," Jordan said.

"Girl, it's twenty degrees with a wind chill near zero. Aren't you cold??"

Jordan shrugged. "This is like spring to me."

"Were you kidnapped to Antarctica or something? Geez! I'm freezing!"

"No. Come inside then," Jordan said, pointing towards the door.

The two walked inside and sat on the couch, the room lit only by the sunlight streaming in through the windows. Jordan poured a glass of orange juice for herself, offering the same to Erica but she declined.

"Why couldn't I hug you? We're still friends, right? We're still the same people."

"I am not the same person I was when I was taken. If you knew where I had been or what I have done these last five years—" Jordan sighed as she sat back down next to Erica.

"I want to know. I've wondered all this time. When I learned you were alive, it was incredible! But then, no one would tell me where you were or what was going on. Please, could you tell me now?" Erica asked.

Jordan observed Erica for a few seconds. She called forth memories from years past, her time and friendship with Erica. Jordan felt saddened by the emotional chasm she felt between them. A part of her wanted to bridge that distance and reconnect with her.

"I must warn you, what I am about to say is going to sound crazy," Jordan said. "If I had not lived it, I probably would not believe it myself."

"Try me," Erica insisted. "You used to trust me about everything."

"Okay. Just remember, you asked me to tell you this," Jordan paused. "Mom and I were taken to another planet by aliens."

Erica blinked several times in a row. "Excuse me?"

"It is the truth."

Jordan could see the doubt in Erica's eyes. And while she understood, it still angered her.

"I used to trust you because you used to *believe* me," Jordan said.

"Jordan, I understand what pain and loss can do to a person. I can refer you to someone who will be completely professional and confidential. She's been very helpful to me."

Jordan huffed in irritation. "Great. You think I need a therapist."

"I think being abducted and held for five years by bad people would mess with anyone's head."

"I was not a captive for five years, Erica. I was taken to an Earth-like planet, along with my mother, and we were released there. Some *extraordinary* things happened—like this."

Jordan showed Erica the palms of her hands, causing Erica to gasp at first. Then Erica ran her fingers along the gems' facets.

"Is this some kind of body art?" Erica asked. "Like piercings but with jewels?"

As Jordan's frustration mounted, the jewels began to faintly glow. By the time she noticed it and turned to Erica, Jordan saw that her former friend's eyes were now fixated on the gems, but she didn't comment on them.

"Okay . . . um, let's say for a minute that I believe your story," Erica continued. "You and your mother were kidnapped by aliens. If you were taken to some other world, how did your Mom get back before you?"

"The ones who abducted us used their technology to send Mom home."

"Why her and not you?"

"They did not know where I was. And it took time for me to find them."

"You found them? Did you fight them? Is that how you got those scars?"

"No. I *earned* these as a huntress," Jordan said, lifting her head proudly.

"Jordan, I'll level with you. I believe that some . . . unusual things happened to you and your mom. I imagine some of them were pretty terrible. I want to understand, and I still want to be your friend. I hope you'll give me a chance to get to know you again."

"I would like that," Jordan said. "It really is good to see you again, Erica."

This time, when Erica stood up and offered Jordan a hug, she accepted it. She was surprised at how tight the embrace was and how long it lasted, as if Erica didn't want to let go. A moment later, though, she did.

We have both changed. I may not have much time on Earth, but I hope I can be a friend to her while I am here.

31

SIDES OF A COIN

THE NEXT DAY, KAYLA MET Erica at a coffeehouse called Java Overload. The winds had let up, but the temperature was only in the high teens. Erica sat at a booth towards the back, away from the windows. Kayla was still bundled up in her coat, hat, scarf and gloves when she sat down to the left of Erica.

"You okay?" Erica said.

"Gimme a minute to warm up, I'll be fine," Kayla said, rubbing her hands together.

"I'll go order you something to help with that, my treat. Any preference?"

"A big caramel macchiato?"

"Coming right up!" Erica said, smiling as she stood up.

A few minutes later, she returned with two of the sweet coffee drinks and placed one in front of Kayla.

"Copycat," Kayla said.

"It looked good, so I ordered one, too," Erica said with a grin. "I can't help it if my cousin has good taste."

"I suppose not," Kayla said, returning the grin. "So . . . did you see Jordan?"

Erica sat down and put her drink on the table. She took a sip of it and looked at Kayla with a confused expression.

"Yeah," Erica said.

"I thought this might be about that," Kayla replied with a nod. "What did she tell you?"

"Not much. But she did say that she and her mother were . . . taken by aliens. I still don't know what to think of that."

Kayla consumed some of her coffee, giving herself a moment to consider how to respond.

"It's true," she said.

Erica almost spat out her coffee. "What?"

"Mark and I were there when she, um, arrived," Kayla said in a hushed whisper.

"Why do you say it like that?" Erica said.

"It was incredible, Erica! A portal of light just appeared in midair and Jordan came out of it, dressed in furs and animal hides. It was wild!"

"Furs and animal hides?" Erica repeated, raising an eyebrow.

"Yes. I was scared to death, but they recognized each other right away and were so happy. They even started speaking another language to each other!"

Erica's brow furrowed in confusion. "Another . . . language?"

"Their mom taught some of it to Mark when she returned. I think it's called Mok-something. It's what the tribe speaks, the one that took them in when they were taken to that other world."

"You believe it then?"

Kayla chuckled. "After seeing a person appear out of nowhere, it's not so hard. Besides, you saw her hair and her eyes. Those weren't contacts and she didn't dye her hair. Something happened to her. Did you see the crystals in her hands?"

"Yes."

Mark walked into the coffeehouse. After spotting Kayla, he joined them at their booth. He gave his girlfriend a quick kiss on the lips and sat down on the other side facing the two of them.

"Hey there, Erica," he said. "You took off yesterday before I could come downstairs and say hi."

"Sorry, I had work. I just wanted to see for myself that Jordan was back."

"And now you have. What do you think?"

Erica took a long and contemplative sip from her coffee. "I'm not sure. Kayla was just telling me—"

"I told her about the light portal," Kayla said, interrupting. "And how Jordan looked when she stepped through."

"It was intense, that's for sure."

"What does it all mean, Mark? You are her brother, you probably know her better than either of us. Who—or what—is Jordan now?"

Mark turned his eyes downward to Kayla's cup of coffee, which was housed in a tall mug. She smiled and handed it over to him. He took a big gulf before giving it back, taking time to mull over Erica's question.

"Besides being my sister and your friend . . . does it really matter what she is?"

That surprised Erica. She raised both eyebrows. "Are you serious?"

Mark put up a hand to prevent a rant and nodded slowly. Then he continued. "Look, obviously she's changed. She's not a teenager anymore. She's lived on that other planet for nearly five years. She even married someone there."

"She's married?" Erica gasped.

Mark nodded again. "That world has become more her home than Earth. She's going back tomorrow."

Erica's eyes widened. "That's possible? She can do that? Wait— you're saying she *wants* to leave here to go back there?"

Mark heaved his own sigh of frustration. "Yes. And she's never coming back."

Erica's hand that was holding her coffee mug suddenly lost all its strength and fell to the table in front of them, spilling her beverage. She sank backwards into the booth.

"But she . . . just got back," Erica said slowly, the pain in her voice very evident.

"You could have saved that part for later, genius," Kayla said under her breath, elbowing Mark in the ribs.

"Sorry," he replied softly.

Erica took a deep breath and seemed to rally her strength. She scooted out of the booth and stood up.

"I should get going," Erica said, her voice strained. "You two enjoy the rest of your day."

Mark stood up, regret evident in his eyes and expression.

"Erica, please stay," Mark said. "I didn't mean to upset you."

Erica feigned positivity but she was clearly rattled. "I'll be fine. I'm glad we were able to talk. Thanks."

"Come by tomorrow morning and spend the day with us," Mark added, looking at Kayla then Erica. "I happen to know Jordan wants you there. She wants to see you again before she has to go."

"She—she does?"

Mark nodded. "She was happy to see you."

Erica smiled briefly. "All right then. I'll . . . be there."

"Good. I'll let Jordan know," Mark said.

Erica nodded as they said their farewells. She barely heard them as she turned and walked out of the coffee house. The temperature was still frigid outside but not as chilling as the fear surrounding Erica's heart. It was a terrific effort just to focus enough to make her legs walk to the parking lot across the street. Once safely inside her car, she was finally able to release the tears and sorrow that were threatening to consume her from within.

———

Jordan stood back a couple of feet from her father's barbecue grill and watched with immense satisfaction as the flames licked the chicken breasts they were cooking. Dad watched her in both awe and amusement.

"I had no idea you knew how to cook, much less grill," he said.

"Well, on Algoran, we used more of a rotisserie method. But sometimes you just have to season the meat and grill it over a fire however you can," Jordan replied. "I learned this out of necessity. After Mom became ill and lost her sight, she could not cook anymore, so I did what I had to."

"I'm looking forward to tasting your handiwork tonight."

Jordan put her index finger to her chin and looked thoughtfully at the meat, as if judging her own cooking.

"Chicken is thinner than Sasstonn or zala beast," she added. "I hope it is not too dry."

"Sasstonn and—? You know what, don't tell me," Dad said. "I'm sure your chicken will be fine."

Jordan smiled at that. "You are grilling the sausage, right?"

"And the burgers, yeah."

That surprised Jordan, who raised an eyebrow. "You are making hamburgers, too?"

"Why not? This is a special occasion. I considered making hot dogs, but—"

"But you remembered I do not like hot dogs."

Dad laughed and then crossed his arms, looking at his daughter with mock indignation.

"Jordan, how can you like sausage but hate hot dogs?"

"If you made those instead, I would probably eat them now. One of the first things I learned on Algoran was this: a member of the tribe, especially a hunter, never wastes food."

"Good rule."

Jordan picked up some metal tongs and turned two of the chicken breasts over on the grill. There were fresh sizzles and white smoke rose briefly as their juices dropped onto the charcoal beneath.

"Zoska, my best friend, taught that to me when she trained me as a huntress," Jordan continued. "She said it could make the difference between life and death."

Her father opened up a medium-sized plastic container filled with ropes of sausage and his own ready-to-cook, hand-packed and freshly seasoned hamburger patties. He placed one sausage rope and four one-third-pound burger patties on an unused portion of the grill.

"How long have you and Zoska been friends?" he asked.

"Over four years. She has been there for me since the beginning," Jordan responded. "Zoska is married, too, and about to have her first baby."

"That's a big responsibility. It changes everything."

Jordan nodded, smiling as she looked at her father. "So I have been told and seen with other women from the tribe. Zoska has had more than a few words with me about it."

"I hope you've taken her advice to heart then."

Jordan picked up on his unspoken hint and blushed.

"Are you trying to say or ask something, Dad?"

"Do you and Bopol plan on having kids? Is that possible?"

Jordan nodded, continuing to blush. "Yes. And yes, it is."

"I wish I could see them," Kevin said.

That evoked a sympathetic and wistful expression from Jordan.

"Someday, I will tell them all about you, Mom, and Mark. I promise," Jordan said, becoming teary-eyed.

They continued the cooking in silence for a while.

32

DEPARTURE

WHILE HER FATHER FINISHED GRILLING the last of the burgers, Jordan went inside to change clothes and freshen up before her unofficial going away party. After her dad had declared Mom and Jordan legally deceased, he had gotten rid of their clothes and most of their belongings. Only the most memorable keepsakes had remained: old photos, a duck carving Jordan and her father had made together, a music box and a few pieces of jewelry.

Earlier in the day, Kayla had asked Jordan if she could take her to get a few clothing items, so she wouldn't be stuck in her mother's workout sweats for the rest of her visit. Jordan found it awkward, but she agreed. At the mall, Jordan realized how much her fashion sense had changed to accommodate the harsher climate of Algoran; she wasn't used to thinking beyond the practical anymore. So, while she could aesthetically appreciate the flowing skirts, cute blouses, and the latest blue jeans that Kayla showed her, Jordan couldn't see herself wearing most of them. She felt like they would tear like tissue paper the moment she stretched or needed a good run. As a result, she kept to more utilitarian choices: simple blue jeans and a couple of solid color blouses.

She did pick out one basic navy blue, short-sleeved dress. Jordan considered getting one that was long-sleeved, to cover the scars on her arms, but decided against that. She was pleased with the marks she had earned as a huntress. And since this party was in her honor, she wanted to be true to herself. She would also share stories of how she acquired them.

After showering and drying off, Jordan undertook the ordeal of shaving her legs. It had been completely unfeasible on Algoran, especially since there were no compact razors nor any need for them. However, she felt it was an extremely small sacrifice to look nice for the evening. The jagged scar from the mosdon strike caught her attention and Jordan was reminded of how close to death she had come. From that experience, words replayed in her mind once more:

"Do you truly believe in the power of the God you call out to?"

Is this God?

"Do you believe that God can restore your life to you?"

Yes. Yes, I do!

"Will you trust in that power?"

Yes.

There was no question in Jordan's mind that she had changed that day. She had survived, and the direction of her life was now radically different than before. She had succeeded in her mission, even getting back to the world of her birth. However, she knew her sense of purpose and where she belonged was on Algoran. Thinking again of her husband, missing him so much, she desperately longed to return. But her loved ones on Earth deserved a proper goodbye and she was determined to give it to them.

Jordan chose to wear the blue dress for the occasion. When she put it on, it was loose enough that she could move freely in it while not looking unattractive. She put on a matching piece of jewelry from the scant collection her father had brought to her. And then, she worked for half an hour at taming her hair.

Kayla had arrived early and knocked on the door of the guest room, where Jordan had been residing. When Jordan opened the door, she was basically ready for the evening.

"Wow, Jordan, you look great!" Kayla exclaimed.

"Thanks," Jordan replied, her face heating slightly. "I was not sure I would look okay. It has been a while since I dressed up. I'm out of practice."

"Everyone's gonna love it," Kayla assured her.

Jordan sat down on the bed and looked at Kayla.

"Hm, speaking of everyone, could you call your cousin, Erica? I would . . . like it if she could be here, too."

"Honestly, I thought she'd be here already. Mark invited her yesterday."

"I probably made her uncomfortable," Jordan said, her frustration evident.

Kayla sat down next to Jordan. She looked at Jordan sympathetically.

"It may not be you. Erica's . . . been through a lot since you've been gone."

"Like what?"

"I can't really go into details, but I think she wants to tell you herself. It's just hard for her. That's all I can say."

"Please call her and tell her I will not judge her on her past," Jordan replied, suddenly melancholy. "I have no right to."

The memory of those she had killed descended on her like a burdensome weight. It was one she felt she would never be free of.

"Sure. I'll call her and convince her to stop by, if I can. I don't know if she's working or not."

"Even if she can stop by after work, that is fine. I will still be up."

"Sure, I'll tell her. Give me a minute."

Jordan's curiosity prompted her to follow Kayla as far as her bedroom door. Once Kayla was in the hallway, she took her phone out of her purse, turned on its speaker and dialed a number as Jordan overheard. On the fifth ring, Erica answered.

"Hey, where are you?" Kayla said, sounding exasperated. "Jordan is leaving tomorrow, you know!"

"I know," Erica replied sheepishly. "I didn't know if I could . . . face her again."

"You need to get over here now! This isn't something you can shy away from. If you don't talk to her, you'll regret it for the rest of your life."

Erica was silent.

"I made it a little easier for you," Kayla continued. "I told her you've been through things but I didn't tell your business. Believe me, she's not going to think less of you. She *wants* to see you!"

Erica remained silent.

"Do I have to come over there and get you??"

More silence.

"Erica . . . I don't want you to end up like your dad," Kayla said softly. "You have to do something about this. Tell her everything. Don't leave anything unsaid . . . because you won't get another chance like this."

Jordan heard light sobs on the other end of the phone.

"Okay," Erica finally said.

"Okay what?" Kayla asked.

"Come get me," Erica said. "I want to see Jordan, but I'm not okay to drive."

Jordan's heart went out to Erica. She didn't know what Kayla meant about Erica's father but it didn't sound good. She was glad Erica had finally agreed to come over.

Thirty minutes later, Jordan greeted Erica with a hug and a laugh. Erica still looked nervous but was more composed than when Kayla had spoken with her before. The rest of the family was in the dining room ready to begin supper.

"I am so glad you could make it, Erica!" Jordan said.

"Thanks. You look great, Jordan!"

"Thank you! We have a lot of catching up to do."

"Yes, especially since my cousin tells me you're a married woman now," Erica tried to smile.

"It is true."

Jordan noticed Erica not-so-subtly staring at the variety of scars on Jordan's arms and laughed inwardly. She had long ago embraced the jagged and painful-looking disfigurements, even learning to treasure them as the rest of the Mokta did.

"This may sound strange to you, Erica, but do you see this one?" Jordan pointed to a long scrawl on her left arm. Erica nodded squeamishly. "I got this fighting a mighty Sasstonn, one of the largest I have ever seen! I planted my javelin in its neck before it knocked me off. My fellow hunters had to finish it off and save me."

"Didn't that hurt?" Erica asked.

"More than you can imagine," Jordan answered. "It took me a week and a half to recover."

"She speaks the truth," Mom interjected. "I feared for her . . . that she might die."

"I believe that!" Erica added. "Weren't you scared, Jordan?"

"I was having too much fun to be scared and there was too much at stake. That Sasstonn provided a winter's worth of meat for our village."

Jordan could see that Erica was having a difficult time processing what she had said.

"Wow. You're like some kind of warrior or something," Erica said.

"I am just a huntress."

"Compared to everyone here, you're like Wonder Woman!"

Jordan had to search her memory then she understood the compliment. Or was it really one?

After a moment's awkward silence, Jordan joined her father in making plates of food for everyone. Silverware and glasses of water had already been placed at each seat. After making one for herself, Jordan sat down next to Erica while Dad sat next to Mom.

"Jordan, I have . . . missed your cooking!" Mom said. "The seasoning . . . is perfect."

"Thanks, Mom."

"Even if the chicken is a little dry."

Jordan sighed.

"Just kidding," Mom added, chuckling. "It is good, really."

"The meat has a bold flavor, a little spicy but that's all right," Erica said. "And Jordan, the chicken isn't dry at all. It's surprisingly tender."

"Thank you, Erica," Jordan replied.

Following dinner, Jordan was glad that Mark and Kayla volunteered to clean up. She knew it had been a long day, so she wasn't surprised when Mom and Dad went to bed early. Jordan invited Erica to the guest room where she'd been staying.

"I know yesterday was awkward," Jordan said as they entered the room. "I wanted us to be able to talk more freely."

"Thank you."

"I know you have had your doubts about me. You probably wondered if I am really the same Jordan you grew up with."

Erica said nothing but her answer was confirmed in her eyes and the troubled look on her face.

"I can understand that. What do you think now, after spending some more time with me tonight?"

Jordan sat next to Erica on her bed. The minimally decorated room was illuminated by two lamps. Jordan had felt that the overhead light was too harsh and bright, so she eschewed using it in favor of the softer lamp bulbs. There was a dresser with a mirror, a medium-sized window, the bed and a couple of small, generic pictures on the beige wall. It reflected the contrast of how Jordan had changed. She was as out of place in this room as she was on this world and they both knew it.

"I think you've been to another world, a world that's your home now. And you've become an incredible woman," Erica admitted. "I don't know if I can relate to what you've been through, but I still want to be your friend. I want to know who you are now."

Jordan smiled. "Thank you for that."

"I know you're leaving tomorrow, that you're going back to—what was it called? Algoran? You're going back to Algoran and your husband."

"That is right."

"Is there some reason you can't stay here longer?"

"Yes. I have been away too long already. It is not just that I miss him, I *want* to be with him. He is a part of me and I do not feel the same when we are apart."

"I can sort of understand that."

"Can you? Do you have someone special?"

"I did. It didn't work out."

"I am sorry to hear that."

Jordan could tell by the awkward silence that she'd wandered into a sensitive topic without meaning to.

"I do not really know anything about your life these last five years," Jordan said humbly. "But I would like to."

"I'm glad you want to know. I wish I could say it's been great but it hasn't."

"What—what happened?" Jordan asked sympathetically.

Erica shared her parents' tragedies and how they had impacted her. Jordan listened, occasionally acknowledging Erica's words but never interrupting. And while Jordan did not hear any resentment towards her from Erica, Jordan's heart was hurt nonetheless. Without the comfort and support of a best friend, Erica's depression and loss had spiraled out of control. It was to Erica's credit that she had taken charge of her life again, but the cost had clearly been monumental.

Jordan pulled Erica into a side-hug, like she had when they were pre-teens, letting Erica lean against her. When Erica began crying, Jordan felt her own tears running down her cheeks. And though it didn't solve any of Erica's problems, there was some healing that came from them reconnecting emotionally.

Hours later, after midnight, Jordan walked with Erica to the front porch of the house. Any awkwardness had vanished. They had forged a new bond, in some ways stronger than what they had shared as children.

"Well, as you can see, I'm still the emotionally dependent friend you've always known," Erica said with a mixture of humor and regret.

"I do not see it that way, Erica. You are someone who has survived her own challenges, things that break other people. And you are still here. That says a lot of good things about you."

"I wish we had more time. I want to know more about you."

"Arrive early tomorrow. I am going around noon. We can talk some before I leave."

"Thank you. I'll be here."

———

When Erica arrived at ten o'clock the next morning, the sun was shining, the temperature had risen into the thirties and there was only a slight breeze. As Jordan's father opened the door and let her in, Erica saw that Jordan had already dressed in the furs she had arrived in, which her mother had made herculean efforts to clean and deodorize. The furs made Jordan look much more intimidating than the blue dress had. Leaning against the nearest wall was Jordan's equally fearsome twin-bladed javelin.

She embraced Jordan and they sat down on the living room couch. She told Erica about the terrain and climate of Algoran as well as a few things about the Mountain Mokta tribe and its customs. Erica asked her more about Bopol and Jordan was happy to elaborate. She also shared a few hunting tales. Noon came sooner than either of them expected.

"I need a few minutes, Erica. I already talked to Mark and Kayla," Jordan said, standing up. "But I need to say goodbye to my family."

"Of course."

Jordan approached her father first. To Erica, he looked weary, as though he accepted the reality of the situation but was still pained by it.

"I don't suppose I can talk you into another day? We haven't gone fishing in a while," he said tearfully. "I bet you are great at catching fish."

"Do not tempt me, Dad," she replied, a smile on her lips but her voice was shaky. "I would hate to make you look bad."

"You think you're that good, huh? I'm glad I taught you something useful as a kid."

Erica teared up as Jordan pulled her father into a bear hug. "You taught me more than you know!" Jordan said. "I am really going to miss you."

"I'm gonna miss you, too. I'll look up in the sky every night for you."

"Then I will do the same. It will be our special time, okay?"

"Deal."

"I love you, Dad."

"I love you, too, Jordan. Be well."

Erica felt privileged to be a part of this gathering. She saw Jordan nod and step backwards, turning to look for her mother, who was waiting several feet away. Janice opened her arms, bidding her daughter to come to her. She looked sad and anxious, but Erica thought she was obviously trying to be strong for Jordan's sake. Jordan returned the hug but more gently.

"My only regret now is . . . that you will not get to know your Mokta grandchildren," Jordan said.

"I will . . . see them in my dreams," Janice replied. "And know them in my heart. But your father . . . and brother, they need me."

"I need you, too," Jordan answered softly.

"You are . . . so strong. You have chosen your path, your mate," Janice said, smiling through her own tears. "You will be . . . fine."

"I will still miss you, Mom," Jordan said, crying once more as she put her hand on her mother's cheek.

"You will . . . see me . . . in your children," Janice said as Jordan hugged her one last time. "That will be enough."

Erica felt nearly overwhelmed with emotion. Jordan looked at her family, probably for the last time, happily smiling while tears dampened her cheeks. Jordan's gaze was conveying her pride in each of them, her deepest love, joy and gratitude. After a time, Jordan turned and pressed the blue button on a device. A portal opened in the hallway and Jordan walked through, waving to the family as she went.

Erica waited several seconds, and then made a mad dash through the portal just before it closed!

33

APPREHENSION

JORDAN HAD EXPECTED A FEW seconds of disorientation from the flashing lights of the tunnel before emerging into the ghost town of the Onchei. Instead, she felt like she was being rapidly swept along under the dark currents of a raging river. Unsure of her direction and surrounded by sparkling energies which were colder than any lake or mountain top, she was instantly and unceremoniously tossed onto damp, rocky ground, stunning her and stealing most of her consciousness. Jordan thought she heard Erica groaning, which didn't make any sense to her.

Through semi-blurred vision, Jordan looked around and saw that the walls of the surrounding cavern were made of deep blue crystal. Strained by the effort, she went limp and closed her eyes. She could still hear sounds as she drifted in and out of a waking state.

Someone was walking towards her, fury radiating from every footfall. She could sense that it was SnowFire, her presence setting off alarms inside Jordan. She tried to muster her strength so she could form a defense, but it was useless. She was too weak from the impact.

"This is one of the reasons I let you live, huntress!" SnowFire said in Mokta. "You have fire and spirit, even if you have no taste for blood. Return to our people and prepare for the day you will be Chieftess."

Jordan felt herself being enveloped in the energies of the transport tunnel again. The cavern vanished in a flash of light.

SnowFire walked over to where the other young woman was. She watched as Jordan's companion, who was just as stunned and near-helpless as Jordan had been, managed to turn from her back to her stomach and was struggling to rise. SnowFire stretched her thin, strong fingers to grab her cheek, turning the young woman's head so she could look her into the eyes. The woman gritted her teeth and stared at her defiantly.

"What is your name, newchild?" SnowFire asked in English.

"Erica," she said, still struggling. "Not that it's any of your business!"

"You have your own fires, Erica of Earth," SnowFire said. "Let us see where they lead you."

Jordan fell from the sky a dozen feet above the Onchei City and rolled as best she could, trying to protect herself from further injury. She was mostly successful, but her head impacted against a jutting solid object before her spinning stopped. Sore, dumbfounded, and feeling faint, her nerves still abused and numb from the previous impact, Jordan was unable to move or even open her eyes. Her forehead felt wet and some kind of liquid was dripping onto her nose. She heard the stamping of footsteps rushing towards her as she passed out.

Sometime later, Jordan opened her eyes and saw the semi-blurred face of her beloved Bopol, bringing a smile to hers. She felt woozy, even somewhat nauseous. Reaching up, she discovered a cloth bandage wrapped around her head. To her senses, everything seemed to be moving in slow motion. Bopol scooped her up in his powerful arms and began to carry her. Though wounded, she relaxed. Seeing past the pain, her trust in her mate was complete.

"You worried us, Jorr-Don. You were gone for days and returned hurt. What happened?"

"Everything went fine on Earth. I got to see my family. And this time, I was able to say goodbye to them."

Through the haze of her vision, she saw Bopol nod to acknowledge her words. She instinctively smiled as he gently leaned his forehead forward to touch hers. It confirmed he was real and not a dream.

Trying not to move any more than necessary, Jordan slowly craned her neck to the left and right as they slowly ventured forward. The blurriness in her vision was passing but even so, she could only see empty buildings surrounding them.

"Is my friend okay?" she asked. "I mean, have you seen any other people from Earth around here?"

Bopol looked confused. "You arrived alone. Did someone else come back with you?"

"Yes, my friend Erica! I—" Jordan said, concerned as she leaned forward in a rush. A fresh wave of vertigo stopped her. She had to cease her efforts.

"You are safe. Be content with that," Bopol said, holding Jordan close. "I have missed you being close to me like this. You must get better."

It would have been easy for her to embrace sleep once more. But Jordan's thoughts returned to her concern for Erica. She jerked her head to force herself back to an alert state, despite how nauseous it made her. She opened her eyes and looked up at Bopol.

"What is wrong?" Bopol asked.

"Something happened while I was traveling back. It is something I need to share with all of you."

Did Erica follow me through the portal? That is the only way she could be here.

Jordan felt that Erica was still with SnowFire, wherever that was on Algoran, and that scared her a great deal. While she didn't think SnowFire would have reason to do any harm to Erica, there was no good that could come from it, either. There were just too many unanswered questions and that was truly unsettling.

SnowFire had no presence on Earth, I am sure of it. Erica, why?

It was mid-afternoon in the Onchei village. The bodies were gone but the air still had a certain staleness and odor to it. While not as toxic as before, it was a reminder of the carnage that had occurred. Bopol helped Jordan stand and walk to where the Chieftess, Zeetra and the rest of the hunting pack were.

Bopol helped Jordan sit down next to Zoska, who put her arm around Jordan and squeezed with pride and happiness. Jordan smiled as Reiban nodded in approval, sharing his mate's sentiments. Jordan was pleased as Kitranor stepped forward and put her hand on Jordan's cheek.

"Welcome back, my daughter," Kitranor beamed. "We have done our best to pass the time in your absence, but we found no more survivors in the area. When you are well enough, we should go back home. For now, tell me, did you see your gemta?"

"Yes. She is doing well and living with my torkomm and brother. She is happy there."

"That is good. I am glad she is well," Kitranor said, somewhat reluctantly.

Jordan saw the Chieftess' mixed reaction to her news. She decided to steer the conversation in a different direction, hoping to make Kitranor feel better.

"Using the device Zeetra gave me, we can be back in the village in a few heartbeats," Jordan said. "But there is a problem."

"What is wrong?" Kitranor asked.

"When I went through the portal to return here, I landed somewhere else first. And SnowFire was there."

Kitranor's breathing stiffened and the others were stunned silent. Zeetra looked apprehensive to hear SnowFire's name.

"Go on," the Chieftess said.

"One of my friends from Earth followed me through the portal without my knowledge. SnowFire sent me here but my friend did not come with me. I am afraid for her. She does not understand how life is on Algoran. I feel that she is my responsibility, but I do not know where she is."

Kitranor ruminated on Jordan's words while Zoska, Reiban, and Bopol remained silent. Jordan followed Kitranor with her eyes as the older woman walked over and sat down in front of her and Zoska.

"Did SnowFire say anything before she sent you here?" Kitranor asked.

"She said I should return to our people and prepare to be Chieftess."

Kitranor nodded, accepting Jordan's answer.

"SnowFire is as the legends say she is. And she has confirmed your future role as Chieftess. No one will oppose you, when the time comes," Kitranor said.

"With respect, Chieftess, that is for the future. I fear for my friend, Erica, right now."

"I understand. Like you, I do not know what SnowFire will do or where she may send your friend. But wherever this Eri-kaa ends up, she will be the only other child of Errrth on our world. We will find her."

Kitranor leaned forward and gripped Jordan's shoulder. "We should return to the village. Healer Latas and my son Rizok have watched over it while I have been away, but we should go back now."

"One thing first," Jordan said, spying the Onchei woman nearby. "Your name was Zeetra?"

"Yes," Zeetra replied, disquieted by Jordan's presence.

"How can we make sure none of this technology can be used by anyone after we leave this place?"

Zeetra crossed her arms thoughtfully and nodded.

"I took care of that while you were gone. I created a magnetic energy pulse that disabled all of the machines within this territory. Creating such a large pulse also burned out the machine that sent it out."

Jordan needed more convincing.

"Show me the machines then. Prove to me that they no longer function."

She still couldn't walk around on her own, but Jordan asked Bopol to carry her wherever she needed to go. It took an hour for Zeetra to demonstrate that the machines in the vacant city were all non-functional and powerless.

Jordan asked Zeetra to change the coordinates on the still-operational portal-making device to take them to the Mokta village. After Zeetra made the adjustments to the device, Jordan opened a portal to the Mokta village and they all walked through.

34

NEW POSSIBILITIES

THE SMALL GROUP EMERGED FROM the portal of light on the path that led to the Mokta village. The sight of the majestic mountain beckoned. The scents of familiar flowers and trees were comforting after traveling and being away for so long. To Jordan, Bopol, Reiban, and Zoska, the sounds of the mountain streams and the twittering birds solidified what they all felt: their quest was over, they were home. Kitranor was relieved but Zeetra felt some apprehension.

"So, *this* is what you experienced when you were brought here, Jorr-Don?" Zoska said, looking all around in amazement.

"It was far less pleasant back then for me and my mother, but yes."

"Zoska! Do you not remember how frightened and sad they were when they arrived?" Reiban reprimanded.

"Forgive! I did not choose good words," Zoska answered, chastened.

Jordan sighed. "It is all right. Having passed through these portals by my own choice now, I know that they are just a tool. They are not good or bad."

Jordan handed the transport device to Kitranor. The Chieftess accepted it with some hesitation.

"Chieftess, I had wanted to destroy this when I got back to Algoran. But it is the only thing that can send Erica back to Earth, so we should keep it for now. Can you have this hidden away in some place only

Chiefs and Chieftesses have access to? It is dangerous, and no other tribe or people must know of it."

Kitranor nodded. "There is such a place and I can put it there myself. But I disagree with you. I think this box should be destroyed. Your friend chose to come live on Algoran. We should end the danger. Now."

"You are my Chieftess, but this is my friend's life. Without help, I do not see how she can survive on our world. If we can send her back to Earth, we should do that."

"You are the future Chieftess. I must consider your wishes," Kitranor added respectfully. "The box will be hidden."

"Thank you."

Kitranor's gaze was a warning in itself. "Do not thank me, child. You may one day regret this choice."

Jordan was pained by Kitranor's words. She knew the Chieftess was right, but she couldn't ignore Erica, especially after reconnecting the way they had.

Jordan called out to Zeetra. The young Onchei turned her head towards the sound.

"This has been a difficult time for us both," Jordan said as she approached Zeetra. "However, you have proven yourself in my eyes and everyone here. Even if Chieftess had not already declared it, with what you have done to distance yourself from your people's former goals and aid us, you have made yourself Mokta."

"Yes!" Reiban exclaimed. "Come, Zeetra, experience what it means to be one of us!"

"You need never feel alone again," Jordan said with a softer tone. "We will be your new family and people."

When Zeetra spoke, it was barely above a whisper. She looked conflicted.

"You Mokta have all shown forgiveness and been kind to me," she said. "Perhaps someday, I will feel like one of you. For that, I thank you."

Chieftess Kitranor put her arm around Zeetra and led her forward towards the village. "We may not have machines like what you knew or tall buildings, but we have food and shelter. Most importantly, we have each other. You will be accepted, eventually. We are used to taking in people from many places."

Jordan observed Kitranor trying to inspire Zeetra concerning the need for hopes and dreams, even while still grieving and healing. Jordan's own bitterness towards Zeetra faded as she found the strength to forgive her, if not her people. Zeetra began to nod and it looked like Zeetra accepted the Chieftess' words, even if she didn't fully agree with them.

————————

Jordan and Bopol sat next to each other in a wooded area a quarter mile from the entrance to the Mokta village. The others had gone ahead but Chieftess Kitranor had specifically asked these two to wait behind until she sent for them.

"I understand why Chieftess is doing this, but it makes me feel like I did something wrong," Jordan said, looking self-conscious.

Bopol lovingly stroked her hair. "You have done more for our people than they might be able to take in. However, Chieftess is wise with her words and she knows the people."

"I did not do this alone. I cannot take credit like that," Jordan said, turning to look at him. "But I can see why Chieftess is the one to tell them that the Qui Tol are gone. And that I have changed."

Jordan nuzzled her head against Bopol's chest and he responded by wrapping a protective arm around her. She was still unsettled but comforted by his love. A slight breeze blew cool air between the trees.

"I am not sure who I feel sorrier for, myself or Zeetra," Jordan lamented.

"You have little to be concerned about, Jorr-Don. However, Zeetra may have a difficult time adjusting, even with Chieftess' support. I do hope she can enjoy life here, though."

"You think the people will fear her?"

"Yes."

"Will they not fear me, too?"

Bopol hesitated before answering. "Perhaps."

Chieftess Kitranor approached the entrance to the village with Zeetra at her side while behind them, Reiban assisted Zoska in her ponderous walk. The cool winds seemed to push them forward, blowing the leaves in the trees. The village sentries made eye contact with the Chieftess, who looked at Zeetra and nodded reassuringly, so the sentries allowed them to pass. Many villagers stopped what they were doing to gape at the return of their leader and the stranger she brought. Others reacted with surprise to the very pregnant Zoska. Most slowly gathered close to the Chieftess, seeking an update or explanation from her. They did not have to wait long.

"My people, it is good to be home!" Kitranor bellowed. "I bring news—much news! First, the Qui Tol all perished in a recent battle, except this one next to me. She was away, returning our sister, Januss, to Errrth. Januss is well and with her mate and son once more. I have offered for this female, Zeetra, to join the Mokta and she has agreed."

At that revelation, there were murmurings and looks of dissatisfaction, concern and anger among the growing crowd. Some people began to point at Zeetra with hostility.

"How can we trust a Qui Tol, Chieftess?" a tall male exclaimed. "If the rest of her people are dead, she should join them!"

"Zeetra has gained my trust. She is alone now and has become like one of the abandoned people the Mokta have helped in times past, like Jorr-Don and Januss."

There were nods but some of the tribe crossed their arms and looked on with distrust and unhappiness. Out of nowhere, a javelin was thrown at Zeetra, personifying some people's great anger at the Qui Tol. Kitranor lunged and caught it. Fuming, she broke the weapon over her knee.

"That is enough! We have law for how to treat the abandoned ones. If you harm or maim her, you will be exiled from this village. If any one of you kill her, and it is not justified self-defense which you can *prove* then you will die by my hands without mercy. We have always taken in the abandoned without pre-conceived judgment. That is the law! We are Mokta!"

After an initial stunned silence, numerous people began to chant "We are Mokta!" Others joined in gradually until almost all gathered were shouting the chant. Satisfied, Kitranor extended her arms and quieted them by opening her hands and lowering them slowly.

A moment later, a short elder female wearing a red robe approached within a few feet of the Chieftess and bowed her head respectfully before speaking.

"What of Januss' daughter, Jorr-Don?" she asked. "Did she return to Errrth also?"

"Jorr-Don went to Errrth but chose to return to us! She is nearby and will join us soon," Kitranor replied. "She has chosen to be the mate of my son, Bopol, which fills me with great happiness!"

There were stirrings of excitement then. Many were delighted at that announcement.

"My new daughter set upon a mission with Bopol, Reiban, and Zoska to find the Qui Tol, learn their reasons for bringing her and Januss to us and whether it was possible to go home. They were mostly successful," the Chieftess said, stirring more cheers and shouts among the people. "Along the way, they met many people and did great things. Then something truly incredible happened. The journey was perilous, and Jorr-Don faced death. But she was saved . . . by SnowFire."

Kitranor's divulgement elicited gasps and looks of disbelief.

"SnowFire is one of our most sacred and feared legends," Kitranor continued. "Had I not seen Jorr-Don with my eyes, heard her words and those of her pack, I might not have believed, either. But my new daughter has convinced me. She has also changed in appearance. Her hair is the deepest blue and her eyes are like the ice . . . yet she is still the same woman inside."

The elder female was still close and attempting to remain as respectful as possible, but she clearly had doubts. "Forgive, Chieftess, for I know you are sincere, but how could this be possible? How could this figure walk among us when our own ancient stories say she left thousands of cycles ago?"

"Just because Snow and Fire left us, it does not say she left our world. I believe there will be new stories about her someday. Those stories could answer any questions we may have now," Kitranor declared. "One thing is certain, however: SnowFire herself has stated that someday, Jorr-Don will be the next Chieftess."

The elder female's eyes widened. She bowed and stepped back.

The crowd began to talk among themselves, some muttering, others afraid but most were simply confused. There seemed to be a general reluctance among the people, but most accepted the Chieftess' words. Some didn't like the news, but they had to acknowledge its relevance. Kitranor understood their confusion and, to a degree, shared it. But she had a duty to perform.

"Jorr-Don was wounded recently but she will fully recover. Healer Latas will see to that," the Chieftess said. Latas, who had approached and stood at her side, nodded in response. "But she and the others are very tired from their journey. I ask that you allow them time to recuperate. We will speak again soon, and they will join us at that time."

With that, the people began to return to what they were doing before. But now, they had much more to think and be concerned about.

———————

Days later, Kitranor came to visit Jordan, who was resting in the new hut she shared with her mate. Bopol was keeping steady watch over her, providing all her needs. As the Chieftess entered, Jordan sat up.

"Chieftess?"

"How are you, child?"

"The cut on my head is nearly healed and I am recovering from the soreness."

The Chieftess startled for a moment, remembering how incapacitated Jordan had been when she arrived back from Earth. She knew even the heartiest Mokta would not have recovered this quickly.

Jordan must have picked up on her discomfort. "I think I heal faster than before. Time will tell."

Their understanding of the circumstances, of this new ability of Jordan's, was mutual and silent.

"Agreed. What is important is that you are getting better."

Jordan nodded, then she looked towards the open doorway.

"Have there been any sightings of my friend, Erica?"

"No. I have had some of the scouts look all throughout our territory, but they have seen nothing unusual."

"I understand, Chieftess," Jordan said, worried.

"I will have them expand their search to include other regions. If there is another like you, another young woman from Errrth, they will hear of it or see it themselves. But it may take time."

"Yes, Chieftess."

Jordan looked at her for a moment and smiled briefly. Then Jordan turned her gaze to the ground, clearly troubled.

"What is it?" Kitranor asked.

"For many reasons, I am glad Bopol asked me to be his mate . . . and that I chose him. You have always been like another gemta to me, ever since I was brought here."

"And you have been like another daughter to me," Kitranor replied.

"I said what I needed to my gemta . . . but I am still sad."

The Chieftess hugged Jordan, who responded with a weary acceptance and silence.

"You will always carry these feelings, but they will become a lighter burden someday," Kitranor said, "You are young and have many experiences ahead of you. They will make good stories, I think."

"I already have one!" Jordan said, brightening at the chance to share a tale from the hunting pack's journey.

"What is that?" Kitranor said, surprised.

"A story, Chieftess!" Jordan said proudly. "It all began when we entered the Kastadi lands . . . "

EPILOGUE

ERICA MELENDEZ AWOKE IN AN unfamiliar hut made of wood and plant-like materials. It was cold, and she could hear a rushing wind outside. Her stomach communicated its hunger through loud growls. They focused her attention, bringing her to full consciousness. She was no longer in the clothes she had worn when she'd left Earth. She was in some kind of hide skin shirt and pants.

As she tried to stand, her legs buckled. She was on all fours when she heard someone enter the hut in a hurry. It was a woman, taller, and a few years older than her. The woman had light green hair that was shaved on one side; she had rose-pink-tinted skin and her clothes were similar to Erica's. When the woman spoke, it was in a language Erica had never heard before.

Looking sympathetic to Erica's inability to understand her words, the green-haired woman got down on all fours to see if Erica was all right, turning her head from side to side slowly, scanning Erica with her eyes. Expressing curiosity and concern, the woman pointed at herself and said "Kalami," pronouncing it "kah-LAH-mee."

Erica nodded and repeated the name. Then Erica pointed at herself and said her own name, which the woman repeated.

Kalami pointed at her mouth and said a strange word. When Erica didn't understand, the woman repeated the word and rubbed her belly, as if asking *Are you hungry?*

Erica's stomach groaned, and Erica nodded enthusiastically. Kalami nodded in return and walked out of the hut. She returned with a medium-sized bag. When Kalami opened it, there were what looked like fruits and vegetables of different shapes and colors. Erica grabbed a soft red piece of produce about the size of grapefruit and bit into it to taste it. She chewed it for a moment savoring its tender textures and sweet flavor. It tasted like cherries dipped in chocolate and had a minty aftertaste. One by one, Erica cautiously sampled every item given to her. Kalami offered her a bowl of water and Erica drank it completely.

Erica could feel some of her strength beginning to return. She didn't fully trust her circumstances or these people, but to give herself the best chance of survival, she had to accept their kindness.

She was still hungry and very thirsty but wanted to see if she could keep down what she'd just consumed.

"More water?" Erica said, holding the bowl in front of her and asking with her eyes.

Kalami nodded in understanding. She left and soon returned with more water. Erica listened and watched as a few villagers passed nearby the hut's opened doorway. She couldn't tell what they were doing, and she was still somewhat disoriented by this new environment and how she felt physically. No one sounded rushed or alarmed. Everyone seemed to be going about their normal routines.

Kalami continued watching over Erica during the next week in ways that varied from a motherly to sisterly fashion. Kalami spent most of each day with her, trying to communicate or provide food and water or just be there to provide company.

Kalami had spoken to her calmly, even knowing Erica couldn't understand her. Erica understood the warmth and peaceful sound of her voice. It acted as a soothing agent, verbally massaging the fears and alarm she felt. Sometimes it took a simple phrase. But more often, it took relating stories or descriptions of the world around her to do the job. Erica didn't need to know what the words meant, only the intent, patience and emotional state of the person speaking them.

When Erica was strong enough to stand up and walk, Kalami took Erica by the hand and led her outside the hut. As they walked in the direction of a stream flowing on the outskirts of the village, Erica was amazed by her surroundings. In addition to the huts, there were dozens of Kalami's people involved in numerous tasks ranging from building new huts, selling various wares and tending to children or animals. Passing by a few adolescent males who were displaying their new hunting gear to one another by the river, she felt her face blush as they paused one by one to gaze at her in silent awe.

The village was located in a meadow just below the tree line on a mountain. The grass was a light blue color and she could see what looked like bales of it rolled like hay to her left. Medium-sized animals that reminded Erica of sheep, if sheep had light orange wool and were twice as long, grazed and purple-hued hawk-like avians soared overhead.

It felt good to walk outside. The air was thinner and colder than she was used to, but it was refreshing, making her body feel lighter. It sharpened her senses, particularly smell and hearing. Sometimes gusts descended the mountain, hitting them with an oppressive chill. Erica thought her eyes might be playing tricks on her, as the atmosphere had a greenish tint which was arduous to adapt to, as was the sight of this world's twin stars.

About twenty minutes into their stroll, they arrived at the stream. Kalami got down on her knees and scooped up some of the liquid into the bowl. With Algoran's day stars brightening everything from overhead, Erica got her first good view of herself reflected in the stream's waters. Even with the verdant sky, she could tell that her hair was the deepest blue she had ever seen, and her eyes were now ice-colored. There were nickel-sized blue crystals embedded on either side of her neck. She put her hands on them to verify she wasn't hallucinating.

I've become like Jordan! Whatever happened to her, it's happened to me!

Nearly overwhelmed with emotion and fear, she looked to Kalami, who was calm and had obviously been aware of Erica's physical appearance this whole time. Kalami conveyed acceptance and the cheer of a simple glance. For the first time, Erica realized that the way she looked now had significantly elevated her status with Kalami's people. Without context, it was hard to understand.

Kalami didn't have to say anything. Erica needed and was grateful for everything Kalami was offering, even if it was just her continued calm and acceptance.

The first couple of months on Algoran had been the most difficult. Erica felt terribly isolated and alone. She had wondered if her impulsive action of following Jordan through the portal had been an awful mistake. But Kalami and others from the village did their best to reassure her, keeping Erica engaged and involved. Throughout it all, she never lost focus or gave up hope. Erica knew that, no matter how long it took, she would find Jordan again.

Kalami set her eight-year old son and four-year old daughter to sleep for the night, covering them with their fur blankets and kissing their necks. She gazed at them for some time with gratification, pride and love. Once she heard each of them cease their nervous squirming and start to breathe deeply, she knew she could relax and focus on other matters. She walked outside the hut, where her mate, the tall and barrel-chested Daraz, awaited her.

"They are asleep. Binoz was already tired and easy to please but Makazi wanted me to tell her the Water Flight story twice to make her happy," Kalami said in their language.

"You spoil the girl, my Heartpath."

"I can't help it. She is our youngest and you know I always wanted a girl."

"Just don't complain when she is a tyrant by the Age of Emergence."

Kalami laughed. "She might only be a *slight* tyrant?"

"Not if *I* have to deal with her," Daraz insisted. "How is The One doing?"

"Ere-Kah? She is exactly as she should be. Now that we can communicate together in the Ullvarr tongue, it has been much less troublesome, for her and us."

"Have the roots and herbs been working?"

Kalami rested contentedly against her mate's back and shoulders.

"I have been testing her responses," she answered. "The mixture I created causes her awareness to be dulled just enough to make her more susceptible to impressions and commands."

She was slightly startled when he turned around to face her in his excitement.

"Excellent! We need to bind her fate to our people's."

She ran her hand along his muscular arm as she spoke. "I have already introduced her to Vakar's family, Dearest Love Scent."

"Vakar! He is a good warrior and handsome as well. But does he like her at all?"

Kalami chose her next words very carefully, deliberately appearing thoughtful.

"She is fair to look at, if softer than some. It did not take much convincing," Kalami said. "Vakar knows the SnowFire legends as well as any of our tribe. He understands the benefits, both personally and politically. So, he has agreed, at least tentatively."

Daraz grinned. "You are a sorceress, my mate!"

"I am not!" she insisted with fake modesty. "I just know how to listen and talk to people. And to our fortune, our young legend is more than willing to tell us all about herself and her beloved Jorr-Don."

Daraz quickly stifled the rage sparked by her speaking Jordan's name, even though her voice had been filled with contempt. Kalami sensed his anguish and she sympathized, gently putting her hands on his shoulders and kissing his cheek then his lips.

"Sorrows, Daraz."

He took a deep breath and released it. "I will be fine. It just brings back the memories."

"All will be well. When our efforts have reached their conclusion, that cursed huntress will suffer for killing your mother. And we will use her friend to bring it about."

SNEAK PEEK OF JORDAN'S ARROW

Erica Melendez had been living among the Ullvarr for nearly a year already. She had grasped their language enough to have moderate conversations and start learning people's names, occupations, and family relations. Kalami, the woman who had helped and guided Erica since her arrival, had made her welcome among her household. Her husband, Village Leader Daraz, and most of the village showed a mixture of pleasantness and wariness with certain degrees of insincerity. Even so, they had allowed her to become a member of their community and were trying to get to know her.

High quality, vibrant clothing was handmade for her which looked and felt like fine silk. A new hut was built for her as well. It was beautified by a lush flower bed near its entrance. She did not know all the types of these remarkable blooms, but their petals radiated lively shades of red, orange, white, and lavender. Inside the hut, Ullvarr artists had made bright and cheerful paintings directly on the walls and laid a plush bird feather mattress on the wooden floor. The shelves against the opposite wall were stocked with separate bowls of fruit and water. A stone chest was filled with more of the gorgeous clothing which had been made for or given to her. The wide oval window allowed both day and moons' light inside. Two wooden chairs and a table lent themselves for conversation or a meal. Each day, someone would bring

Erica fresh supplies of fruits, vegetables, and dried meats to snack on between the community meals in the morning and evening.

Yet, without the presence of friends or regular visitors, the hut usually made her feel lonely.

Sometimes Erica's main problems were with herself. She didn't entirely trust her own perceptions. It wasn't just the physical changes she'd experienced, gaining blue hair, icy-colored eyes, and the strange gemstones fused to her neck. Ever since the first day she'd appeared near this village, it felt like she was a second or two out of phase with everything and everyone else. This sensation didn't feel like an illness. Sometimes she could filter it out or ignore it, but it was always there.

Having so much time to herself gave Erica opportunity to reflect upon her life and how she'd come to be here. She thought about her parents, how their marital strife had led to a prison sentence for her mother and suicide for her father. She relived the regrets of not fully committing to her fiancé and how it had ended that relationship prematurely. The culmination of these events had been sufficient reasons for her to forsake the world of her birth, leaping through a spatial portal which led to Algoran.

After being separated from her once-best friend, Jordan Lewis, on arrival, Erica wondered why she hadn't located her yet. Jordan told Erica she'd traveled across nearly all of Algoran just to find a *possible* way back to Earth. And she'd succeeded in that. Didn't Jordan already have knowledge about this world's tribes? Wasn't locating a lost friend just as important as finding a way home? Erica instinctively felt like Jordan was alive and well. And yet, where was she?

Erica wanted to be fair towards Jordan. It seemed like a big planet and she didn't know how far away Jordan was. Did Jordan return to the tribe she knew? Did she get sent to another part of the world, the way Erica had? There were plenty of things to consider but no ways to confirm them. Despite her efforts, she found herself resenting her childhood companion more often than not. Someday she would find Jordan herself. And when she succeeded, she would demand answers.

One evening at twilight, Kalami introduced Erica to Vakar, the head of the Ullvarr warriors. Kalami explained to them that Vakar would essentially become Erica's bodyguard. He had just finished training some new recruits from the village. The meeting was only semi-formal and Vakar was still drenched in perspiration from his exertions, breathing deeply. At almost a foot taller than her, he was very muscular and handsome, sporting long green hair, shaved on the right side like the rest of these rose-pink-colored people. This man was somewhat reserved, not shy but deliberately quiet. She could tell that he was trying to assess her in some way.

She was certain that Kalami was encouraging the two of them to become mates. Erica wasn't ready for such a commitment. However, she had to admit to herself that, looking at this glistening and robust male, the idea was both flattering and tempting.

Whenever Vakar did speak, it was brief and with sincerity. Erica had sensed a certain reluctance from him towards her but since she felt the same, she didn't think much of it. She imagined that the expanse that loomed between them, being from two different worlds' cultures, could lessen over time. As things stood now, they were barely more than polite acquaintances. And that suited her just fine.

During one of their early chats, Kalami had asked if there was any-one else who looked like Erica. She had even using the word "SnowFire" and gestured towards Erica's blue hair and the gemstones fused to her neck. It had felt like Kalami was probing Erica for knowledge about the mythical figure.

Erica happily talked about Jordan and how she had similar features. But she still had a poor grasp of Ullvarr words. Erica realized afterwards that she must have sounded to Kalami like she didn't understand the question and was rambling on about her close friend. Kalami tried to be polite but was clearly disappointed in the outcome. The topic was never brought up again.

Erica desperately wanted to know what her physical changes meant. Who was SnowFire really? She knew that SnowFire had saved Jordan's life by transferring her own blood and it had changed Jordan. Had SnowFire done the same to Erica?

Once Erica was more fluent in the language, Kalami brought her to meet with Daraz. As Village Leader, he had offered to answer any questions she might have. Like others she had seen, she slightly lowered her head and did not look directly in his eyes. She kept her arms relaxed and her feet together. Her phrases were short and to the point. She knew he was a busy man and did not have time for lengthy dialogues.

"I am thankful for your time, Great Leader," Erica humbly offered.

"This meeting is long overdue, Ere-Kah. Relax!" Daraz replied with a magnanimous smile. "Ask me anything."

Inside the Leader's Chamber, a large hut with a wooden floor and decorative weapons displays on the walls, Daraz was sitting on a grand wooden chair that resembled a throne. He wore his Leader robe, which was made from animal furs and embedded with valuable-looking gemstones. Kalami stood proudly at his side.

"Why am I important to the Ullvarr?"

"A fine question! Good! Good!" he clapped his hands joyfully. "Ere-Kah, did you know that you fell from the sky to us?"

"No, Great Leader," she responded, her eyes widening and her stance stiffening.

"You told Kalami you are from another world, yes?"

"Yes . . . Great Leader."

Daraz stood up then and began to almost strut around the room. Under any other circumstances, Erica might have allowed herself to be entertained. On Earth, this behavior would be ridiculous.

"We—I feel that you were *sent* to the Ullvarr, like a gift from the twin stars themselves!" Daraz continued, stopping and swinging around towards Erica, lifting his hands and his eyes towards the ceiling. "And it is our duty to protect, treasure, and honor you."

He turned away from Erica and towards his throne.

"I do not understand, Great Leader. I may be from another world and maybe I fell from the skies," Erica interjected. "But would you tell me: does this 'special honor' have anything to do with SnowFire?"

Daraz froze like a statue but Kalami could not prevent her mask of calm from being briefly shattered by Erica's inquiry. Erica was not sure why it alarmed her so much but it didn't take a genius to understand that they were hiding something.

Daraz slowly faced Erica, his facade returning. He attempted to regain the upper hand.

"It is true that you resemble that figure of another people's legend," he declared confidently. "But that holds no special meaning for us. We are simply glad to have you with us. You are unique and we only want you to feel welcome among the Ullvarr."

"I do, Great Leader," Erica added quickly. "And I would like a more active role in the village. My time passes slowly and I am sometimes lonely."

Daraz's smile returned. He took Kalami's hand in his and looked at her.

"Teach her our written language. And see if perhaps she might make a good teacher for the children," Daraz commanded. "I feel they might enjoy learning from our Ere-Kah, yes?"

Kalami's eyes broadcasted that she did not approve of either idea but she complied nonetheless.

"Of course, Great Leader," she acquiesced. "I will make arrangements to give her the necessary instruction."

"Excellent, My Heartpath!"

Then Daraz returned his attention to Erica. She was surprised by his solution but not disappointed.

"Will these things please Ere-Kah?" he asked, looking sincere.

"Yes, Great Leader," she responded, giving the traditional bow with a circular hand gesture as she rose back up. "Thank you for your time."

Daraz smiled and nodded. Then Kalami quietly led Erica out of the chamber.

That night, Erica quietly exited her hut and tiptoed stealthily into the nearby woods. It was made more difficult by the intoxication-like symptoms she constantly felt. Even so, she pushed past it. She was fed up with the facade from everyone, it had to end.

I have spent too much time here already, she thought, ironically, in Ullvarr. *I do not know what they want with me but it does not feel right. And I've got to find Jordan!*

She was frightened at the prospect of leaving the village but excited and determined to make a life for herself away from them.

Her vision quickly adjusted to the moonslight and she tried to listen out for any predators. Then she just stopped. She could not move any parts of her body but her eyes and mouth. In front of her, there was a blue and white glow that hovered in mid-air. That radiating light formed into a woman with long blue hair and ice blue eyes. This had to be SnowFire!

The figure before her said nothing but was grim and foreboding. Her eyes conveyed a mixture of anger and sadness.

"I know who you are! What do you want?" Erica shouted in frustration. "Why have you stopped me??"

The Spirit of the Mountain said nothing. She just looked at Erica with some degree of understanding, considering the situation.

Then she pointed in the direction that Erica had come from.

"You—you want me to go back? Why?"

SnowFire did not answer Erica. She just continued to insist, unmoving.

Erica struggled to move forward to no avail. However, when she tried to turn around, she could move. SnowFire literally would not let her leave the area.

She made one more thrust forward, even knowing what would happen. She screamed as she struggled with all her might against SnowFire's invisible force. All her strength, pride, and anger made no difference. In the end, she collapsed to her knees, spent and defeated, wanting to cry.

Despite the outcome of this encounter, Erica would try again sometime soon. She had to, whether she succeeded or not.

———————

Weeks passed with Erica and Vakar becoming accustomed to their new roles. Erica strolled across the land one morning wearing flowing robes of blue with silver, her wrists adorned with bejeweled bracelets. Vakar was ever at her side. She drank in the magnificence of the sub-alpine forest with amazement and appreciation. Its bright blue grasses and flowering plants in every color imaginable gently danced in the afternoon breeze, lifting her spirits. Small creatures with long thin legs, tan fur, and light brown wings fed near a stream which snaked towards the snow-covered mountains in the distance. The air was cold but fairly tolerable to her. The suns were on full display in the nearly cloudless green-tinted sky.

This day, Vakar's expression was nearly unreadable. She tried to start conversation with him numerous times, asking about his family or his role as a warrior, but his answers were always abrupt and, in few words, giving her little room to develop a dialogue. His eyes mostly looked ahead, except when he was making sure she kept pace with him. He was treating the experience of being in her presence like a duty only. He always stayed within a foot or two of her, ever ready to protect her from any threat with his daggers or raw strength. At least he never complained.

"I am not familiar with all of Algoran's seasons, since I'm always so, um, sheltered and protected," Erica began. "Is it always cold like this? Does it get warmer?"

"This is the warmest time. It will become much colder in the coming moonturns," Vakar responded, his words curt and dry.

"I think Algoran will make Colorado seem warm."

"Kolloh-RAH-do?" Vakar attempted to repeat. "A village on your world?"

Erica smiled with her eyes, taking care not to laugh. "Well, it's a part of a vast land there. It is where I was born."

He turned to look at her, as this subject did interest him.

"Do you . . . miss that place?" he asked.

"I do not," she responded. "I chose to leave there and I do not regret that decision."

"I see. That is good. Many of the villagers already consider you Ullvarr."

Erica gave a wan smile. "Thanks."

"Concerning the change of seasons, I will have our best clothesmaker prepare proper robes and dresses for you before the colder days arrive."

"That is very kind."

Vakar grunted in acknowledgement.

"You are the leader of all the warriors," Erica noted. "You teach them exercises and stretches, yes? To help them become better at what they do?"

"Yes."

"Do you think you could teach me?" Erica asked, her enthusiasm evident, pleading with her eyes. "I think it would help me. I am not very active and the village gives me so much food and drink. I know I was not a thin woman before, when I arrived either, but now . . . "

Without thinking about it, she rested one of her hands upon her widened stomach, lowering her gaze and slightly blushing as she awaited his reply. Surely Vakar could see how self-conscious she was and how awkward it was for her to make this request. Could he see her need for training, to instruct her? Had he been ordered not to?

"I would, if it were permitted," Vakar replied stiffly, his eyes looking at the trees ahead. "But I am not allowed to risk injury to you."

Erica lowered her head, feeling obstructed and dejected once more.

"I should just accept my walks and shut up?" she scowled.

"I would not have worded it that way, but—"

"I get it," she interrupted. Then she sighed.

A short while later, Erica and Vakar walked through the stone archway which marked the west entrance to the Ullvarr village. She glimpsed the simple but enduring efficiency of the huts. Each was single story but varied in width and function. Some were for storage but most were for families. With Erica now inside the safety of the community, Vakar excused himself as he saw Daraz walking nearby. With a nod, Erica let him go. She watched the two men walk off, no doubt to discuss village business or security.

———

Vakar followed Daraz into the Leader Chamber. He closed and secured the door behind them.

"The princess did not seem very pleased upon your return," Daraz scoffed. "Did you say or do something to upset her?"

"I answered her questions with the information you provided me," Vakar replied. "Can I help it if she does not like it?"

Vakar did not bother to hide his resentment from Daraz about being forced to comply with the rules and instructions he was given. He and Daraz had been friends for many cycles before Daraz came to power. So, Vakar felt he could be honest, even blunt, if he needed to.

"She would not be focused on what she *cannot do* if you shared your heart and pursued her. Those were my orders to you," Daraz fumed. "If you had followed them, she would only be concentrating on being your mate and the mother of your children!"

"I cannot give my heart to that—*thing!* She disgusts me!"

"Remember your place, Vakar!" Daraz barked, standing to his full height, glaring at him threateningly. "You are the head of the warriors but I am Leader."

Vakar clenched his fists. Stress lines furrowed into his brow. But as he contemplated Daraz's words, he had no choice but to acknowledge their truth. His body relaxed.

"I . . . ask forgiveness," Vakar remarked, chastened.

Daraz had to be an example to the whole village. Vakar backed down. But he still needed some convincing.

"Ere-Kah appeared to us from the skies almost a cycle ago, a gift from the twin stars," Daraz insisted. "You could be mated to an avatar for SnowFire! Do you not see the honor given to you?"

"What I *see* is that she is pale, weak, whiny, and fat!" retorted Vakar. "And worse, since she is a host for the one called SnowFire, I see that she is a monster."

"We can turn that to our advantage," Daraz countered. "With her presence, the other tribes and villages will fear us. We can conquer them with hardly a battle. Ere-Kah will secure the Ullvarr's place as a great people on Algoran."

"The Ullvarr are *already* a great people, Daraz."

"Not in number or power. We are not even the sole masters of our land."

"The Kastadi are a powerful ally, are they not?"

Daraz looked down as though contemplating Vakar's words. "Yes," he admitted. "But we should not have to depend on anyone."

Vakar nodded. "So, what should we do now?"

"You need to put aside your dislike for Ere-Kah and ask her to be your mate. Then keep her satisfied and begin your family."

"I would die before having offspring with her!" Vakar said, outraged.

Daraz backhanded Vakar across the face with his hulking fist, hammering him back and to the ground. He then stomped on Vakar's chest, vacating the wind from his lungs.

"You are a fool! That female possesses more power than you could ever hope to have—and Kalami tells me that she already *favors* you!" Daraz raged. "Any child you have with her will be valued above all Ullvarr who have ever lived! Can you not see that? You should want as many offspring with her as possible. You would be securing your own future!"

Vakar was stunned silent.

"Are you, a warrior, going to tell me you are ruled by your own worries?" Daraz continued. "You should *have* no fear!"

Vakar clamored to his feet, anger still simmering behind his eyes.

"I understand your words and purpose, Leader," Vakar wheezed, slightly bent forward as he tried to recover from the pounding he'd received. He made himself look up and into Daraz's eyes. Vakar's sweat accented his pallor. "But hear me on one thing."

"What is it?"

"My only fear is that Ere-Kah SnowFire will one day be the *death* of the Ullvarr people."

Daraz had no answer for that.

TO BE CONTINUED IN

JORDAN'S ARROW

For more information about
Allen Steadham
&
Jordan's World
please visit:

www.allensteadham.com
allen@allensteadham.com

www.facebook.com/jaspecfiction
@Mindfirenovel
www.instagram.com/allensteadham

For more information about
AMBASSADOR INTERNATIONAL
please visit:

www.ambassador-international.com
@AmbassadorIntl
www.facebook.com/AmbassadorIntl

If you enjoyed this book, please consider leaving us a review on
Amazon, Goodreads, or our website.